Love Blooms with the Duke

Suddenly a Duke Series
Book Six

Alexa Aston

Dragonblade Publishing, Inc. is an imprint of Kathryn Le Veque Novels, Inc.
P.O. Box 23
Moreno Valley, CA 92556
ceo@dragonbladepublishing.com

Produced in the United States of America

First Edition August 2023
Print Edition

ARE YOU SIGNED UP FOR DRAGONBLADE'S BLOG?

You'll get the latest news and information on exclusive giveaways, exclusive excerpts, coming releases, sales, free books, cover reveals and more.

Check out our complete list of authors, too!

No spam, no junk. That's a promise!

Sign Up Here

www.dragonbladepublishing.com

Dearest Reader;

Thank you for your support of a small press. At Dragonblade Publishing, we strive to bring you the highest quality Historical Romance from some of the best authors in the business. Without your support, there is no 'us', so we sincerely hope you adore these stories and find some new favorite authors along the way.

Happy Reading!

CEO, Dragonblade Publishing

Additional Dragonblade books by Author Alexa Aston

Suddenly a Duke Series
Portrait of the Duke
Music for the Duke
Polishing the Duke
Designs on the Duke
Fashioning the Duke
Love Blooms with the Duke

Second Sons of London Series
Educated By The Earl
Debating With The Duke
Empowered By The Earl
Made for the Marquess
Dubious about the Duke
Valued by the Viscount
Meant for the Marquess

Dukes Done Wrong Series
Discouraging the Duke
Deflecting the Duke
Disrupting the Duke
Delighting the Duke
Destiny with a Duke

Dukes of Distinction Series
Duke of Renown
Duke of Charm
Duke of Disrepute
Duke of Arrogance

Duke of Honor
The Duke That I Want

The St. Clairs Series
Devoted to the Duke
Midnight with the Marquess
Embracing the Earl
Defending the Duke
Suddenly a St. Clair
Starlight Night (Novella)
The Twelve Days of Love (Novella)

Soldiers & Soulmates Series
To Heal an Earl
To Tame a Rogue
To Trust a Duke
To Save a Love
To Win a Widow
Yuletide at Gillingham (Novella)

The Lyon's Den Series
The Lyon's Lady Love

King's Cousins Series
The Pawn
The Heir
The Bastard

Medieval Runaway Wives
Song of the Heart
A Promise of Tomorrow
Destined for Love

Knights of Honor Series
Word of Honor
Marked by Honor
Code of Honor

Journey to Honor

Heart of Honor

Bold in Honor

Love and Honor

Gift of Honor

Path to Honor

Return to Honor

Pirates of Britannia Series

God of the Seas

De Wolfe Pack: The Series

Rise of de Wolfe

The de Wolfes of Esterley Castle

Diana

Derek

Thea

Also from Alexa Aston

The Bridge to Love

One Magic Night

PROLOGUE

London—March 1801

W ILLA FENNIMORE WINCED as Theodosia ranted about some trivial matter. Her mother berated the new housekeeper as Willa stood off to the side, feeling sorry for the woman. If Theodosia wasn't careful, the housekeeper would quit less than a month into her service.

Not that that mattered. Servants came and went with alarming frequency in the Fennimore household. Either Ambrose became too attached to the young, pretty ones—and his wife fired them—or Theodosia argued and castigated them into quitting.

Willa had known nothing but chaos her entire life.

She was barely ten and five and felt at least double her age, sometimes believing she was the only true Fennimore adult. In truth, she ran much of the household because her parents couldn't bother to take the time to do so. Ambrose was the fourth son of an earl and one of London's most celebrated playwrights. He had married Theodosia, who was an actress of great renown these days. Together, they had produced Willa and then promptly ignored their parental duties. For the most part, Ambrose overlooked her, while Theodosia had lately begun pretending she was Willa's older sister. At thirty-five, Theodosia was still a breathtakingly beautiful woman, but a woman aware of the clock ticking on that beauty. Her mother was constantly pushing for her husband to write new material for her, afraid she would not be able to remain on the stage as she grew older.

Theodosia had been her husband's muse for the sixteen years they had been together, causing him to produce over a dozen plays in which she played the leading role. The new theater season was about to embark, thanks to the London Season starting in a month's time. If there was one thing members of Polite Society enjoyed doing, it was spending a night out at the theater.

At least with the Season approaching and new plays going into production, Willa would be totally left on her own. She had raised herself for the most part, having only had a governess for a single year when she was seven. Up until that point, Theodosia had brought her daughter to the theater and left her to roam it while she worked. Willa had become part of the theater family from a young age, with everyone from actors to prop masters to scene decorators looking after her. Once she learned to read and write, the governess was let go. Actually, fired by Theodosia because she suspected her husband was far too interested in the attractive, young woman. It was a pattern of her parents' marriage—Ambrose's roving eye and Theodosia's hysterics when she discovered his unfaithfulness.

Willa liked her father to a degree but would never have put up with him as a husband. As for her mother, she avoided Theodosia for the most part, not enjoying the drama the actress created off-stage.

"I quit!" the new housekeeper declared, throwing her hands in the air.

Willa shook her head, not even remembering the woman's name. She sighed, thinking this was but another loss due to her mother's mercurial nature.

The servant stormed from the room, Theodosia shouting at her, her language worse than that of a sailor.

In other words, a typical day in the Fennimore household.

Her mother finally calmed after pacing a bit and turned to Willa. "Come, Willa. We will go to the theater now."

They left the house and walked the half-mile to the playhouse, where Ambrose's latest play was being produced. Although they could have easily afforded to hail a hansom cab, Theodosia insisted they walk, claiming the exercise was good for them.

Actually, Willa enjoyed walking and spent a great deal of her time moving about the streets of London by foot. On her own, she visited museums and frequented parks and bookstores. She felt intimately acquainted with London after having spent her entire life living in the great city.

They arrived at the theater, where the first rehearsal would begin in a couple of hours. Still, the hustle and bustle within reflected the closeness to opening night. While Theodosia went off to find her dresser, who was working on costumes for the play, Willa made the rounds, visiting with everyone. She talked to the prop master, who had put her to work when she was five, lining up props and handing them off to actors as they entered and exited the stage. She talked with two workers painting a backdrop for the second act, which took place outside a Parisian café. The smell of paint would always be in her blood since she had helped paint background scenery for years.

She moved to the conductor of the orchestra and spent time visiting with him, telling him about the latest piece she had composed on the pianoforte. Willa was self-trained in music, having spent many hours listening to orchestras rehearse. She had been composing music for a few years now, despite the fact she could not read it. It all was stored in her head. That was something she decided she would like to learn this year.

Everything Willa learned was self-taught. Once she knew how to read, Theodosia had told her to pursue whatever topics interested her. Willa took her mother at her word and explored all kinds of subjects. One of her favorites had been languages. Though many of the people who worked in the theater were English by birth, a growing portion was immigrants. Willa had an ear for languages and over the years, merely by lingering in the theater for hours and hours each day, had picked up French, Spanish, and Italian. All three were romance languages and seemed to come naturally to her. A new carpenter from Dusseldorf had just started working at the theater last month. She had spent weeks begging him to teach her German. Although she found the language a bit guttural and it didn't flow as well as the romance languages, she was picking up phrases here and there from him.

After two hours had passed, she went backstage to her mother's dressing room and stood at the open door, measuring the temperature of the room before entering. Theodosia was in a heated discussion with her dresser. Nothing new there. Their voices began to escalate, and Willa decided it was time to go home to the solace of the gardens. Gardening was the single thing that soothed her when nothing else could. Felton, their gardener, came two or three days a week and had become her friend over the years. He had taught her everything she knew about plants and flowers. She found there was nothing like digging in the dirt to soothe her soul.

Leaving backstage, Willa came upon Ralph Baldwin, the director of Ambrose's latest play, as well as the new owner of this particular theater. She liked him because he was always friendly to her, and the questions he asked made it seem as if he were truly interested in her replies.

"Have you come from Theodosia's dressing room?"

"Yes, Mr. Baldwin. She is in a row with her dresser right now. If she asks—not that she will—tell her that I have gone home."

The director placed his hand on her shoulder and gave it a squeeze. "I am sorry, Willa."

"For what?"

His hand fell away, and he shrugged. "For you not having a child-hood like most of us enjoyed. For having parents who don't act as parents to you at all."

"Do not feel sorry for me, Mr. Baldwin. I learned long ago that it does no good. I realize my parents should never have become parents. Theodosia was too young and selfish to ever have a child. Ambrose only thinks women are good for fucking."

He overlooked her crude words. "You have raised yourself, haven't you?" he asked.

"I have—and I believe I have done a fine job of it," she said saucily, winking at him.

Unexpectedly, he pulled her into his arms and hugged her tightly. Pulling back, he rested his hands on her shoulders and said, "You know if you ever need anything, you can come to me, Willa. I may not be your legal godfather, but I would like to think I could help."

"Thank you," she said, moved by his words. "The theater is full of good people, people who have helped me all these years. People such as you, who show me on a daily basis that you care. Thank you."

She turned away, her throat thick with unshed tears. Usually, she did not show such emotions. Her upbringing had been chaotic, and Willa found she enjoyed order in her life. She had learned to disguise her emotions at a young age and take pleasure from order, realizing she was a private person and did not want to share much with others. While she felt liked, she had never experienced love and doubted she ever would. Ambrose and Theodosia were too selfish to love anyone but themselves—and possibly, each other, upon occasion.

As she left the theater, she heard Mr. Baldwin calling for order and for someone to retrieve his lead actress. Willa knew the director liked to take rehearsals from the beginning, so they would start with Act 1, Scene 1.

What did surprise her was that her father was not present this morning. She knew he had been at the readings of the play the past few weeks, as the actors gathered in a large room about a table and read aloud from their scripts. Ralph Baldwin had given them suggestions and had them read a scene again, trying to perfect as much as they could before they began blocking the actions of the play and then adding in the words, stage directions, and props.

It was unlike Ambrose not to be at a first rehearsal. Then again, he might be starting a new work. Sometimes, her father got an idea and would work around the clock for days, barely taking time to even eat and only getting a couple of hours of sleep before he was back at his desk, scribbling away, as inspiration filled him.

After only having gone half a block, she heard someone calling her name and turned. Surprisingly, it was Jemima James who hurried after her.

"Are you going home?" the actress asked.

"Yes, why?"

"Do you mind if I accompany you? I need to discuss a scene with Ambrose. I am still not quite certain of my character's motivation."

Willa had heard this very excuse before and said, "Shouldn't you take that up with Mr. Baldwin? He is the director, after all. He can tell you how to play the scene, Jemima."

The pretty actress pursed her lips a moment. She really was quite attractive. From what Willa recalled, Jemima was only three years older than she was and had been acting a good five years or more on the stage because of her mature looks and figure. Jemima had been the understudy to Theodosia in two other productions and served in that capacity again for the new play. This time, though, she was also cast as the second female lead. Willa suspected Ambrose had written the role for Jemima.

"It's just that Ambrose created my character. Oh, I know that Ralph could walk me through things. But I need Ambrose's advice on it. Since he didn't appear at the theater today, I wasn't able to ask him."

Willa started moving down the pavement again, and Jemima fell into step beside her.

"You are welcome to see if Ambrose is at home. If he is, though, he is probably working on something new and won't wish to be disturbed. I am merely warning you that you might not be able to see him."

"It's worth taking the chance," Jemima said breathily.

That was when she knew her father stayed home deliberately today. The first act was full of Theodosia and her two male co-stars. Jemima did not even appear until the second act. If Ralph Baldwin kept to his usual pattern, the company would only be rehearsing scenes in the first act today, keeping Theodosia tied up.

And leaving Jemima free.

Guilt washed through her. By bringing Jemima home with her, Willa felt she was betraying her mother. Yet, in a way, she couldn't blame Ambrose. Theodosia's rages were becoming more and more frequent. She had even begun to wonder if her parents might consider divorcing. True, it would create a scandal—but scandals oftentimes sold tickets.

They arrived, and Willa used her key to let herself in. They hadn't had a butler in some months and no longer had a housekeeper as of this morning. She didn't see any other servants about.

"Let me go and see if Ambrose is in his study working," she told the young actress.

"Why do you call your father Ambrose?" Jemima asked, her curiosity obvious.

Willa didn't care to share with this woman that both her parents had rejected the traditional titles of Mama and Papa. Her father hadn't truly wanted children and insisted from the time she began walking and talking that his daughter address him by his Christian name. Naturally, her mother followed suit. From what Willa knew, Theodosia had become with child soon after she met Ambrose and had insisted they wed. Something had gone wrong during the birthing process, however, and Theodosia had been told by the midwife it would be impossible for her to have more children in the future. That was perfectly acceptable to the actress. She wanted to be eternally youthful and remain on the stage as long as she could.

It took some time before Willa understood how unwanted she truly was. Still, she respected her parents' wishes and addressed them as Ambrose and Theodosia. She didn't bother to correct anyone when they mistook Theodosia and her for sisters.

"It's a theater thing," she said airily. "Having been brought up in the theater, it is natural for me to call them by their first names. Wait here. I will return shortly."

She left Jemima in the foyer and went to her father's study, not bothering to knock. If he were truly working, he wouldn't hear the knock anyway. Opening the door, she saw him standing at the window, looking out at the gardens.

"Jemima James is here to see you," she informed him.

He turned, and she saw the gleam in his eyes, confirming this was no random meeting but a planned assignation.

"Is she? Whatever for? Rehearsals started today. She should be there, watching Theodosia, since Jemima is her understudy."

Continuing with the farce, Willa said, "Jemima says that she is having trouble developing her character's motivation and thought to go straight to the source. Shall I bring her to you?"

"No, I will fetch her myself."

That meant they would be going straight to his bedchamber. No need for the farce to play out with Theodosia tied up all day.

"What will you be doing?" he asked, wanting to establish her whereabouts.

"I will join Felton. We are going to prune the rose bushes today."

Ambrose's nose crinkled in disgust. "I don't know what you see in spending time with that man."

Tired of holding her tongue, she tossed back, "That man has had a good deal of raising me. I enjoy his company and gardening, Ambrose.

It is quite soothing and calms me."

He laughed harshly. "Then I wish Theodosia would take it up. She has been more volatile as of late."

"Might you think about being faithful to her for once?" she challenged. "It couldn't hurt."

His brows arched. "What are you saying?"

"Just that Theodosia becomes enraged every time you take up with a new lover. Such as Jemima James."

"You are challenging me?" he asked angrily.

"No, Ambrose. I am simply trying to give you some advice. But you are going to do as you choose."

Worry filled his eyes. "Will you tell her?"

"I never have, have I? No, that is between the two of you. Conduct your affairs as you see fit, and leave me out of your quarrels."

Storming from his study, she went upstairs to change into an old gown, covering it with a large gardening apron Felton had given her for her birthday last year. She took several deep breaths, pushing her anger away. It did no good to be upset with her parents. They were like spoiled, unruly children who made everything about them. She couldn't wait to leave their household. She planned in a few years to ask Felton if she could come to work for him. It would infuriate her parents since both assumed she would follow in their footsteps and make the theater her world when she reached adulthood.

That was the last place she would wish to be.

By the time she reached the gardens, her anger had subsided, and she greeted her friend, who handed her a set of gloves.

"How are you today, Felton?"

He looked up, shading his eyes. "Right as rain, Miss Willa. You ready to prune?"

"Of course. Test me."

His eyes lit with amusement. "All right then. Why do we prune roses?"

She smiled. "There are four reasons to do so. We want to remove dead and diseased branches."

"And those are called what?"

"Canes," she replied. "We also want to revive the plant and encourage it to bloom. We prune to control the shape of the rose bushes and their size and should cut stems crossing or rubbing against one another. Last, we must foster airflow through the shrub."

"How much should be removed and retained?" the gardener questioned.

"We will cut about one-third of the old branches and leave the other two-thirds in place. This will encourage fresh blooms."

"You've learned your lessons well, Miss Willa. Why do we prune in March?"

Knowing it to be a trick question, she laughed. "Sometimes, we do so in March, Felton. It is best to wait until the forsythias bloom before we prune our rose bushes. Pruning might take place in late February. Throughout March. On rare occasions, even early April."

Her friend smiled. "Can't pull a fast one on you, Miss Willa. Let's get started. What's our first step?"

"We must remove the leaves surrounding the rose bushes," she told him. "So we can see all the stems." Grinning, she added, "We might even find some pests hiding under them."

"Disease, too," he added.

They began clearing the leaves and then tested the wood, cutting into it. Brown meant the wood was dead and green signified it lived. She cut the dead wood back to the base of several bushes in the section they worked. Felton liked to prune a section at a time before moving to the next grouping. She began opening up the centers of the plants and sawed away any thin, weak growth.

As they worked in quiet in companionable silence, Willa felt at one with the earth. She would enjoy devoting her life to plants and flowers.

Then familiar noises started up, and she winced. Glancing up, she saw her father's bedchamber window open, knowing the sounds came from there.

"He's got a new one?" Felton asked.

"Another actress," she confirmed. "She is only a few years older than I am."

The gardener shook his head. "He'll never learn."

The noise grew louder, and Willa wanted to put her hands over her ears. She forced herself to continue working, though, as Jemima's scream of pleasure came from the open window on the second floor. Ambrose's shouts also let them know he was enjoying the illicit lovemaking. Sometimes, Willa believed the danger of discovery encouraged Ambrose to keep bringing new lovers to the house.

Then the quiet enveloped them again. The couple probably had fallen asleep.

She and Felton worked for several more hours with their saws and shears, pruning the canes so that the new stems would grow outward in the direction of the buds. They sealed the new cuts and began picking up all the leaves and cut branches, placing them in two nearby wheelbarrows. Felton would burn these so if they contained any disease or pests, the roses would be protected from both.

Pushing herself to a standing position, Willa surveyed their progress and was pleased. Before she could say anything, though, she heard a familiar shriek and loud cursing come from the window of her father's bedchamber.

Theodosia was home.

And not happy.

"Another tart?" her mother shouted, her trained stage voice carrying from the house to them.

Felton shrugged and stood, taking the handles of one of the wheelbarrows and rolling it away.

Willa knew she should take the other and follow him, yet couldn't.

She was drawn into the drama playing out above her.

She listened as her mother hurled insult upon insult at Ambrose and Jemima, cringing at the language and volatility. Thinking she should go and interrupt the tirade, Willa removed her gardening gloves and apron.

And then the deafening noise came, so loud that Willa recoiled, dropping to her knees and covering her ears. After a moment, the fog in her brain cleared, her incoherent thoughts becoming crystal clear.

It had been a gun that sounded.

An awful gnawing ran through her. She heard screaming. Two women screaming. Theodosia and Jemima.

"Look what you've done," Jemima shouted. "You've killed him. And almost me!"

"You both deserved it," Theodosia retorted, venom in her voice.

Willa saw her mother appear at the open window and realized she was trying to reload the gun. Jemima came into view, blood all down her front. She grabbed for the pistol and Theodosia jerked back—and fell through the open window.

In that moment, her gaze connected with her mother's. Willa saw the panic.

And madness.

Then Theodosia hit the ground with a thud. Felton was suddenly there, and both he and Willa ran toward the body. A low, guttural noise came from her mother, the sound a dying animal made.

And then quiet once more occurred.

Felton eased Theodosia onto her back. It was obvious she was gone. Her neck was at an incredibly odd angle. Her eyes bulged in horror.

"Look away, Miss Willa," Felton said gently, sweeping his hand down to close the dead woman's eyes.

She couldn't, though. She had never been close to death.

Another scream sounded from inside the house. A footman rushed outside and took in the situation, shouting, "I'll go for the doctor."

No doctor would be able to bring Theodosia back to life.

Numbly, Willa stood and said to Felton, "Stay with her. I'll go see Ambrose."

She went inside and trudged up the stairs. A housemaid flew by her, also screaming. Willa headed down the corridor and went through the open door of her father's bedchamber. She saw Jemima staring down at the bed, holding her hand to her shoulder.

Going to her father, horror ran through Willa as she saw the bullet her mother fired had gone through his right eye. He lay naked on the bed, his one good eye staring at the ceiling.

Willa looked at Jemima, who wore Ambrose's tan banyan, now covered in blood. Dully, the woman said, "The bullet passed through him. It struck my shoulder." Then fear filled her face. "I did not mean for her to fall, Willa. We fought over the pistol. I thought . . . I thought she would kill me."

Jemima gulped, tears streaming down her face. "I did not mean for her to fall."

"She would have," Willa agreed, making a quick decision. "No one needs to know the two of you struggled. You had no role in Theodosia's death. She took her own life after she killed Ambrose."

Confused, Jemima asked, "What?"

"You were never here," Willa told her. "I will send a doctor to see to your wound. Do not tell anyone what happened here today."

"You would protect me?"

Nodding, she said, "There is no point in destroying your life, Jemima. The play may or may not shut down. If Mr. Baldwin decides to continue, you will be cast in the lead role since you are the current understudy. The part is a good one. You and I both know it could make your career. But if you are associated with this tragedy, you might be blackballed from the acting community."

Jemima began to weep. "Why are you helping me? I caused this."

She took Jemima's hand in hers. "No, they caused it. They were locked in a vicious cycle for years. A cycle of love and hate. I will not let their behavior take you down."

The actress lifted Willa's hand and kissed it. "Thank you. Thank you, Willa."

"Go home. If anyone asks why you were not at the theater today—and I doubt they will—say that you were ill. No, say that Theodosia told you that you were not needed since only Act 1 would be rehearsed today."

"But I am the understudy. I should have been there to watch her performance. To take notes."

Willa shrugged. "Say that Theodosia was jealous of you. Told you to stay away. No one would doubt that."

"All right," Jemima agreed. "I owe you a great deal, Willa. My life. My career."

"All I ask in return is that you stick with this story," she insisted. "They quarreled. Theodosia shot Ambrose and then killed herself. They could be poison to one another, but they also thrived with one another. She could not have lived without him."

Pausing, Willa thought a moment. "Did you see any servants while you were here?"

"Only a maid. She ran in after Theodosia fell. She saw Ambrose's body and left, screaming. I don't think she ever looked at me."

"Good. Let me help you dress."

Willa went to her father's wardrobe and removed a white shirt, tearing it into strips and wrapping it about Jemima's shoulder to stanch the bleeding. She got the actress back into her shift and gown, tossing the rest of her garments into the wardrobe and closing it after removing Ambrose's greatcoat.

Slipping it about Jemima's shoulders, she said, "Go home. I will send the doctor to you. You cannot stay here."

Quickly, she led Jemima from the bedchamber and down the back staircase, asking for the girl's address.

"Lie down when you get to your room," she advised. "The less you move about, the better your chances are. I don't think your wound is serious."

Jemima snorted. "Well, it hurts like Hades."

"If the bullet had struck bone, you would be in much greater pain. I saw no evidence of bone being shattered, so it is merely a flesh wound. Keep your mouth shut. I will do what I can and encourage Mr. Baldwin to keep the play going, and you recast in Theodosia's role."

As they stepped outside, Jemima said, "I will never forget your kindness, Willa."

She watched Jemima hurry away and returned to Felton, who sat by the body.

"Mr. Fennimore?"

"Dead in his bed," she said succinctly.

"You sent the girl away?"

"I did. No sense in her being a part of this tragedy." She shook her head. "Theodosia would want the newspaper headlines reserved for her and Ambrose. I told Jemima to keep quiet."

"So, your mother shot your father as they argued and then took her own life?"

"Yes."

"What will you do now, Miss Willa?"

She swallowed painfully, knowing how her life would now change. Still, she was free of the two people who had been responsible for her. She would make her own way in the world.

Turning to Felton, she said, "I would like to—"

She paused, mid-sentence, seeing his face twisted in pain. His hands flew to his heart, and he grimaced.

"Felton?" she asked, panic flooding her. "What is wrong?"

"It hurts, Miss Willa. My chest. It's burning like it's caught on fire."

"No," she whispered, dread filling her, knowing everything which had taken place was too much for him.

He began swaying, and she caught his elbow, trying to steady him. "Here, Felton. Let's ease you to the ground. I will summon the doctor. Everything will be all right. I promise."

He gasped in short spurts, and Willa saw beads of sweat form along his brow.

"Dizzy," he managed to say. "So dizzy. And tired."

He whimpered softly, and she knew this was the end for him. Bitterness filled her, knowing a good man's demise was the fault of her parents. She tightened her grip on him, but he groaned and collapsed, falling to the ground.

"Felton! No!" Willa shouted, dropping to her knees, shaking him. "Felton!"

But her friend and surrogate father was gone.

A darkness spread through her, cold and raw. Felton had been her hope. Her salvation. The one person who truly cared for her.

Willa Fennimore was now alone in the world.

CHAPTER ONE

Spring Ridge, southern Kent—January 1813

ALEXANDER HUGHES GLANCED out the carriage window at the rolling countryside. They would arrive at Spring Ridge soon, a place he had not visited since childhood. He looked back at Rollo, who sat across from him. Rollo was the eldest of the four Hughes brothers. The Duchess of Brockbank had given birth to three boys in the first three years of her marriage—Rollo, the heir apparent; Peter, now a major-general in His Majesty's army; and Stanley, who held the living at Sherfield, the closest village to Spring Ridge.

Those three sons' roles were destined by their birth order. Heir. Military. Clergy. Xander, being a fourth son, weas left with no defined place.

Other than murderer.

That was the word his father had used to describe his youngest son because Xander's birth had killed his mother. Brockbank had only spoken to his fourth son a handful of times over the years, and once Xander left for university, he had never laid eyes upon his father again. After graduation, he accepted his quarterly allowance from Mr. Crockle, the family solicitor, and kept rooms in London, which he shared with his friend, Gil, Viscount Swanson. Xander never saw or had any contact with his brothers because they were so much older than he was. He had nothing in common with them.

He glanced at the woman sitting next to Rollo, the wife Xander had just met early this morning. He had not even been invited to Rollo's wedding and had only discovered he had two nieces this morning when their traveling party left London for Kent. Frankly, he was surprised that Rollo had even suggested that Xander accompany them to Spring Ridge. Xander would attend the deceased duke's funeral and leave quickly after its conclusion, while Rollo and his family remained in Kent.

He would tolerate the proceedings and return to his life, one of ease. As a fourth son and gentleman, he had no true profession or responsibilities and spent his days at White's, reading the newspapers and visiting with friends, as well as dining at the club twice a day. Afternoons were oftentimes spent with his latest mistress, while evenings found him in the gaming hells of London.

The only change to his routine was when the Season began each spring. Xander attended most of its social affairs, dancing with the new girls making their come-outs, squiring some of them to the theater or opera and garden parties. With his limited income, however, he doubted that he would ever wed. His role in Polite Society was to look handsome and be charming at events. He conformed to that role with ease.

"I hope that Stanley is waiting for us at Spring Ridge," Rollo said.

"I am certain your brother will be there, Brockbank," Pamela said, reminding Xander that he should start thinking of the couple as His and Her Grace.

It was hard to imagine his brother as the Duke of Brockbank. Their father had been a large, imposing man. Xander took after him, being three inches over six feet and possessing broad shoulders and a muscular frame. Rollo, on the other hand, was much shorter and stout. Any muscle he'd had turned to fat long ago. He supposed Rollo would be trying for an heir now since he only had the two girls. Cecily and Lucy had been very curious about Xander, having never met this uncle before. He was glad his nieces were riding in a different carriage with the servants, because he didn't really like children. Not that he had been around any, but the thought of children made him uncomfortable.

The vehicle came to a halt, and as a footman opened the door, Xander saw a man waiting for them, quickly realizing it was Stanley. He, too, was short and stout, his face full and ruddy, looking much like Rollo.

Xander allowed his brother and sister-in-law to exit the carriage before he did. Rollo and Stanley were thumping one another on the back in a joyous reunion. He and Pamela stood off to the side as outsiders. Xander had not heard Pamela say more than a handful of words since they'd left town. She seemed truly subservient to her husband.

Stanley turned his attention his younger brother's way. "Hello, Brother," the clergyman said. "I am sorry we finally meet up again under such difficult circumstances."

"Yes, the duke's death was a tragedy," he said, always knowing the right thing to say whether he believed it or not. If anything, he knew how to fit into any situation. He was smart and affable and realized also that he was a bit lazy. It was a good thing Rollo was the one to inherit Spring Ridge and all the other entailed properties. Running such an estate had no appeal to Xander. He enjoyed life in town.

The four of them went inside as footmen brought in their luggage. Lorry, the butler, greeted them, fawning over Rollo and Pamela, even as he ignored Xander. The butler had been their father's closest confidante and friend for decades. He supposed Lorry also thought him a murderer.

A woman moved toward him. "Good morning, Lord Alexander. I am Mrs. Dylan, the housekeeper. I will take you to your room as soon as I see Their Graces settled in theirs. I am told you are staying in what was your old room."

He smiled. "No need to escort me there, Mrs. Dylan, since I recall exactly where it is."

He left the group and went to his former bedchamber, noting nothing had changed about it since he had left Spring Ridge ten years ago for university. The same curtains hung at the windows, and the exact same carpet covered the floor. The furniture gleamed, however, and he assumed Mrs. Dylan to be efficient in her duties, keeping the parlor maids in line.

His portmanteau arrived, and Xander unpacked it himself, not having a valet. The allowance provided to fourth sons did not take into account such luxuries. His friend Swanson did have a valet, however, and the servant oftentimes helped Xander in dressing, as well as pressing his shirts and trousers. They also had a woman come in two days a week, one to clean and one to do their laundry. He was already itching to get back to his life in London.

Once he had unpacked, Xander headed down to the drawing room, where he assumed the others would gather. The new duke and duchess were already present, deep in conversation with Stanley.

"Are you settled in?" the duchess asked.

"I am, Your Grace. Thank you for asking."

She smiled tentatively at him and said, "Your brothers wish to go sailing now. I am trying to dissuade them because these gray skies look as if they may turn to rain."

Being on the water was the last place Xander ever wanted to be. He avoided it at all costs. His brothers had taken him out one time long ago in a rowboat. He had been six or seven years of age, and Rollo had told him it was time to learn how to swim. His eldest brother had then shoved Xander from the boat and laughed as he helplessly batted the water. He went under several times, swallowing what seemed like buckets of water, fighting to keep his head above the water's surface as Rollo and Stanley laughed at him.

Finally, Peter had leaned over and grabbed Xander's collar, hoisting him into the rowboat. Of the three, Peter was the only one who ever really spoke to him. The other two, like their father, ignored him. Even at that young age, Xander believed his two brothers hoped he might drown, and they would be rid of him.

He had not been out on the water since that long-ago day. Not to swim. Not to row a boat. Never to sail. He always found an excuse during a house party not to go to the lake and row a pretty girl about. He would feign business that needed his attention or simply remain on the shore, saying he could not leave the company of all the beautiful women present just to spend time with one of them in a rowboat. Women lapped up those kinds of compliments and it endeared him to the guests.

Still, he saw the worried look on Pamela's face and said, "You might want to wait until the weather is better. Her Grace is right. The skies look threatening, and there is a strong wind today."

"The better to sail and challenge ourselves," Stanley proclaimed. He looked to Pamela. "Don't worry about us, Your Grace. I will have your husband back to you in time to change for tea this afternoon."

Rollo and Stanley exited the drawing room, leaving Xander alone with his sister-in-law. She chewed on her bottom lip, and he felt sorry for her.

"I think I shall go up to the nursery and see if the girls are settling in," she told him, excusing herself, leaving him alone, which was perfectly fine with him.

He made his way to the library and lost himself in a book.

A footman appeared and told him tea was being served in the drawing room. He put aside the book. He had missed the filling, scrumptious teas which had been served at Spring Ridge and hoped they hadn't changed.

When he arrived in the drawing room, he saw only the duchess present.

"I thought His Grace and Stanley would be back by now."

Worry filled her face. "No, they have yet to arrive."

Concern now filled him because he had heard the heavy rain coming down and seen lightning from the window he had sat near as he read.

"Perhaps we should send a footman down to the lake to see how they are," he suggested.

"Yes, please do so." She hesitated and then added, "But make sure His Grace knows you were the one who sent him. He thinks me inclined to worry and would be embarrassed to know I sent anyone to check on him."

"Of course, Your Grace," he assured her, ringing for the butler.

When Lorry arrived, he said, "I am concerned that my brothers have yet to return. With the weather turning so foul, I would like a footman to check on them. In fact, I believe I will accompany him," he added spontaneously.

"Oh, thank you," the duchess said fervently.

Xander left with the butler and a footman volunteered to head to the dock with him. Mrs. Dylan gave them rain gear, and they donned it, going out into what now was a violent storm. Knowing a shortcut to the water, he motioned for the footman to follow him, and they cut through the woods, coming out near the dock. Once they reached the dock, Xander stared out at the lake, seeing nothing. Then he looked down the shoreline and froze.

A body.

"Come," he said urgently, and the footman followed as Xander began to run.

The form was face down, and as he reached it, cold fear coiled in his belly. He turned the shape over and recognized Rollo, his face bloated. He shook his brother in vain. Rollo's term as the Duke of Brockbank had been an incredibly short one. Word would need to be sent to Peter immediately. His brother would need to resign his military commission and return to Spring Ridge to take up the mantle of Duke of Brockbank.

Glancing at the lake again, Xander caught sight of what he thought might be another body. The small hope which had been within him now faded quickly. He stood and waded into the water, retrieving his other brother's body, hauling it to shore.

The footman stood agog, and Xander instructed him to bring a wagon down to the shore so the bodies could be brought home.

The servant nodded, still looking dazed as he left.

Xander would have to be the one to tell Pamela that her husband had drowned. Peter would make for a better duke, in Xander's opinion, and he knew his dutiful brother would take care of Rollo's family.

Half an hour later, the wagon arrived, driven by Lorry. Several footmen jumped from it and descended the bank to where Xander sat with the dead bodies. A part of the sailboat had washed ashore in the last few minutes, and he figured lightning had struck the craft. He would tell Pamela that neither man suffered—and hoped she believed him.

The bodies were loaded into the wagon, and he joined the butler, who had come to supervise, and now took up the reins.

"Does Her Grace know anything?" he asked.

"No, my lord. It will be your responsibility to tell her."

"I think we will need to postpone my father's funeral. Stanley would have performed the church ceremony and graveside services. We will have to find someone to do so for the three of them now." He paused, feeling awkward in the butler's company. "His Grace would have liked to share his services with his two beloved sons," he added.

Lorry nodded brusquely. "I agree, Lord Alexander."

"I will write to my brother after I have spoken to Her Grace, and inform Peter of these two new deaths."

"I will see the letter posted as soon as you do, my lord."

The butler's tone toward him had softened considerably, and Xander said, "I know you are grief-stricken, Lorry. You and His Grace were close for so many years. It is a good thing you are with us in this tragedy. I know Her Grace will be depending upon you heavily, along with Mrs. Dylan."

"You must stay, my lord. At least until the new duke arrives. Her Grace is . . . what we might call . . . fragile. She will be in no shape to make any kind of decisions. The running of Spring Ridge will fall to you until the new Duke of Brockbank arrives."

Xander thought it ironic that the family which had, for the most part, disowned him would now need him to hold it together during this time of sorrow. Still, he did have a sense of honor, despite his reputation as one of London's leading rakes, and he knew his obligation to his family was strong.

Even though that family had never shown any interest in him or given him any love.

Once they reached the house, he left Lorry to supervise bringing in the bodies and caring for them. He knew it would take too long to make himself presentable, especially when Pamela was worried about her husband and brother-in-law. Going straight to the drawing room in his bedraggled state, he found the duchess sitting by the fire, wringing her hands.

The moment she spied him, she sprang to her feet and began weeping.

Xander went to her and, despite the fact he was soaked to the bone, enveloped her in his arms. "I am very sorry, Your Grace. Neither Rollo nor Stanley made it."

"But they were both strong swimmers," she wailed, her tears flowing freely now.

"I know," he said gently. "Part of the boat washed up on shore. I believe lightning struck it. Most likely, it knocked them unconscious."

She looked at him with watery eyes. "So, they did not suffer?"

"I doubt they ever awoke," he assured her, knowing he lied but wanting to ease her pain.

She began wailing loudly and said, "Who will tell our girls?" She looked hopefully to him.

Uneasiness gnawed at him, especially knowing he had no experience with children. Still, he was a gentleman and would do his duty.

"If you wish, I can say something to them tomorrow morning. Let them have their dinner and get a good night's sleep. Then I will handle it in the morning."

Collapsing against him, she said over and over, "Thank you, thank you, thank you."

Dread filled Xander. He had never spoken to a child before.

And now he would have to tell two little girls they would never see their father again.

CHAPTER TWO

X ANDER PUSHED AROUND the food on his plate. He usually did not eat breakfast and waited until later in the day before he ate at his club. He hadn't been able to sleep, though, and had come downstairs early. His sister-in-law was nowhere in sight.

She had become increasingly agitated after learning of her husband's and brother-in-law's deaths, and Xander had sent for the local doctor, who gave her laudanum to calm her nerves and put her to sleep. The physician said sleep would be restorative for her and said she would most likely sleep through the rest of the day and night and not awaken until today.

He had written to his brother, telling Peter of the two unexpected deaths. Lorry had confirmed that Crockle had previously written to Peter about his father's passing. Xander knew this would be an unexpected blow to Peter, learning of these two additional deaths. He wondered how Peter would take to civilian life after having been in the army close to two decades. Would he be relieved leaving the battlefield behind—or would he be resentful at losing the only life he had ever known?

Lorry had sent a messenger with Xander's letter but cautioned Xander that they weren't even certain if Peter had received the first note notifying him of his father's death. Dread had filled him, as he realized he might be stuck at Spring Ridge for months until his brother arrived. The thought of spending his time buried in the country with a grieving widow and two small children upset him. He hid his feelings, though, placing duty to his family before anything else.

And that meant going up to the nursery now and telling his nieces of their father's death.

He had learned they were six and eight years of age. He tried to think back to that time in his life and what he had understood about death. Of course, he had always lived with the fact that his birth had been the cause of his mother's death. Growing up, he sensed an empty space within himself and decided it must be because his mother was no longer at Spring Ridge to take care of all of them. While his father spent months at a time in London and usually locked away in his study when he came to the country, servants had been the ones responsible for seeing to Xander's needs. He'd had a tutor for a couple of years before he was sent away to school. He only came home during school holidays, and oftentimes he would write to Mr. Crockle for permission to go home with a friend during these times. It was always granted, and as an adult, Xander wondered if his father even knew he spent time with other families.

He'd liked Gil's family best. Gil was the oldest and only boy and had three younger sisters who worshipped him. Gil's parents, the earl and countess, were very friendly to Xander and treated him as an additional child in their fold. He still dined with them occasionally when they returned to town for the Season and had danced with each of the three sisters during their come-outs. The youngest had made her debut last Season, and all three girls were now wed. He suspected once Gil's father passed that his friend would finally give up his bachelor ways and marry.

Rising, he placed his napkin in his chair and left to go upstairs. He recalled Pamela saying that they were between governesses, and it was the nursery maid who had accompanied them to Spring Ridge to care for the girls. He supposed if Pamela couldn't manage her grief that he might actually have to hire a new governess.

Xander reached the schoolroom, where Cecily and Lucy were seated at a table with a servant, eating their breakfasts. She nodded deferentially to him and slipped from her place, leaving the room. Obviously, she knew what he was going to say. Keeping the two deaths quiet in a household would have been impossible. He was angry, though, at her leaving, thinking it the nursery maid's job to tend to her charges when they grew upset.

"It's you again," the older girl said. "Mama said you were our uncle, but we've never seen you before."

"You're not old like Papa," the younger one pointed out. "How old are you? Papa is forty. That is very old."

"I am eight and twenty," he said, pulling out a chair and sitting in it, feeling far too large to be seated at this table he had once sat at more than two decades ago.

"You don't look like Papa at all," Cecily said, studying him. "You do look like Grandpapa. He's dead, you know."

"Yes, I do know. I came to Spring Ridge to attend his funeral."

"Mama says women and children do not attend funerals," Lucy said solemnly. "Why is that? If a funeral is to say goodbye to someone, why do we have to stay here?"

"A funeral is a very somber occasion," he explained. "I think it best if you simply remember your papa the way he was when he was with you. You might be sad if you went, and he wouldn't want that, would he?"

"I don't like to be sad," Lucy said.

Exactly what he didn't need to hear.

"Where is Mama?" Cecily asked. "She usually comes to tell us goodnight and again to see us at breakfast. Is she sick?"

"In a way," he said carefully. "Your mama is very sad right now. Sometimes when you are sad, it makes you feel bad."

"She didn't like Grandpapa," Lucy said matter-of-factly. "She was afraid of him."

"Most people were," Xander agreed, surprised that the little girl was so astute. "Your grandfather—my father—was a duke. Dukes are very powerful men in England."

"I wasn't a bit scared of him," Cecily proclaimed. Then she frowned. "But I don't think I want to see him dead. We saw a dead bird once. It was lying on the ground. Our governess told us not to touch it. It made us sad to think it would never fly again."

Oh, he needed to escape.

"I have a bit of news which will make you sad," he began. "I think the best thing to do when there is sad news is to simply say it—so I will." He paused, gathering his courage. "Do you remember how hard it rained yesterday after we got to Spring Ridge?"

Both girls nodded, their round eyes studying him with interest.

"Well, your papa and Uncle Stanley decided to go sailing."

"Papa loves the water," Lucy said. "I'm afraid of it, but Cecily isn't."

Her sister nodded. "Papa has taken me out sailing before. I'd like it even better if my belly didn't go lopsided at first."

His nails dug into his palms as he said, "There was an accident. Lightning struck the sailboat."

"Did it hit Papa?" Lucy asked, her voice quavering.

"No, just the sailboat, but the force of it likely knocked your papa and uncle unconscious and from the boat." Xander swallowed. "They drowned. They will not be coming back. They will go to heaven now, as all good people do."

He hoped that would be explanation enough because he was very uncomfortable elaborating further.

Fat tears began to roll down Lucy's cheeks. She stood and came toward him. Without thinking, he scooped her up into his lap. She rested her cheek against him. She felt small and vulnerable to him, and he wished he knew how to make her feel better.

Cecily's eyes grew misty, but no tears fell. "Then Papa is not there. I suppose Uncle Stanley is because he worked in a church, and God would like that." She sighed. "But Papa was not a good man."

"Why do you say that?" he asked, curious why an eight-year-old would have formed such a harsh opinion of her father.

"Because he is not nice. He yells at everyone. The servants. Mama. Me and Lucy." She shuddered. "He doesn't really like us because we aren't boys. I heard him tell Mama that she has to give him a boy because he needs an heir." Cecily paused, looking up at him. "Why can't a girl be an heir?"

"It is the law," he said. "Only sons may inherit titles and entailed properties. Fathers do look after their girls, though. I am certain you and Lucy already have a dowry arranged."

"What's a dowry?" Lucy asked.

"Well, when you are old enough to wed, you give your husband a gift. It's called a dowry."

Lucy frowned. "But what *is* it? I've never seen a dowry, Uncle . . . what is your name again? I forgot."

"It is Alexander—but I go by Xander."

Lucy smiled up at him. "I like that. Uncle Xander."

"What is a dowry?" Cecily demanded, trying to reclaim his attention.

"It is almost always a set amount of money. Sometimes, it can even involve property."

Cecily's bottom lip thrust out in a pout as she thought over his words. "So, we must pay a man to marry us?"

"That about sums it up," he agreed.

"Then I don't think I want to get married," the girl declared.

"Me, either," Lucy chimed in.

Wonderful. Now he had a revolt on his hands.

"Most girls do marry, you know. You will make your come-outs when you are older. You will wear lots of pretty, new gowns. Go to balls and dance with handsome gentlemen. You might even fall in love with one."

"Oh, like Cinderella falls in love with the prince," Lucy said enthusiastically.

"Exactly," he confirmed.

"What if you don't fall in love?" Cecily asked worriedly.

"You can still get married," Xander insisted. "You might just like your husband and respect him. Hold him in esteem." When he saw them both frown, he added, "Admire them. Look up to them."

"Oh," Lucy said softly.

"That is far in the future, though. You will be about eighteen or so when you make your come-outs. You can think about it several years from now."

"Where will we live now?" Cecily demanded. "Mama said Papa was now a duke, and we would live at Grandpapa's house in town and come here sometimes. If Papa is dead, who is the new duke?"

"That would be your uncle Peter. I doubt you have met him because he is serving abroad in the military."

"Mama says Uncle Peter fights to make us safe," Lucy said.

"That's right. He is an officer in His Majesty's army. He and his men protect the people of England. Right now, a very bad man is fighting against our country. Uncle Peter and others are fighting against him to keep us safe."

Lucy frowned. "If Uncle Peter comes home, who will fight for us then?"

"The king has many soldiers and officers who have gone to war. But Uncle Peter is the new duke, so he must come home and be responsible for things here, such as caring for you and your sister."

"Why can't you be the duke?" Cecily asked. "You seem nice."

Xander was far from nice. He had tried to gain his father's attention by acting very badly, both at home and at school. He had been told over and over how responsible his brothers were and decided to go in the opposite direction. His rebelliousness had never gained the duke's attention, though. He continued to be the naughty boy who grew into the naughty rake, gambling and drinking and running through a host of women, not caring what anyone thought of him.

In actuality, he cared a great deal what others thought about him. He knew both men and women were attracted to him. Men wanted to be his friend and run wild with him, while women deliberately allowed him to seduce them. He was wild and moody and never followed any of Polite Society's rules. If he became the duke, he would fight tooth and nail not to be a pillar of the *ton*.

"The oldest boy in a family inherits his father's title. That is why you came here to Spring Ridge, because your papa was the oldest of the four of us and designated as the heir apparent. Since he is gone, Uncle Peter is the next oldest. He will be Duke of Brockbank now."

"I wish you could be the duke," Lucy said wistfully. "I like you, Uncle Xander."

Her words caused his throat to thicken with emotion. "That is very nice of you to say, Lucy. I like you, too. And I like Cecily."

"When will we meet Uncle Peter?" Cecily demanded.

"I have written to him regarding the situation. He is abroad, so it will take several weeks for my letter to reach him. Then he must resign from the army and sell his commission and return to England." Xander paused. "I will stay here at Spring Ridge with you until he arrives."

Lucy threw her arms about his neck. "Good."

"Can we say goodbye to Papa?" Cecily asked.

Recalling the bloated body, Xander shook his head. "No, it is best you remember him and Uncle Stanley as they were."

Standing, he set Lucy down in the chair. "I have some business to attend to. Will you be doing lessons now?"

Cecily giggled. "No. We do not have a governess."

"She left because she didn't like us," Lucy said. "None of them do."

"They like Lucy more than they do me," Cecily volunteered. "They say I am trouble."

He could certainly see that. But how much trouble could an eight-year-old girl cause?

"I will see that we find a new governess for you. One who will like both of you very much and teach you all manner of things."

Xander left the schoolroom and returned downstairs. He knew London had several employment agencies. He would write to Gil's mother and see if she could advise him on which one to use in order to engage the services of a governess.

He thought he would stop by and see how Pamela was doing. She was delicate in nature, as Lorry had mentioned, and Xander would need to keep a close eye on her. Going to the duchess' suite of rooms, he started to knock when the door flew open, and a maid ran smack into him.

"We need a doctor!" she cried, her eyes wild. "I cannot rouse Her Grace."

"Go tell Lorry immediately," he said, racing into the room.

He found Pamela in bed, looking peaceful. No one alive ever looked so tranquil, not even in sleep. Trepidation filled him. Though Xander knew she was gone, he lifted her by the shoulders and shook her forcefully, willing her to be there. For her girls.

"Wake up! Pamela, wake up now. It is Xander. I need you to open your eyes."

He paused, seeing no reaction and realizing how cold she was to the touch. Gently, he lowered her back onto the pillows.

That was when he spied a folded page on the nightstand. Trepidation filled him as he picked it up and opened it.

I cannot go on without my Rollo. Tell my girls I am sorry.

"No!" he cried, the page fluttering to the ground.

Then he spied the bottle on the nightstand and picked it up. It was empty. He opened it and sniffed. The sickly, sweet scent of laudanum filled his nostrils.

He could not believe it. Pamela had taken her own life. His thoughts rushed to the girls he had just spent time with. How could he tell them their mother was gone?

Stumbling from the room, Xander went downstairs, his head pounding.

Lorry rushed to him. "The maid told me Her Grace was unresponsive. I have sent for the doctor."

"He won't be needed," Xander said sadly. "Only another coffin will."

The butler gasped. "No!"

"Yes," he said, shaking his head.

Lorry's gaze met his. "I am loath to give this to you, my lord, but I believe it is something you must see immediately."

"What?" he asked harshly, thinking he could take no more bad news.

The butler retreated to a table near the front door and picked up a folded parchment. Bringing it to Xander, he handed it over, sadness filling his eyes.

Apprehension filled him as he turned it over and saw the seal. Cold sweat broke out along his hairline. Both he and Lorry knew what this was. Xander thought if he did not open it, it would not be true. He squeezed his eyes shut, denying the truth.

"You must open it," the butler insisted.

Opening his eyes, he broke the seal and unfolded the single page. He read it once. Twice. A third time, hoping the words would change.

What had changed was his life.

Refolding the page, he slipped it inside his coat pocket and said to Lorry, "Major-General Peter Hughes was killed in action."

Sympathy—and pity—filled the retainer's face. "I am sorry for your loss, Your Grace."

Numbness filled him, hearing the butler address him.

Xander was the last Hughes standing.

The new Duke of Brockbank.

CHAPTER THREE

London—February 1813

"**I** MUST THANK you again for allowing me to stay with you," Willa told Ralph Baldwin over breakfast.

"You are family, Willa. I would hope you would always stay with me when you come to London." He looked at her hopefully. "And if you decide to stay in town, I would be thrilled. You know this will always be your home."

She did know. Ralph had taken her in a dozen years ago after she had been orphaned. It had not surprised Willa when she'd learned there was no money to be had. While both her parents had flourishing careers, they also spent lavishly. Even as a child, she understood Ambrose and Theodosia lived beyond their means. Her father also had a soft spot for out-of-work actors, of which there were many. Willa had witnessed many occasions when he had slipped money to one, knowing the actor would never be able to pay back what was always termed a loan. And that did not even include Ambrose's many lovers, who often had received extravagant gifts.

It had not surprised her when the solicitor who handled her parents' theater contracts had told Willa that there was very little left for her. She had hoped she would at least have the house and could sell it in order to secure her future, but she learned her father had sold it several years ago and then actually rented it back from its new owner. After her parents' debts were settled, she had only a small sum.

Thank goodness Ralph had taken her in. The director had become more a friend than father figure to her, but he provided her with a good home. Actually, the entire theater family had embraced Willa after tragedy struck. She might have moved into Ralph's residence, but her true home had been the theater. Never had she felt so loved and wanted than in the three years she had remained with Ralph, working daily at the theater in several capacities. Willa had sewn costumes. Painted scenery. Scoured the markets for props. Run lines with actors and prompted them when they faltered on stage.

Yet she couldn't help but want to distance herself from that world. The only people in her acquaintance were theater ones—actors, playwrights, directors, crew members. And she wanted more. She knew life would be difficult if she left Ralph's household.

That proved to be an understatement.

Willa had contracted with the Wainwright Agency, an employment agency that specialized in positions for upper servants. Butlers and housekeepers. Governesses. Companions. She had set out on her own at eight and ten years of age, wanting to support herself and put her education and talents to use anywhere but the theater. Her first job had been one of companion to a marchioness and had lasted just over six years, with all that time being spent in the country. After living in London her entire life, Willa came to cherish the peace and tranquility of country life.

After the marchioness' death, Mr. Wainwright had thought her ready for the ranks of his governesses. She believed being a governess would be a much better use of her knowledge, imparting it to young pupils. While she did enjoy teaching, she had a rough go as she tried to avoid her employer. Lord Dearling had made it clear from the start that he found Willa quite attractive and was forever trying to get her alone. She had spent eight months in his household, doing her best to avoid him. When he finally cornered her one night, she had first told him she had no intention of being seduced by him and would tell Lady Dearling if he tried anything.

He had laughed in her face—and backed her into a corner.

She had screamed as he put his hands on her, his mouth covering hers, his tongue forcing its way into her mouth. As she struggled, Lady Dearling had entered the room, taking a vase and smashing it over her husband's head.

Willa had thanked the countess, only to be told by Lady Dearling that her services would no longer be required and that no reference would be issued. Willa was told to pack immediately. She did not even get a chance to tell her charges goodbye. Instead, she was driven in a cart to the nearby village and given money by the coachman, who told her Lady Dearling wanted her on the next mail coach to London. Humiliated, she returned to town and the Wainwright Agency, where Mr. Wainwright had excused Lord Dearling's behavior, telling Willa that these things happened, especially when a governess was as pretty as she was.

The employment agency owner next sent her to Cornwall and Lord Appleton, a viscount with two children. He was a widower and wed soon after Willa arrived, sending relief through her. All was well for a year. Until Lady Appleton got with child. Suddenly, Lord Appleton was visiting the schoolroom regularly and calling Willa to his study for reports on his children's progress. During their last encounter, he had locked the door to his study without her realizing he did so.

Then it was the same story, with a second verse the same as the first. Lord Appleton tried to seduce her. When Willa fought back, he slapped her hard and shoved her against the door, pressing his body to hers. Revulsion filled her as he pawed at her, squeezing her breast and raising the hem of her skirt so he might slip his hand against her leg.

She was having none of it and kneed him hard in the balls. It was something Ralph Baldwin had told her to do if she found herself in dire circumstances. The look on Lord Appleton's face was priceless as he gasped and then wheezed. Willa knocked him back, and he fell on the floor. She had towered over him, telling him how shameful it was that he behaved in such a manner, especially with the kind wife who carried his child in the same house.

Telling him she was going to pack, she also said she expected him to write a glowing reference and have it finished by the time she returned downstairs. If he didn't, she would tell both his wife and children what a monster he was.

She didn't ask how the viscount had gotten himself into his chair and managed to write the reference. Willa merely read it and encouraged him to sign it, or she would kick him in the bollocks again. Never had a man scribbled his name so quickly on a document and once again, she left without telling her pupils goodbye, returning to Mr. Wainwright.

The man agreed with her that it would be best if she went back to being a lady's companion and sent her to Dover and Lady Berry, a querulous woman who berated Willa day and night for imagined misdeeds. Lady Berry accused Willa of stealing her jewelry. Selling her silver. Hiding her favorite books. Spitting into her teacup. Thankfully, the dowager countess died in her sleep only a month after Willa's arrival. Her son came to the dower house after his mother's death, apologizing to Willa for not having visited, but saying that his mother had been vindictive her entire life, and he could not abide to be around her.

He did give Willa a generous amount far beyond her usual compensation, saying he knew she had earned it. The son also wrote a decent reference and even sent her back to London in his own carriage.

Fortunately, Ralph had once more taken her in. The director had a soft spot for Willa.

"Do you have an appointment with Mr. Wainwright anytime

soon?"

His question startled her from her reverie. "Yes, I do. This after-noon."

He sighed. "I know I have asked you this before, Willa, but would you consider making your debut on stage? You have the right looks and the ability to memorize lines quickly. You were practically raised in the theater. Surely, it would be like coming home to you."

Actually, she had considered it. Ralph—and others—had pressed her many times to take to the stage. Yet a part of her rebelled against the notion. She knew what most people thought of actresses. That they were glorified whores prancing about the stage. After her chaotic upbringing, Willa had a need for calm.

She also had a secret desire for children. If she were to have any, she would need to find a husband—and no husband worth his salt would wed a woman who had walked the boards for a living. Her wish for a normal, pedestrian life had begun to consume her. She hoped one day, whether serving as a governess or companion, she might meet someone who would give her companionship within a marriage. An estate steward. A minister at the local church. Even a shopkeeper in the nearby village. With every position she accepted, Willa yearned that she would meet a man who might see her worth and offer to marry her.

That would not be possible if she took the stage.

"No, Ralph. You know that is not what I want. I am not interested in that kind of life. Yes, while the Season is going on, I could come here every night. Once it ends, though, I would have to join a travelling troupe in order to make a living. I do not wish for a nomadic way of life. In truth, I have found the country to be my taste."

"You might not need to do so, Willa," Ralph said. "Your mother commanded the highest salary of any actress during her day. It was why she was able to keep you here in London year-round."

"But she also had Papa's income as a playwright. He wrote night and day."

When he wasn't carrying on with actresses half his age . . .

"You wouldn't need to leave here," Ralph protested. "I stay in town year-round. You would have a roof over your head and food on your plate. You could pick and choose the roles you wished to play."

Willa shook her head sadly. "I am sorry, Ralph. I simply do not wish to act."

He scowled at her. "So, you think it better to go from household to household, letting men paw at you and old women scream at you? Even if you did find a place you enjoyed, as you did in your first position, the job will always end, Willa. You will keep returning to the Wainwright Agency again and again. Do you wish to grow old alone? Here, you would have your theater family surrounding you."

She swallowed the painful lump in her throat. "I know I am disappointing you, Ralph, but the stage is not for me. I want nothing of the theatrics involved, on or off it. I want to be able to provide for myself and be beholden to no one."

His face softened. "I don't mean to push you, Willa. I merely see so much potential in you. I hate that it is being wasted, you being buried in the country with peevish old women and annoying, spoiled brats." Ralph paused. "Stay as long as you wish. I must leave now for the theater."

"I will go with you," she volunteered.

He cocked a brow. "Truly?"

"Yes. My appointment with Mr. Wainwright is not until early afternoon. I would enjoy visiting with old friends and seeing what production you will start the Season with."

"We will be alternating nights for the first month. A Restoration comedy, along with *A Midsummer Night's Dream.* Shakespeare's comedies are always popular."

"Which Restoration?" she asked, it being among her favorites to see performed.

"John Vanbrugh's *The Provoked Wife*."

Willa chuckled. "Perfect fare for the *ton*. A woman who weds for money and a husband wanting sex. Secret trysts. Spying on others." She thought a moment. "The role of Lady Brute calls for not just a comedic actress, but one who can garner sympathy from the audience as she drops clever ripostes. Who will play Lady Brute?"

Ralph's gaze dropped to his now-empty plate. "It did take some thought in casting the perfect actress for the role."

Immediately, Willa knew who had landed the part. "Jemima James."

He nodded. "If you don't wish to accompany me, I will understand."

She had not seen Jemima since the day Theodosia shot and killed Ambrose, the bullet going through her husband and striking Jemima. Willa had the forethought to send Jemima back to her boardinghouse and a physician to her. She heard Jemima had left London. Ralph later told Willa that Jemima turned up in Bath, acting there and in a few other cities throughout England.

"How long has she been back?" she asked, a blanket of sadness settling over her.

Ralph thought a moment. "I would say a good five years or so. I never mentioned it to you because . . . well, you were in town for so short a time. She has honed her craft, though. I believe she has become the top actress of her generation." He paused. "You could be, as well, Willa."

"No. I will never set foot on a stage."

She was not her mother. She was Willa Fennimore. A woman who wanted much more than Theodosia ever did. All her mother wished for was acclaim from the masses. She lived for the applause. The curtain calls. The flower arrangements flooding her dressing room. She hadn't cared for her only child. She had abused her husband, arguing with him constantly, yet needing him as much as the air she breathed.

Willa told herself she wanted more. Deserved more. Would find more.

"Do you still wish to go with me today, knowing Jemima will be there?"

"No. I hold no grudge against her, but I am not ready to see her yet. She would want to talk about it. I recall she was a great talker. I prefer to remain silent on the subject of my parents' deaths."

Ralph took her hand. "You saved Jemima's life, you know. Not just the physician you sent to her, but also getting her to leave the scene. If she had been discovered there, she would have been embroiled in controversy. She never would have been able to take the stage again. Worse, she might have swung from the gibbet if the courts believed she pushed Theodosia from that window."

"It was an accident," she said softly. "I have always known that. I saw no point in Jemima losing everything." Sighing deeply, she added, "Tell her hello for me, if you would, Ralph. And wish her well for opening night."

He squeezed her hand. "Jemima will be touched. I will do so. Will I see you later?"

"Of course. We can dine together tonight. Hopefully, I will be able to report to you of the new position Mr. Wainwright has found for me."

"Or not," Ralph teased. "If it takes a few weeks—or longer—for him to find you something, I will selfishly have you to myself until then."

He departed and Willa decided to make good use of her time in London. She visited a dressmaker Theodosia had used and found a few gowns already made that fit her with no adjustments needed. She asked that they be delivered to Ralph's. Willa also bought a new pair of boots on the chance she would once more be sent to the country-side. Her current boots had seen better days. She also purchased a few minor things, including two books at her favorite bookstore.

Then it was time to make her way to the Wainwright Agency. The clerk greeted her and took her packages, saying he would keep them safe while she spoke with Mr. Wainwright.

Going to the door, she put a bright smile on her face before knocking and entering and then chuckled to herself, knowing she did a little acting even now.

Wainwright sat at his desk and motioned for Willa to close the door behind her. He was always fastidiously dressed, and she noticed the gray at his temples now ran throughout his hair.

"Have a seat, Miss Fennimore."

She did so, opening her reticule and producing the letter of recommendation from her last post.

"This is from my employer's son. Lady Berry was much too ill to write one herself. I suppose her son was paying for my salary so it would be appropriate for him to write my reference."

She handed it over, and Wainwright took it, reading it to himself. He cleared his throat. "I am a bit frustrated with you, Miss Fennimore."

"Why is that?" she asked, perplexed by his statement.

"You have been a governess to two different families in the last eighteen months or so. Then you only spent a month as companion to Lady Berry."

Her temper rose, but she kept her voice calm. "I cannot help the fact that your client was in poor health when I was asked to be her companion. I have no control over how long someone lives, Mr. Wainwright. As for the two governessing jobs, those—"

"It will keep happening, I am afraid," he said crisply. "You are far too attractive to be a governess. Far too tempting."

Willa no longer wished to disguise her anger. "You are blaming *me* for the roaming eyes of the gentlemen I went to work for? I should blame *you* for placing me in their households, sir. It is demanding enough to hold the position of either governess or companion, but it is quite intolerable to have to deal with men who force themselves upon me. I cannot help what I look like, and I do not see it as a reason—much less an excuse—to be treated so shabbily by you."

"Now, see here, Miss Fennimore. You cannot go blaming Lord Dearling or Lord Appleton for—"

"But I am blaming them, Mr. Wainwright. They were bent on breaking their marriage vows. If they wished to take a lover or mistress, that was their choice, and they should have selected a woman willing to go along with the idea. I will never lower myself and willingly participate in an affair. Now, you either find a position for me where I will be treated with respect, or I will find another agency."

She shot to her feet. "You may contact me at Mr. Baldwin's if something suitable comes up."

He, too, pushed to his feet. "It may be time for us to part ways, Miss Fennimore."

Willa snorted. "I am an exemplary employee, sir, but I will not be treated this way. Please do not bother to send me word of a prospective position. I wish to have nothing to do with you or your employment agency."

She had only taken two steps when the door burst open and the most handsome man she had ever seen dashed into the room. His clothes were slightly askew, and he smelled of sweat and horse, as if he had literally ridden a long way and come directly here.

"I need a governess. Right away!" he declared. Pausing, he looked her up and down. "You will do."

CHAPTER FOUR

H IS LIFE WAS a nightmare.
All because of two little girls . . .

Actually, Xander had enjoyed the life he was now living, as least for the most part. The past several weeks had been busy ones. First, he had seen to the burial of his father and two brothers, along with Pamela. He had contacted the bishop, who had sent a substitute clergyman to perform the funeral services. The living at Sherfield was still open, but the visiting clergyman was holding regular services on Sundays, and Xander thought his sermons quite good. Not that he had much experience in hearing any. Frankly, he hadn't set foot in a church in years. As the new Duke of Brockbank, though, he thought it important to be seen at the parish's services and so had attended a few times, being the last to arrive and the first to leave, not wanting to get caught up in any conversations with the parishioners.

Unfortunately, the clergyman had retired a few years ago and was not interested in the position on a permanent basis, admitting to Xander that he enjoyed retirement and the freedoms it brought. The man of God did not mind helping out for a short while, though, and one of Xander's top priorities was to see the living filled as quickly as possible.

It had been a decade since he had left Spring Ridge, and it felt good to be home again. Left on his own much of the time as a child, he had explored the land and knew every nook and cranny of it. That came in handy now as he went out and about on the estate, accompanied by his steward, meeting his tenants and listening to their concerns. Mr. Key, who had been the steward at Spring Ridge the past seven years, was an agreeable sort and knowledgeable about all estate affairs. He gave Xander access to all the ledgers, and Xander had gone through them with a fine-toothed comb, studying the last five years closely, looking for any anomalies or patterns. He saw which crops performed best and the amount of livestock bred and sold. Mathematics had always been one of his strong suits, and so interpreting the figures within the ledgers proved quite easy.

He had enjoyed school in general, being one of the top students each year. One tutor had called him naturally gifted academically and yet immensely lazy because Xander could earn top marks in most every subject without expending much effort. He was glad now, though, that maths had been an area he excelled in because he could see he would use it quite a bit now that he was the duke. He knew he had other estates he needed to visit and attend to at some point. For now, though, he wished to concentrate on Spring Ridge since it was his ducal seat—and the home of his two nieces.

With Rollo and Pamela's quick, unexpected deaths, which had left Xander as the guardian for Cecily and Lucy, came his current problems. He recalled his first meeting with the girls in the schoolroom and the fond feelings which he had experienced for them. Those had quickly gone by the wayside.

He had done as intended and written to Gil's mother, inquiring about a good employment agency where he could engage the services of a top governess. The countess had actually had a candidate in mind for Xander, writing to him of a young, impoverished local girl from the gentry who would make for an excellent governess. Xander agreed and arrangements were made to bring the young lady to Spring Ridge.

He should have known from the beginning that things would be a disaster. Something about the gleam in Cecily's eyes when they met the carriage bearing the governess didn't sit well with him. The young woman had been timid but articulate, as Xander had taken her into his study and interviewed her upon her arrival, making certain she was up to snuff. She seemed proficient in French and history, though she was a little shaky in mathematics. He had decided he would take on that portion of the girls' education and leave the rest, including reading and writing, to the new governess.

She had lasted all of two weeks.

Coming to Xander in tears, the governess explained how frustrated she was with her charges, revealing the girls would not listen to a word she said and refused to do the lessons she set for them. She further shared that she had never known little girls could be such horrible devils and then wished him well in finding someone who might tame the little heathens.

Xander had been shocked by her words, having spent a portion of each day with his nieces, who were delightful in his company. When he met with Cecily and Lucy and shared what the governess had told him, they both appeared round-eyed and claimed that they were totally innocent of any wrongdoing. He had decided it was the young woman's fault. The girl had been too young and lacking in experience to have taken on two pupils, especially ones freshly grieving their parents. He had decided to find someone with a great deal of experience, hoping a more mature governess could better understand Cecily and Lucy and meet with success.

The next time, he went through Mr. Crockle, who recommended two employment agencies to him. Xander went with the first one the solicitor mentioned, since Crockle said it was the best known in London, and wrote to it regarding his specifications, asking the agency to select a proper candidate to be sent to Spring Ridge at once.

The second governess proved to be just as inept as the first although she was in her forties and told Xander she had been governessing over two decades. She'd told him that she had a firm hand and all her previous charges had adored her.

Apparently, neither Cecily nor Lucy Hughes felt the same as previous pupils.

The woman had lasted a month and when she left, gave Xander such a piece of her mind that he had to stop and remind her that she was berating a duke of the realm. Realizing her error, she apologized profusely and asked that he not send in any reference letter to her agency, not wanting this short assignment to reflect poorly upon her stellar record of employment. Xander agreed to do so and found himself back at square one after the woman had left him with a lengthy list of all the crimes his nieces had committed. To say he was appalled at their atrocious behavior was minimizing the situation.

He had known when they came to Spring Ridge for the duke's funeral that the girls were without a governess. He had not bothered to ask Pamela why, the matter not being of interest to him. Now, he wondered if this were a regular thing. He recalled how Cecily said no governesses ever seemed to like them, her, in particular. He had talked with the girls at length about their behavior and how important it was for them to be respectful to their governess. Xander told them he would try one more time to find them an appropriate governess—and warned them that if they chased a third one off, he would be forced to send them away to school.

Frankly, he did not even know if girls went off to school, not having had any sisters. Cecily was eight. Most boys went off to school at age seven or eight. Lucy, however, was only six. He doubted any school would take a pupil so young. Perhaps it might be best to separate the girls. If Cecily were the poor influence, it might be best for her to go away and learn some discipline. At six, Lucy's character had not been formed as much as that of her sister's. Yet when he mentioned this idea, both girls had wept profusely, and he had been forced to promise that he would not separate them, feeling guilty about even thinking of doing so. After all, they had lost both of their parents less than two months ago. They were still grieving. He supposed acting out against authority was one way they were dealing with their grief.

That meant he needed a governess.

Immediately.

He had ridden to London, changing horses once, going straight to Crockle's office. The solicitor had been surprised to see him but ended an appointment early with the client he visited with to spend time with Xander. He supposed it was one of the advantages of being a duke, that others danced to the tune he set.

Mr. Crockle had been disappointed that the agency he recommended had not sent a suitable candidate. Then he admitted to Xander that this very same agency had sent four previous governesses to Rollo's household. All had failed in forming any kind of relationship with Cecily and Lucy. It seemed the girls were so poorly behaved and unwilling to stick to their lessons that they had barely learned to read or write. Crockle apologized and said perhaps Xander might want to try the Wainwright Agency next, having heard of their sterling reputation.

Xander learned of its location and went there immediately, refraining from stopping by the first employment agency and giving them a piece of his mind for doing such an abysmal job in providing his family with a decent governess.

When he told the clerk who he was and that he wished to see Mr. Wainwright at once, the man had babbled incoherently. Fed up, Xander took matters into his own hands. He strode down a corridor, finding a few empty rooms, and then spied a closed door at its end. He did not care if he interrupted or not. He was desperate. And a duke.

He would not leave here until he got what he needed.

Throwing open the door, he stopped in his tracks so that he would not crash into a woman who was standing and looked as if she were making her way to the door. He glanced at her quickly and said, "I need a governess. Right away! You will do."

The man behind the desk, most likely Mr. Wainwright, asked, "Who are you?"

He turned. "I am the Duke of Brockbank. I am in need of a governess."

Flustered, the man said, "I am Mr. Wainwright, Your Grace, and this woman is no longer represented by my agency. I do have a few candidates in mind and would be happy to allow you to meet them and interview them if you choose."

"I don't have time for that," he said harshly. "I need someone *now*."

Pivoting toward the woman, his first thought was that she was far too beautiful to be a governess. Still, she was here in front of him.

"Are you available?" he asked her.

"I am, Your Grace," she replied, her voice low and measured. "My name is Miss Fennimore."

"Do you have experience with children?" he barked at her.

"I have held two positions as a lady's companion and another two as a governess. I speak French, Italian, and Spanish fluently. I also have a smattering of German. I play the pianoforte. I am knowledgeable in history and science. My charges have thrived with both their reading and writing under my care."

Relief swept through Xander. "You are hired, Miss Fennimore."

"No," protested Wainwright.

Miss Fennimore said, "Mr. Wainwright is upset because I am no longer with his employment agency. That means he is missing out on the fat fee which you would have paid him for him supplying you with a governess. If you would prefer to hire your governess from his ranks, I do understand. Before I accept the position, however, may I know something of the children I will be teaching?"

"I came here today because another agency has failed to provide an adequate governess for my nieces. You seem to have a bit of good sense about you, Miss Fennimore. Perhaps we could leave and discuss my nieces and their needs."

"I would delighted to accompany you, Your Grace." Miss Fennimore looked to her former employer. "Good day to you, Mr. Wainwright."

Wainwright slammed his hand down upon the desk. "You cannot do this!" he declared.

Miss Fennimore smiled sweetly and said, "Just watch us do so, sir." She turned back to Xander. "Shall we?"

The governess sailed out of the office, and Xander quickly followed her. They did not speak until they left the agency's building. He realized he only had his hired horse and no way to take her anywhere—or any idea where *to* take her to discuss Lucy and Cecily.

She seemed to understand his dilemma, a point in her favor for being so astute, and said, "I am a great one for walking, Your Grace. If you would like to walk and talk over the situation, it would be agreeable to me."

"Very well, Miss Fennimore. Give me one moment."

He went to the boy he'd paid to watch his horse. "I will be gone for a while, but you are to remain on duty." He pulled a coin from his pocket and gave it to the lad. "There will be another one for you if you stay at your station."

"Yes, my lord," the boy said, pocketing the coin.

Xander rejoined Miss Fennimore, and they set off. He couldn't remember the last time—if there had ever been a time—that he had strolled down a London street with a woman.

He rarely spent time in the company of women, only his mistresses. He had ended his last affair mere days before Rollo had contacted him regarding traveling to Spring Ridge for their father's funeral. The only other time Xander was around females was at some *ton* event. So to be strolling along the pavement with an extremely attractive woman was new to him.

Xander liked the fact that Miss Fennimore was decisive. If anything, the girls would need a firm hand. Of course, the last governess claimed she had one and that had been nothing short of a calamity.

With Miss Fennimore being a servant, albeit an upper one, he did not offer his arm to her. It seemed a bit churlish not to do so, but he continued moving along the pavement beside her.

"So, tell me about my new pupils. That is, *if* I accept the position you are offering."

He saw a teasing light in her eyes and found that incredibly attractive. He loved nothing better than a sense of humor. Coming from a woman of her looks was most surprising.

"They are my nieces. Cecily is eight years of age and the older. Her sister, Lucy, is six, and follows her sister's lead in everything." He hesitated.

"What is it, Your Grace? Do they have some kind of infirmity?"

"A sadness of the heart," he admitted. "We all had gone to Spring Ridge, my father's ducal seat, in early January. We were there for his funeral. The girls' father had inherited the dukedom and he, along with my brother, who held the living nearby, went for an afternoon sail the day before the funeral. Unfortunately, the weather turned quite foul and violent. They both drowned."

Sympathy filled her eyes. "How very awful for those girls, as well as you. No wonder they are so sad, losing their father and uncle, along with their grandfather. It must be both hurtful and confusing to them."

He swallowed. "I am afraid it is much worse than that, Miss Fennimore. My sister-in-law, the duchess, was emotionally fragile. The death of her husband proved to be too much for her."

The governess drew in a quick breath. "What did she do?"

"She drank an entire bottle of laudanum, which the doctor had brought to calm her nerves. It seems she did not want to continue living without my brother by her side."

Miss Fennimore stopped and placed a hand on his forearm. A quick rush of emotion poured through Xander.

"This is very tragic, Your Grace. I would like to accept this position as governess to Lady Cecily and Lady Lucy. I will do my utmost to do more than teach these girls. I hope to comfort them and help them learn to stand strong."

She removed her hand from his sleeve, and he realized that he had held his breath the entire time she'd touched him.

"I must be candid with you, Miss Fennimore. The girls are acting out terribly since their parents' unexpected deaths. In the last six weeks, since I have been Duke of Brockbank, I have hired two governesses. Neither proved they were up to the task of educating and caring for these girls. In fact, they totally disliked my nieces and resigned their positions, in large part based upon the poor behavior they witnessed. I am afraid if you do come to Spring Ridge that you will have quite the challenge ahead of you."

Their gazes met, and he was lost in her mesmerizing, amethyst eyes.

"I, too, had a chaotic childhood and can sympathize better than most with your nieces. I also lost my parents quite unexpectedly. I have known loss and tragedy, Your Grace. I believe I am qualified to not only teach your nieces, but I can help them work through their problems."

Her words surprised him. "Then it seems you would be the ideal person for this position, Miss Fennimore."

"We must come to terms, Your Grace."

"Terms?" he asked.

"Yes."

He realized she meant her salary. "I am willing to compensate you generously, Miss Fennimore. Frankly, I have no idea what the going rate for a governess of two needy girls might be, however. Perhaps you could give me an idea what you might earn in my employ."

She smiled at him, and he was entranced by it, telling himself he would need to act the proper gentleman with her. He needed a capable governess for his nieces and would do nothing to alienate this competent woman.

"Then let me outline for you what I require, Your Grace."

Miss Fennimore detailed the salary she would require, which would be paid quarterly. She also asked to have off every other Wednesday afternoon from two until five, as well as one Sunday a month, the choice being left up to her as to which Sunday she would select.

"Anything else you might require?" he asked, thinking her quite shrewd. She probably was asking more of him than she had received from previous employers, but he was willing to pay any price at the moment, as long as she cared for the two little girls.

"I expect you to be a gentleman in every action you take and that I be afforded the courtesy and respect due to me as your nieces' governess."

Xander supposed Miss Fennimore wished for him to be a good example for Cecily and Lucy. He could easily agree to that. His conduct would be impeccable in his nieces' presence.

"I accept your terms, Miss Fennimore. The most pressing question I have is, when might you be able to start?"

"Immediately."

CHAPTER FIVE

X ANDER MADE ARRANGEMENTS to pick up Miss Fennimore in two hours' time, obtaining the address where she was staying. She mentioned that it was the home of the man who had become her guardian after her parents' deaths. It was quite close to the theater district. He knew so because so many actors and actresses lived in the area because of its close proximity to many of the well-known theaters. He had spent many an afternoon or late evening with various mistresses in that area and so it was well-known to him. He worried for a moment that the new governess might have some connection to the theater world and then shrugged it off. She seemed intelligent and pleasant enough and spoke as a lady should. Especially with her having lost her own parents as a child, she would sympathize more with Cecily and Lucy. Xander hoped that bond would make a difference and Miss Fennimore would be successful in taming—and teaching— his wild, willful nieces.

He reclaimed his rented horse from the boy who held it and rode it to the rooms he shared with Gil. He had written his friend to let Gil know how his status had changed and that Gil had sole access to their rooms. Xander hoped to see his friend now as he entered the building and headed up the staircase.

Fortunately, his old friend was home and greeted him warmly.

"You are looking rather ducal, Brockbank," Gil teased, addressing

Xander for the first time with his new title.

He couldn't help but wonder if Gil would ever call him by his Christian name again and doubted it. "I still feel like an imposter," he admitted.

"Have you returned to town for the Season? I know it doesn't start for another month or so, but you are not one to bury yourself in the country."

"True," he said quietly, thinking of the time he had spent there these past few weeks and suddenly becoming upset. He had been doing for everyone *but* himself. "Lots of responsibilities and things to learn about my new position."

"Have you come for your clothes? I thought you might have sent a servant by now to take them to the Brockbank townhouse."

In truth, Xander hadn't given the Season a thought. He had been so wrapped up in learning about the estate and settling into his duties there. Now, though, a bit of resentment began to fill him. He was a duke. He had a quite capable steward to manage things for him at Spring Ridge. He had now engaged the services of a new governess. He would wait a couple of weeks and see how Miss Fennimore fared and then make his way back to town for the Season—and beyond. Just because he was a duke did not mean he would give up his bachelor ways. He had spent a lifetime breaking Polite Society's rules and had no intention of settling down and becoming a staid duke. Let others run Spring Ridge and care for nieces he barely knew. He would live his life as *he* saw fit and not bend to the will of others.

"I will send someone for my wardrobe, Gil, and have it sent to my townhouse. I am only in town for the day and about to leave to accompany a new governess to Spring Ridge. I should return in plenty of time for the Season, however."

His friend nodded and said, "I suppose you will need to look for a duchess now. I am about ready to search for a wife myself."

The thought of marriage was distasteful. "No, I have no intention of wedding this Season. Or for many to come," he said flatly. "Yes, I will need an heir at some point, but I do not plan to find a wife for at least a decade. I have too many wild oats still left to sow."

"I see," Gil said thoughtfully.

Xander thought Gil wanted to say more to him but kept silent.

"I simply came by to put on fresh clothes before I return to Spring Ridge. I rode on horseback to town but must accompany the governess."

"That means you'll need to rent a post chaise," Gil said.

"I plan to do so. I must return the horse, though, which I changed out halfway here. I can do so at a local stable, and they will see it returned for me."

"Let me do that for you," his friend volunteered. "I don't mind making myself a bit useful to a duke," he joked. "I also would not mind an invitation to Spring Ridge. I wish to see where my good friend will be spending a majority of his time in the future."

Xander stiffened. "Why, I will continue to remain in town for most of the year. That will not change."

Gil gave him a knowing look. "You say that now, Xander, but you have far too many duties to do so. I will wager you have not even had a chance to visit your other estates."

"It is something I know I need to do," he agreed. "For now, however, I will make certain Spring Ridge is running seamlessly and then return for the Season. I can always visit the other properties in the next year or two."

"Before you leave, Xan, I do want to express my sympathies to you for the loss of so many in your family."

He had written his friend regarding the circumstances of all four deaths and begged Gil not to mention Pamela's suicide to anyone. He had put out the story at home that she had accompanied her husband and brother-in-law and that all three had been drowned during the storm. That way, he had been able to bury Pamela in the church graveyard next to her husband. Neither the local doctor nor his physician challenged him. It was the first instance of seeing the power of a duke in action, rewriting events to protect his family's name and reputation.

Xander had not bothered to send a death notice to the London newspapers of Rollo's death, knowing his appearance as the Duke of Brockbank would set tongues wagging as it were. He would merely reference the boating accident and lump Pamela in with his two brothers. The bulk of the gossip would focus on wild Xander Hughes now being a duke, and he did not mind taking it on, hoping no one would discover the true circumstances of Pamela's death.

"I am handling it," he said tersely. "It is not as if I were close to any of them."

"How about your nieces? Cecily and . . . what is the other girl's name?"

"Lucy. I will admit that becoming their guardian has been by far my greatest challenge. They are delightful young girls, and I have actually enjoyed being in their company. Outside my sight, however, the girls are holy terrors and plague their governess and my staff to great distraction."

"Angels turning into demons," Gil mused. "Well, if anyone can tame a wayward female, it is you, Xander. You charm everyone you meet."

"I hope the new governess I hired today will make a difference. She, too, lost her parents, and I believe that will help her form a bond with Lucy and Cecily." He brightened. "Besides, they will spend their time at Spring Ridge. I have no plans to bring them from the country to town."

He had never been brought to London as a child and knew none of his three brothers had, either. Children of the *ton* were to be rarely seen in Polite Society. If Miss Fennimore was as good as he believed, he would not have much to do at all with the girls until they made their come-outs years down the line. With Cecily being eight, she would make her debut in a decade. Perhaps he should consider marrying a year or two before that so that Cecily would have guidance from his wife as she made her come-out to Polite Society.

Still, the thought of marriage was something new and foreign to him. He had doubted he would ever speak vows with a woman, not having the income to establish a household and properly care for a wife and children. With his circumstances changing now, it would be necessary to wed in order to provide an heir.

Tigers did not change their stripes, though, and once he had that heir, Xander planned to go back to keeping a mistress. His would be a marriage of convenience, with the right woman who possessed the appropriate social connections. Since he was now a wealthy duke, he could even afford to buy his mistress a house of her own. That would be far more convenient and discreet.

"I am off to change," he told his friend.

"Remember, if you get lonely during the next few weeks, send for me. I would be happy to keep you company and see Spring Ridge."

He clapped his old friend on the back. "I will keep that in mind."

As he started toward his bedchamber, Gil said, "Give me the address so I can see your horse returned to the proper stables. I shall do that now."

"Let me show you what he looks like. I paid a boy to watch him."

They went to the window, and he pointed out to Gil which horse was his.

Stripping off his clothes in his bedchamber, he went to Gil's bedchamber, returning with a pitcher of water which he poured into a basin. He washed and then dressed in fresh clothes, leaving his dusty ones on the floor for servants to deal with.

He then took a hansom cab to his father's residence, having obtained the address from Crockle earlier today. Asking the driver to wait, Xander went and knocked upon the door.

A footman answered his knock. "Good afternoon, my lord. How might I help you?"

He saw the black band of mourning on the footman's arm and said, "I need to see the butler. Whoever he is. I am the Duke of Brockbank."

The servant's eyes widened. "Of course, Your Grace. Please, come inside. I'll fetch Mr. Sewell."

The footman hurried off, leaving Xander standing in the immense foyer. He glanced around, taking in the paintings and looking up at the grand chandelier hanging above him.

This would now be his home.

A lean, dignified-looking man with gray at his temples appeared and bowed before Xander. "Your Grace, I am Sewell, your butler. My condolences to you. Is your carriage outside? I must see that your luggage is brought in."

"No, Sewell, I was merely in town for the day on business with my solicitor. I am returning to Spring Ridge within the hour. I have no time for a tour of the townhouse, but I would ask that a footman be sent to the rooms I formerly shared with Viscount Swanson. See that my things are packed up and returned here if you would."

"Of course, Your Grace," Sewell said deferentially. "Might I inquire as to your plans for this Season?"

"I will be returning to town for the Season. In fact, I will most likely spend a majority of my year in town. I prefer it to the country."

"I understand, Your Grace. We will be prepared for your return."

Xander gave Sewell Gil's address and then took his leave, returning to his hansom cab. He directed the coachman to take him to a place where he might rent a post chaise. He entered the offices and a clerk looked up, flashing a helpful smile.

"What might I do for you today, my lord?"

"It is Your Grace—and I am in immediate need of a post chaise to return me to southern Kent."

"Now?" the clerk squeaked.

Xander met the clerk's gaze. "Now," he commanded.

"I will see to it at once, Your Grace." The clerk scrambled to his feet and disappeared.

He watched as the clerk and two other men hurried to and fro from the office, going outside and returning a few times. The clerk entered the building again and vanished down a hallway, returning with a gentleman in his mid-forties.

"Good afternoon, Your Grace. I have been informed that you are in immediate need of a post chaise to take you to Kent. The horses are being harnessed as we speak and one of my best drivers will be your coachman."

The man hesitated and then added, "May I inquire as to your title, Your Grace?"

"I am the Duke of Brockbank. Send your bill to a Mr. Crockle." Xander provided his solicitor's address.

"Thank you, Your Grace. Let me walk you to your vehicle and introduce you to your driver."

They went outside, and he met the coachman, a burly man with a gap-toothed smile.

"I hear we're off to Kent, Your Grace. Can you give me a bit more direction as to your destination?"

Xander did so, naming a few of the towns they would pass through on their way to Spring Ridge.

"I am familiar with the direction you wish us to go, Your Grace," the driver said.

"We are making one stop in the city before we leave," he said. "I have hired a governess for my two nieces. She will accompany me this afternoon."

Xander gave the driver the address Miss Fennimore had provided. He saw the coachman's brows shoot up.

"That's in the theater district, Your Grace."

"I know," he snapped, not needed a driver's opinion on anything.

Getting into the post chaise, he slammed the door and settled against the cushions. The vehicle took off. He began questioning himself once more, wondering about Miss Fennimore's background. He had tried to put off thinking about the governess, but her image now danced before him. She was a remarkably beautiful woman, and he told himself though he was a rake, he was not the sort of man who would seduce his help.

It might be what chased him back to town early, avoiding temptation.

Traffic was light for this time of day, and they reached the address quickly. Xander exited the post chaise and told the driver, "I will go inside and retrieve Miss Fennimore. She will have a trunk of her belongings most likely. See where you wish to store it."

He moved to the door and knocked. The door opened, and Xander saw it was not a footman who answered it, but a man he recognized.

"Ralph Baldwin," he said, tamping down his surprise.

"*You?*"

He frequented the theater, especially the one owned by this man. Xander's last mistress had earned the starring role in the final production last summer at Baldwin's theater. He had spoken to the director on a few occasions and even attended several parties Baldwin also came to, finding the man likeable.

"Hello, Mr. Baldwin. I am here to retrieve Miss Fennimore."

The director shook his head violently. "You will do no such thing! You cannot be the Duke of Brockbank. You are, what? A fourth . . . or fifth son? I read of your father's passing in the newspapers, but you simply cannot be Brockbank."

Xander almost regretted now not having sent a death notice to the London newspapers regarding the deaths of his brothers and sister-in-law.

"I assure you that I am now Brockbank. I am a fourth son and did have three brothers in line before me. One, a major-general, was recently killed in battle. The new duke and my third brother drowned in a recent boating accident. That is how I came to be Brockbank and named guardian for my two nieces. I am here to collect Miss Fennimore, who has promised to come to Spring Ridge as their new governess. Where is she?"

Baldwin's eyes narrowed. "If you believe I will let Willa go off with a rake such as you, you are sadly mistaken, Your Grace."

"What's this?" a female voice demanded, and both men turned.

Miss Fennimore stood there, arms akimbo. "You do not speak for me, Ralph," she corrected sternly. "There are two little girls who need me. I have already accepted the post His Grace offered to me."

"Had I known the guardian of those children was *this* man, I would have told you to turn down the position, Willa. I am forbidding you from leaving this house."

The governess' eyebrows shot up. "I have never taken orders from anyone, least of all you, Ralph." She moved to the director and took his hands in hers. Softening her tone, she said, "I know you have my well-being at heart, but this is my decision. Not yours. I plan to go where I am needed. This man needs my services. If he is the rake you claim him to be, he will soon be gone from Spring Ridge anyway. The Season will be starting next month. He will no doubt wish to be a part of it, returning to whatever mistresses he left behind."

"You will not change your mind, Willa?" Baldwin asked, his face pained.

She shook her head emphatically. "I will not, Ralph." Then she leaned up and kissed his cheek. "I love you. I don't wish to quarrel with you. You have always had my best interests at heart. I am a grown woman now, however. You are no longer my guardian. Stay my good friend, and let us part in peace."

He embraced her. "Take care, Willa. Do what you have been hired to do—and watch yourself with this man."

"I know how to take care of myself, Ralph. Good luck with the new comedies this spring."

Xander watched this scene unfold, curious as to how the famed director and theater owner had come to be the guardian of this beautiful, poised woman.

Miss Fennimore turned to him. "I am ready, Your Grace." She motioned to a footman, who carried two valises from the foyer to the waiting vehicle.

"Goodbye, Ralph. I will write to you once I have settled in," Miss Fennimore said.

With that, she went through the open door. Xander started to follow, but Baldwin took his arm.

"Harm one hair on her head, and I will beat you to a bloody pulp—and then kill you. With pain and great pleasure."

"Message received," he said lightly, pulling away from the director and going to the post chaise.

Climbing into it, he settled next to Miss Fennimore—and reminded himself that this woman was forbidden fruit which he would never be allowed to pluck.

CHAPTER SIX

WILLA TRIED TO ignore the rush of warmth caused by the Duke of Brockbank sitting with his side pressed against hers.

The duke was a handsome one. She hadn't known he was new to his role.

Or a rake.

Would she have taken the position if she had known about the latter?

Doubtful.

She had come late to the conversation her new employer and former guardian were having. Willa had no illusions about Ralph being an angel. Far from it. The theater world was known for its hedonistic parties, particular ones held after the opening and closing nights of a play. Ralph was a mature but still incredibly attractive man. He had never tried to hide from her that he enjoyed the company of women.

What he had done was respectfully not bring any of his conquests home after she came to live under his roof. Willa knew the director still attended parties and assumed he merely went home with various partners, seeking his pleasure away from home when she had lived under his roof. She never judged him, knowing he was a good man. After all, he had taken her in when he had no obligation to do so. He was also kind to his actors and crew, even if he did lose his temper every now and then.

It worried her, though, that he found the duke so objectionable. Apparently, the Duke of Brockbank must frequent the theater world, most likely taking on lovers who were stage actresses and possibly making some of them his mistresses. Still, if Ralph called out the duke as a rake, Brockbank must be a very wicked man.

What if he were worse than Dearling or Appleton?

Her former employers had forced her from their homes, and her bitterness toward them still remained with her. She had liked all of her pupils very much and especially believed she made inroads with Dearling's youngest daughter. It had eaten away at her, not being able to tell her charges farewell either time she had left her posts to return to London.

Determination filled Willa, and she turned to the duke.

"Your Grace, I must make something very clear to you immediately, before we even leave the city limits. You are to listen carefully and if you do not agree, I will ask for this vehicle to be turned around at once." Pausing, she drew on her courage and years of maturity. "I have accepted the post as governess to your nieces. That is the only position I am interested in. I am not to be ogled by you. I am not your plaything. I certainly have no interest in becoming your mistress.

"If you are the rake my former guardian says you are, I want it made known that I am not the type of woman who will engage in any untoward behavior with you. Lady Cecily and Lady Lucy are my chief and only concerns. You will leave me alone and allow me to do my best for them. Duke or no duke, I wish to have nothing personal between us. Is that understood?"

She swallowed, trying to calm herself. She had just spoken to a duke of the realm in a scathing tone. No servant should ever speak to her employer in such a manner. Yet Willa wanted this man to be utterly clear of where she stood in the matter.

As she gazed intently into his startling, ice-blue eyes, she couldn't help but be aware of him as a man. He was quite tall, at least three inches over six feet, and had thick, abundant hair black as night. His impeccably tailored clothing revealed his large, muscular frame. He oozed a sensuality she had never been exposed to, something hidden and potent.

Why was she just now noticing this about him? Why hadn't she simply told him she was not interested in the post he offered to her?

And yet all she could think of were two, orphaned little girls, ones who had lost their parents in tragic ways. Those girls now needed stability and yes, even love, in their lives. She doubted this rogue even saw his nieces much. The *ton*, especially its gentlemen, were not known for spending any time with children.

"Let me be perfectly clear as well, Miss Fennimore. I may have a reputation for being a rake of the worst kind—but I would never take advantage of someone on my staff. You will be treated with the utmost respect by me at all times. Yes, I will wish to see you regularly to learn of the girls' progress, but in no way will I ever force myself on you."

He shook his head. "I will admit something to you that no one else knows. My three brothers were all much older than I was, my mother having died in childbirth. I received very little attention from anyone in my household. I wasn't even an afterthought to my brothers, who were ten to twelve years my senior and away at school. The duke called me a murderer for having killed my mother."

She gasped, pity for him filling her. "That was wrong of him."

Brockbank shrugged. "It is what it is. Suffice it to say that I have had no relationship with my father or my brothers for all these years. I did rebel when I was a boy, acting out because I sought my father's attention. I never gained it, however. I have never been one for rules. I am as untrusting a man as you will ever meet, and I never thought to wed before this dukedom dropped into my lap."

His gaze grew more intense. "I understand why Lucy and Cecily are acting out. They are lost and alone, incredibly sad because they have lost their parents without warning. Their ill behavior screams of the attention they desire. I have tried to give it to them. I hope you will do the same. Together, we must help these girls learn to get on with their grief and behave as proper young girls. I am their uncle and now their guardian. I will lead by example. That means I will never treat anyone—especially their governess—in a questionable manner. If I show respect to you, I hope they will mirror my behavior. Hopefully, you will set them on the right road. If you can, I will then leave the three of you in peace at Spring Ridge and return to town for the Season. In fact, I will most likely spend a great deal of my time in London."

Willa didn't like hearing that and spoke up. "Is it wise for you to abandon them so soon after they lost their parents, Your Grace? Actually, your nieces lost more than their parents. They lost their grandfather and their uncle, as well. No wonder they are so troubled." She hesitated and then said, "They should not have to turn around and lose you, as well, Your Grace."

He waved away her words. "They will not be losing me, Miss Fennimore. I will merely be going to town. Besides, I had not even met them before we went down for the funeral."

She found that odd. Then again, if this man had not been close to his family for his entire life, it was little wonder that he had not met these girls.

"I will reiterate what I just said. Even if you are new in their lives, you are their guardian. If you leave, they will look upon it as another time they are being abandoned. They need to know they are safe and secure."

"They will be. At Spring Ridge."

She snorted. "I doubt you have any experience with children, Your Grace. I do. I am telling you that any progress I might make with Lady Lucy and Lady Cecily might suffer an irreparable setback if you up and leave for London, and they stay behind."

His cheeks spotted in anger. "I did not hire a governess to tell me what to do, Miss Fennimore. I believe I am the employer here. I am the one who tells you how my household will be run."

Anger sizzled through her. "If you truly care for your nieces as you say you do, you *will not leave them*. Take them—us—back to London in a month. It is not as if you might see them anymore than you would in the country. How often do you see them now?" she demanded.

"Once a day, usually. They come down to the drawing room or library, and we read and talk for an hour after teatime. I am busy the rest of the day with estate matters."

"We could easily adhere to the same schedule in town, Your Grace. Pick any hour of the day when it would be most convenient for you to spend some time with the girls. I will arrange our schedule around this hour. But I beg you—do not leave them for months. They will see it as a rejection of them, no matter what you tell them."

The duke sat back against the cushions, obviously lost in thought. After some minutes, he looked to her. "All right. I agree. Let us see how they progress under your care. If they do, then we will all travel back to town together in a month. My father's townhouse . . ." His voice faded and then he said, "My townhouse is quite large. I would welcome having the girls with me in town."

"I think it a wise decision, Your Grace."

He didn't reply and merely looked out the window for the next couple of hours. Willa didn't mind. She had done two things. Made it crystal clear that any advances from the duke would be unwelcomed. And that he needed to put the welfare of his nieces above everything. Although she would have preferred remaining in the country, she thought it important for her yet unseen charges to have family about them, even if it was an uncle they had only recently met.

Besides, the duke was right. His townhouse would be enormous and his social schedule full. If he made time for even half an hour with his nieces each day, it would be more than enough. It would convince the girls that he wasn't going anywhere anytime soon. She supposed she must accompany her pupils when they saw their uncle, but she could leave them in his care for an hour. Other than that, Willa doubted she would ever see him, much less spend any time alone with him beyond the weekly report he required.

They stopped to change horses, and he said, "It will be another hour before we reach Spring Ridge. Shall we stretch our legs for a minute?"

"Yes, I would like that."

The duke climbed from the carriage and handed her down. Willa moved away from him, walking at a brisk pace to get her blood flowing again. She stood at a distance and watched the horses being traded out.

When she returned to the carriage, Brockbank offered her his hand, assisting her into the vehicle once more.

"You are right," he said, joining her. "I thought to leave them where they were becoming accustomed. Spring Ridge will be their home until they make their come-outs and wed. I had hoped the place would be growing on them."

"I am certain it is, Your Grace," she said gently. "Still, they have gone through quite a bit, losing their family members and coming to live in a strange place." Willa paused. "You have, as well."

He scowled. "No, nothing like Cecily and Lucy have. They are mere children. I am an adult."

Facing him, Willa said, "Just because you are a mature adult does not mean that these changes have not been difficult for you. Perhaps even more so. You indicated you were not close to your family. Part of you may regret never healing the rift between you and knowing it is too late to ever do so with their passings. Your entire life has been altered by these deaths. You are a duke now and hold immense responsibilities to a great many others. You are in charge of several estates. You will take your seat in the House of Lords. You have become a guardian and must see to the safekeeping and welfare of two children who are lost."

Without thinking, she placed her hand over his, feeling a spark and his heat. "You need to go easy on yourself, Your Grace. Take small steps as you learn your new role in the world."

She started to remove her hand, but he placed his free one over it. "You are right, Miss Fennimore. My life has changed—is constantly changing—in ways I have yet to learn. I understand that you believe my nieces require stability. Perhaps I do, as well."

Her heart hammering, she asked, "Will you not attend the Season then?"

"I haven't decided. I believe I will wait before I make that decision. Whatever it is, I promise that I will take Cecily and Lucy with me to town. And you, Miss Fennimore. I am sure you would like to be there to see Mr. Baldwin on a more frequent basis."

Willa's mouth had grown dry. "That would be lovely. We have been close for many years, but all of my posts were in the country, far from London. To see Ralph regularly—even have the opportunity to attend the plays he directs—would be wonderful."

The duke removed his hand, and she pulled away from him, placing her hands in her lap.

"I would be happy to escort you to opening night of any of his plays."

A thrill shot through her, followed by a sinking feeling. Had she misjudged this man? She thought he would not try to seduce her, but this offer would put her in close proximity with him. She did not want to be seen with him in public by others. Those of the *ton* would think her a lightskirt, and she might ruin her reputation with that one appearance by his side. The duke himself did not know who her parents had been and her connection to the theater world. If he did, he might think her totally unsuited for being his nieces' governess.

"Thank you for your kind offer, but I must decline," she said firmly, not elaborating on her reasons for dismissing his generosity.

They continued in silence, but Willa was now aware of everything about him. The subtle spice of his cologne. The closeness of their bodies. Worse, for the first time in her life, she felt a deep yearning for something she knew was out of her reach.

She wanted this handsome duke to kiss her. And maybe more.

Willa shoved aside such wicked, impossible thoughts, turning her head to stare out the window at the countryside. The sun was slowly dipping below the horizon. Based upon what the duke had told her, they should be arriving at Spring Ridge shortly. She was eager to meet Lady Cecily and Lady Lucy and explore the land with them.

They slowed and turned up a lane, driving for several more minutes until they reached the house. The duke bounded from the post chaise, helping her to the ground. Willa couldn't help but stare at the enormous structure which was to be her new home.

"Welcome home, Your Grace," the butler said, eyeing her with interest.

"Yes, welcome, Your Grace," a woman echoed. "I am Mrs. Dylan, the housekeeper at Spring Ridge."

Willa realized the woman was speaking to her. "Hello, Mrs. Dylan. I am Miss Fennimore and will be governess to Lady Cecily and Lady Lucy."

Obvious relief washed over the woman. "We are very happy to have you here, Miss Fennimore."

"This is Lorry," the duke said, indicating the butler. He looked to the housekeeper. "Has a room been made up for Miss Fennimore?"

"Yes, Your Grace. The same . . . as before."

Willa smiled reassuringly at the servant. "I know I am not the first governess to take on the girls. His Grace explained that the children recently lost several family members and are acting out. I, too, lost my parents when I was fifteen so I understand how death can affect children. Might I meet the girls now?"

Mrs. Dylan shook her head. "I am sorry, Miss Fennimore. They have already had their milk and bread and a housemaid just put them to bed as we speak."

Disappointment filled her, but she said, "It is good they are keeping to a regular schedule."

"We will need to eat, Mrs. Dylan," Brockbank said. "Have something brought to the winter parlor for us. I wish to speak to Miss Fennimore regarding the girls' schedule and what she will be teaching them."

"Of course, Your Grace. Perhaps you might give Miss Fennimore a quarter-hour to freshen up."

Willa gave the housekeeper a grateful smile. "I would like that, Mrs. Dylan."

"Then I will see you shortly," the duke said, striding into the house.

Mrs. Dylan took Willa to the top floor, showing her the schoolroom and the bedchamber which would be Willa's, and telling her she would take meals in the schoolroom with her charges except for supper, which would be provided on a tray sent to her room.

"The other door connecting to the schoolroom is where the young ladies sleep," the housekeeper said, her eyes misting with tears. "Oh, Miss Fennimore, we are so very happy you've come to be with us."

She took the older woman's hand. "I know the girls have been badly behaved. His Grace did not hide the fact from me. I hope in offering them stability and comfort, they will stop acting out so much. We must give them time, though. They are very young to have experienced such tragedies."

Mrs. Dylan pulled a handkerchief from her apron and mopped her eyes. "You're right. I know you are. For them to lose their father and uncle in the boating accident, was a huge loss. And then their mother went and . . . well, she drowned with them."

The housekeeper averted her eyes, almost as if she had something to hide, piquing Willa's curiosity.

"I will have hot water sent up to you, Miss Fennimore, and have a maid ready to escort you to the winter parlor."

Mrs. Dylan hurried from the room.

Something wasn't quite right. Brockbank had revealed to Willa that the girls' mother had died after she downed a bottle of laudanum, not being able to deal with the deaths of her husband and brother-in-law. Yet Mrs. Dylan pretended as if the duchess had drowned. Why would she say such a thing?

She decided to take it up with His Grace. If something odd was at play regarding the woman's death, Willa needed to know what had actually occurred. She worried that the woman's daughters might have been the ones to discover her body. If so, no wonder they were so traumatized and acting poorly.

Yes, she would ask the duke about his sister-in-law's death at supper this evening.

And hope he spoke truthfully to her regarding the woman's death.

CHAPTER SEVEN

X ANDER WENT TO the winter parlor, which was one of his favorite rooms at Spring Ridge. He liked how small and intimate it was. He associated work with his study and had not wanted to dine in what was considered the small dining room, since it seated a good dozen people. He and Miss Fennimore would have needed to shout at one another to speak and be heard.

He paced about the room, waiting for the new governess. She certainly had pulled no punches with him, dressing him down as she made her strong opinions known. It amazed him how passionately she fought for two little girls she had yet to meet. She also made him see things from the girls' point of view. They had lost everything they had known, all the stability of their home and their parents' presence, even if Rollo had not seemed to be a part of their young lives. If he did leave for the Season and have them remain behind in Kent, it might do irreparable harm to them.

Miss Fennimore looked to be in her mid-twenties, but she was far wiser than he. He supposed it was her experience with children and possibly her own past history of losing her parents and having to mature early. Xander decided the experience had made her stronger and more mature than others her own age.

She entered the room now, wearing the same gown she had for the journey down to Kent. Any other woman of his acquaintance would have taken the time to change gowns. Not the practical Miss Fennimore—and he liked her even better for it.

The problem was that he was attracted to her. Any man would be. She was a foot shorter than he was, with a very curvy, enticing frame. He judged her practical, loose gowns tried to hide this, but he had seen evidence of her curves as she had moved and felt them when her body was pressed against his in the post chaise. She possessed magnificent, sable hair he longed to comb his fingers through, and every time she looked at him with those enchanting, amethyst eyes, he felt desire shoot through him. But it wasn't only her beauty that intrigued him. It was the way she presented herself, a sureness and steadiness that he admired. He thought she would be perfect for Cecily and Lucy and only hoped they would take to her.

"Ah, come in, Miss Fennimore. I hope you found your bedchamber to your liking."

"It is quite large and convenient since it is just off the schoolroom. Mrs. Dylan told me your nieces are on the other side of the schoolroom and that we will breakfast together there each morning."

"Some things never change," he commented. "I also took all my meals at that table when I was a boy. I was not in the room next to the schoolroom, however. My bedchamber was on the floor below. I did not realize Pamela had put the girls near the schoolroom. That was a good decision on her part."

"Speaking of the duchess," Miss Fennimore began. "There was something odd that Mrs. Dylan said to me regarding Her Grace."

The door opened, and Lorry came in, followed by two footmen carrying trays with their supper.

Xander said, "You may remove the chessboard, Lorry. We can eat at that table."

He and Miss Fennimore watched as the table was set and their dishes placed upon it. He dismissed Lorry, telling the butler they would need nothing else.

"May I seat you, Miss Fennimore?"

"Yes, thank you, Your Grace."

He did so and took the seat to her right instead of across from her. They ate in silence for a few minutes, Miss Fennimore finally complimenting on how tender the roast beef was.

"I have discovered Spring Ridge has an excellent cook, even more talented than the one here during my years of growing up. I took my meals at my club in London, but it is nice to be spoiled and come downstairs to what Cook has made each morning."

"What did you do in London?" she asked, slicing another bite of beef.

Xander watched her bring the fork to her mouth and couldn't help but stare at her full, bottom lip. He wanted to sink his teeth into it.

"Your Grace?"

She startled him from his reverie, and he cursed inwardly. He had promised both himself—and her—that he would not take advantage of her. He would hold himself to that promise.

Even if it killed him.

"I hope you will enjoy living in the country, Miss Fennimore."

"I actually prefer the country over town," she replied. "I spent my entire childhood in London, only leaving when I accepted a position as a companion to a marchioness."

"Which do you prefer—companion or governess? You said you have held posts of each twice."

"I suppose it is an easier life to be a companion. I enjoy the company of children, though. I would answer your question by saying that I prefer being a governess and cannot wait to meet your nieces tomorrow morning."

A muffled giggle sounded, and his gaze met Miss Fennimore's. He looked across the room and noticed a tiny leg sticking out, surprised that he had not noticed it before now.

"Cecily? Lucy? Make yourselves known at once," he said sternly.

Moments later, his nieces appeared, rising from behind a large settee.

"Come here," he commanded.

The girls slowly moved toward him. When they reached him, he asked, "What were you thinking?"

As he expected, Cecily took the lead. "Mrs. Dylan told us the new governess might come today. We heard the carriage after the maid put us to bed and looked out the window. We were just curious about her, Uncle Xander."

Before he could reply, Miss Fennimore took charge of the situation. "Why, I think it is lovely that you wished to welcome me, even though it was past your bedtime. Being curious is a wonderful trait to possess. I assume you are Lady Cecily?"

The girl nodded and then pointed to her sister. "This is Lucy."

"It is very nice to make your acquaintance, my ladies," Miss Fennimore said in a friendly fashion. "Would you care to join us since you are already up and about?"

Xander thought this was the absolute wrong thing to do, but he kept silent, leaning on the governess' experience.

The girls sat at the two empty chairs, and Miss Fennimore said, "My name is Miss Fennimore, and I have come to Spring Ridge to serve as your new governess. As I mentioned, curiosity is something we can work with. Tell me—other than me—what are you curious about?"

The girls sat, dumbfounded by the question.

"That is all right," the governess said brightly. "We will explore many topics together and see which ones you wish to pursue."

Cecily looked at her with suspicion. "You mean you aren't going to tell us what we will study?"

"Heavens, no," Miss Fennimore declared. "Why would I do that?"

Her words shocked Xander, but he held his tongue.

Lucy said, "All our governesses have told us what to study."

"Well, I do not believe that is the best way to go about educating oneself. Once I learned to read and write from my governess, my mother told me that I could explore whatever subjects I might be interested in."

Cecily thought a moment, and then asked, "What were you interested in, Miss Fennimore?"

"*Estabo interesado en tantos temas diferentes. Je m'intéressalis à tant de sujets différents. Ero interessato a così tanti argomenti diversi. Ich habe mich für so viele verschiedene Themen.*"

She smiled warmly at his nieces. "I said the same thing in four languages. Spanish. French. Italian. And German. That I was interested in many different subjects. I found that languages were something which fascinated me, and so they were things I pursued with a passion."

"What else, Miss Fennimore?" Lucy asked.

"I also enjoy music and play the pianoforte although I never had a formal lesson. We had a pianoforte in our home. I simply taught myself how to play the instrument. I was almost an adult before I actually learned to read music, and I have even written a few compositions on it. If you would like to learn how to play it, I would be happy to teach you."

Xander observed how Cecily's eyes lit up. "No one has ever offered to teach us music."

"That is in the past, Lady Cecily. We will move forward from this moment on. I will assess each of you to see how well you read and write. That will always be something which we work on since reading and writing are the foundations of so many other things, and you want to master them both. We will be able to explore whatever you are interested in. Perhaps languages. History. Architecture. And—"

"Drawing?" Lucy asked, bouncing with excitement.

"Ah, drawing. So, you are a budding artist, my lady?"

The girl nodded. "I like to draw."

"Then we will have you draw all manner of things. Plants. Animals. Even people. There are also different things to use as you draw. You can sketch in pencil. We can also get you some drawing paper and charcoals. I will let you try different types of paints, as well."

Miss Fennimore turned to Cecily. "Is there something you enjoy, just as your sister likes to draw?"

"I like to make up stories."

"Then you must be quite creative, Lady Cecily. Did you know that people actually earn a living from their writing? Some write about facts. Things that have occurred and their articles appear in newspapers. But then others use their imagination as you like to do and write novels. Then, of course, there are playwrights."

Cecily's brows knitted together. "What is a playwright?"

"A playwright writes plays. Those are stories performed on a stage. We can read some plays and then have you write one of your own. We can even act it out for your uncle and the servants if you would like. Of course, if there are more than two roles, which obviously you and your sister would play, we might need to engage some of the servants to speak the words you write."

"We could do that?" Cecily asked, her eyes round with wonder.

"My lady, we can do anything you wish. I have no set course of study in mind. My position is one of guiding you in your studies, but *you* will decide what those studies are. We will even walk about this estate daily and learn each time we do so. For example, we might go down to a pond and spy a frog. If you are interested enough, we can learn all there is to know about frogs. Or we might walk through the gardens at Spring Ridge. I spent much of my girlhood with our gardener. Felton taught me quite a bit about gardening. I enjoy working with my hands, digging in the dirt and planting things. I enjoy trimming hedges and pruning plants. I think working in the gardens can teach many lessons to you."

"I want to learn like this," Lucy proclaimed, warming Xander's heart.

"You aren't like any other governess we have had, Miss Fennimore," Cecily said. "They told us what we had to learn and gave us no choices."

"I have found it is wise to let my pupils explore their own interests. The more you explore this world, the more you will be interested in it and your tastes will broaden. Why, you may eventually choose to study things you aren't particularly curious about, but you decide you wish to learn a little about the topic simply to better educate yourself."

"I cannot wait for tomorrow morning!" Lucy said enthusiastically. "I will think about what I want to learn."

Cecily frowned. "What if Lucy and I want to study different things?" she challenged.

"Just because you are sisters does not mean you will be interested in the same things. I will tutor you in what you wish to learn. Of course, as you share what you learn with one another and tell your uncle about what you are discovering, you might realize that you do become interested in an area which your sister is pursuing. We have many lessons ahead of us—and many years of learning. That is, if you wish for me to remain here."

"What do you mean?" Cecily asked, suspicion reflected in her eyes.

"It will be *your* decision if I stay as your governess," Miss Fennimore declared. "If you enjoy the way I teach you and you like our lessons, I hope that you will allow me to stay with you for many years. If you decide we do not suit one another, however, then I will accept your decision and simply return to London and find another post."

"No!" Lucy said. "I don't want you to go, Miss Fennimore."

Xander bit back a smile. This woman was very clever, giving his nieces the power over her.

"We will see if we like you," Cecily declared. Then she smiled. "But I think you will want to stay with us, Miss Fennimore."

"I am glad that I have made such a good impression upon you,

Lady Cecily. You and Lady Lucy have also made a very good one on me. I think we shall get along splendidly."

Lucy looked hesitant and asked, "Even if we sneaked out of bed to see you?"

"What did I say earlier?"

"Curiosity is good," Lucy said. She paused, and then added, "So, you won't punish us?"

"I shall never punish you, my lady," Miss Fennimore shared. "If you choose to do something wrong, I will call out your misbehavior, and you will decide how you should make amends."

Cecily's jaw dropped. "You won't punish us? Ever?"

"As I said, I will discuss with you why your behavior was inappropriate. Did it harm you? Did it hurt someone else? I hope I will teach you not only different academic subjects but life lessons," Miss Fennimore shared. "I want you to know how to treat others—and how to treat yourselves."

"You are very different, Miss Fennimore," Cecily said.

Lucy yawned, and the governess said, "I think it is time for the two of you to be in bed. We have a busy day tomorrow, getting to know one another and deciding on what topics we shall first explore this week."

She looked to Xander. "Your Grace, if you will please excuse me, I will see the girls to bed."

He had been entranced by the way this woman had drawn in his nieces and wasn't ready to leave her company.

"I shall accompany you, Miss Fennimore." Grinning, he added, "I may even have to chain these two to their beds so they will not get up and roam about again."

The girls giggled, and he relaxed, knowing he had made the right decision in hiring Willa Fennimore.

The four went to the top floor of the house, and he tucked Cecily into bed as Miss Fennimore did the same for Lucy.

"Thank you for letting me come to Spring Ridge," the governess told the girls. "I look forward to our time together, no matter how long it will be."

"Forever!" Lucy said, a sweet smile on her face.

Xander noticed that even Cecily was smiling. He leaned down and kissed her brow. "I will see you in the morning. Goodnight."

He switched places with the governess and also kissed Lucy. His niece looked at him and asked, "Will you come to breakfast with us, Uncle Xander? You might have some ideas about what Miss Fennimore can teach us."

Once again, Xander felt a tug on his heartstrings and said, "I would be delighted to join the three of you at breakfast. Goodnight."

He followed Miss Fennimore, who exited through the door which led to the schoolroom. Xander closed it behind him. He caught her elbow and turned her to face him.

"Though your methods are quite unconventional, I am sold on them."

Desire rushed through him as he looked at her beautiful face. For a long moment, they gazed upon one another and then she said, "I believe this method will work with your nieces, Your Grace. Since I am already at my room, I will bid you goodnight."

He reluctantly released his hold as she moved away from him, going through the door which led to her bedchamber. Xander watched her close it and stood there.

His nieces had taken to Miss Fennimore with ease. The problem was, so had he—and Xander was helpless to do anything about it.

CHAPTER EIGHT

WILLA HAD RISEN and was ready to dress for the day when a knock sounded at her door. She was surprised to find a servant with a jug in hand.

"Hot water for you, Miss Fennimore," the servant said cheerily.

"Thank you."

"And breakfast will be in the schoolroom in ten minutes' time."

The maid left, and Willa put the hot water to good use. It was the rare household which thought to provide hot water in the morning for a governess. She would have to take Mrs. Dylan aside sometime today and let the housekeeper know how much she appreciated her thoughtfulness.

She dressed and brushed her hair, winding and pinning the locks up so they would stay out of her way. Going through the door which adjoined the schoolroom, she found her new pupils already seated.

"Miss Fennimore!" cried Lucy, rushing to Willa and hugging her.

She hugged the girl back, blinking rapidly so no tears fell.

Cecily smiled. "Good morning, Miss Fennimore." She did not leave her seat.

It did not surprise her. Lucy was younger and would be more needy. Cecily, though only eight, seemed much more self-sufficient. Still, she was a little girl who had carried a heavy burden. Willa would do everything in her power to help Cecily heal from her losses.

As she took a seat, Lucy asked, "Will you eat with us every morning, Miss Fennimore?"

"I plan to do so. I like to start my day with my charges and talk about what we will be doing."

"I am here, too," a voice said.

She looked up and saw the duke, dressed like an elegant country gentleman but with a rakish smile on his lips.

Willa had dreamed of him last night. Of his lips on hers. His hands caressing her body. Her cheeks grew warm at the thought. She pinched herself, trying to dispel the images flitting through her head. This man was a duke. Her employer. She was a governess. Nothing untoward could ever occur between them. After all, he had promised to respect her.

She had made no promises to him, however.

That thought caused her face to flame, and she looked down, hoping no one noticed. They didn't. The girls were happily claiming their uncle's attention, jabbering away. It was good they were so comfortable with him, especially having only known him a short while.

Glancing up, she saw he nodded, as if carefully listening to them.

But his eyes were on her.

She went hot all over.

Fortunately, two maids arrived with trays in hand. One saw the duke present and said, "We did not know you were dining here, Your Grace. We only brought breakfast for Miss Fennimore and the little ladies."

"I will eat downstairs today." He paused. "I do believe I will plan to have my breakfast in the schoolroom each morning. It will be a good start to my day, spending time with my nieces. I will let Mrs. Dylan know."

"Would you like me to bring you a cup of tea?" the maid asked.

"No, thank you. You may go."

The servants left, and the girls began eating. Willa felt nervous in the duke's presence and worried about him starting his morning with them each day. Then again, she could report to him at this time with her pupils present, and it would be unnecessary for her to see him alone. Relief filled her, and she lifted her teacup, sipping the hot brew.

"What has been decided?" Brockbank asked. "Will you study ancient history? Or learn how to do sums?"

"Nothing that boring, Uncle Xander," Cecily said.

"I will have both girls read aloud to me," Willa said. "I want to get an idea of their vocabulary and reading comprehension. Then they will take a brief spelling test and produce a writing sample for me."

"That all sounds boring," Cecily repeated, sighing dramatically.

"I told you I would need to gauge where you are in your academic progress. We will always work on reading and writing and all that goes with it. Grammar. Spelling. But as Shakespeare said, 'The world is your oyster.' Do you know what that means?"

Both girls shook their heads.

"Shakespeare was a famous English playwright. Remember, we talked of how people earned a living writing, and playwrights write the words for plays. One play Mr. Shakespeare wrote was called *The Merry Wives of Windsor*. In it, his lead character, Falstaff, uses that expression." She looked to the duke. "Are you familiar with this play, Your Grace?"

"I have seen it performed but do not recall much about it," he replied.

Willa thought him one of those gentlemen who came to the theater with other things on his mind than watching a play being performed.

To the girls, she said, "The way Falstaff used the phrase differs a bit from today's meaning. When I say that the world is your oyster, I mean that you have a bright future full of many opportunities, if only you look for them."

"Why oysters?" Cecily asked.

She smiled at the girl. "You see, pearls are hidden in the center of many oysters, and they are quite valuable."

"Mama had a pearl necklace," Lucy said, her mouth turning down.

"She must have looked beautiful wearing it," Willa said quickly, causing the girl to smile. "When I say that the world is your oyster, I wish for you to be open to new experiences and learning about new ideas. If you are willing to learn and try new things, you have a better chance at finding happiness, as well as learning something along the way."

"Where do you find oysters?" Lucy asked. "I might be interested in them. If I could find enough pearls, I could make a pearl necklace just like Mama had."

"They are mostly found along the coast, where the sea is," their uncle told them. "We might make a trip someday soon to look for some."

The girls clapped their hands enthusiastically.

"We can hunt for some along the shoreline. They are quite tasty," he continued. "They can be grilled or fried. Either way, I think you will like them. As for your mother's pearls, I will check with the maids and Mrs. Dylan and see if they are here at Spring Ridge or at your former home. Your mother's jewelry belongs to you now. You can wear some of it when you make your come-out."

Lucy frowned. "What's a come-out, Miss Fennimore?"

She laughed. "I think your uncle could tell you far more about that than I can. It's most likely a subject *he* is interested in." She smiled at him and saw he knew how she teased him.

The duke laughed. "When a girl reaches the age of eighteen or thereabouts, she makes her debut into Polite Society. She gets to attend balls and dance the night away, until her feet are sore. She also goes to other social events—parties, musicales, teas."

"Did you like your come-out, Miss Fennimore?" Cecily asked innocently.

"Oh, I did not make my come-out. Only a handful of young ladies do so each year. The wealthiest gentlemen and those who bear titles, such as your uncle, introduce their daughters to society. They go to a plethora of amusing events and while they are enjoying them and meeting new people, they might also find a husband."

"Your father isn't wealthy?" Lucy asked.

"No, he was not, nor did he hold a title. He was merely Mr. Fennimore. A small group of men bear titles such as duke, marquess, earl, viscount, and baron. Those men and their families make up what is called Polite Society. Daughters and sons from those families marry one another, and then their daughters one day make their come-outs, and the process begins all over again."

"Do we have to do this?" Lucy asked, whining.

"You may not think you want to do so now, Lady Lucy, but by the time you are eight and ten, you will be ready to meet others and attend all the wonderful events."

The girl frowned. "It doesn't seem fair. You didn't get to go to anything like that. You aren't married. You are a miss."

"And I am quite happy being Miss Fennimore, I assure you. It is not only titled people who wed. Anyone of age may legally wed in England. They just meet their future husbands and wives at places other than balls."

"Like where?" Lucy pressed.

"Oh, they might live next door to one another. Or they could attend the same church. Or their fathers might work together and introduce them. Marriage is for every class, not just those who are wealthy."

"Will you ever marry, Miss Fennimore?" Cecily asked.

"I doubt I will," Willa said honestly. "I enjoy being a governess and helping children. Besides, if I married, I would have to leave you."

"Then don't marry," Cecily said. "We like you."

"Finish your breakfast, and we will make a list of things you might wish to learn more about," she told them.

They did so, Willa fetching parchment and a quill and inkwell, noting their ideas.

"We have quite a list here," she told them. "And don't forget—we can add to it at any time. Whatever you wish to learn about, we will place on our list."

She glanced at what she had written based upon their conversation, pleased at the variety. She and the duke had asked the girls questions, nudging them a bit, helping to round out the list.

"We didn't mention horses," Cecily said. "I might want to ride one. And learn about them. I saw a horse having a baby horse last summer. At least I started seeing it, but Mama rushed me back into the house. I wish I could have watched the baby being born."

"A baby horse is called a colt," she said. "We can check the stables to see if there are any horses due to give birth this spring and if there are any suitable mounts for you to ride."

"Do you know how to ride, Miss Fennimore?" Lucy asked.

"No, I lived in London and never had the opportunity to learn. I have held a few posts in the country, but usually, a governess does not ride. It is something reserved for family members. I am certain we can find a groom to teach you to ride if you express an interest in it."

"Could you teach us, Uncle Xander?"

"Perhaps, Cecily. I do have a lot of business I am working on now, though. We will see."

She thrust out her bottom lip. "Mama always said that. That meant no."

The duke looked taken aback. "Well, I am different. If you truly wish to learn to ride, we can set a day and time."

A bit mollified, Cecily said, "I will think about it."

Willa almost burst out laughing. Cecily Hughes would certainly be a handful, not only as a child, but as a woman.

"I suppose we should get to our reading and writing," she said.

"We have put it off long enough."

"Can't we go walk outside some instead?" whined Cecily. "You need to see Spring Ridge, Miss Fennimore."

"I think that an excellent idea," the duke seconded. "I am happy to accompany you."

Lucy sprang up and hugged her uncle's neck. "Thank you, Uncle Xander."

Cecily smiled triumphantly at Willa. "See, Miss Fennimore? This is what *we* want to do. You said we would be deciding what we wanted to learn about."

"I did, but thank you for the reminder, my lady. Let me fetch a bonnet and my spencer. You girls need to do the same because I suspect it is cool outside."

Willa returned to her room, unsure why the duke had agreed to go with them. She was torn between wishing for his company and then not wanting him present at all.

She returned to the schoolroom, finding only the duke present.

"You do not have to go walking with us, Your Grace."

"No, I insist. You were right. These girls have had everything torn from them. They were uprooted from their former lives and need to know I will be a steady presence for them."

"Before they return, I must ask you something I started to address last night after we arrived. Mrs. Dylan. She . . . well, she spoke to me briefly about the recent deaths at Spring Ridge. She lumped Her Grace in with the others, as if the duchess had been a part of the boating accident."

"That is at my request," he told her. "If it had been known that Pamela killed herself, she could not have been buried in hallowed ground. I wanted Rollo and his wife to rest beside one another and the girls to be able to visit their graves."

"Did you speak to your nieces about why you did so?"

"No."

"They do know their mother wasn't out on the water that day, don't they?"

"They do. They do not question it, though. I doubt anyone has brought the matter up in their presence."

"I think at some point you should speak to them about it. Sooner, rather than later. They need for you to tell them the truth."

He let out an exasperated sigh. "It was hard enough telling them of the deaths of their father and uncle. Telling them about their mother's death was almost impossible."

He stood and began pacing the room. "I said . . . that she died in her sleep. That she was sad and sick, and she passed on."

Willa pursed her lips. "I totally disagree, Your Grace. You were wrong. It might make them afraid to be sad. They might believe if they are sad about their parents' deaths, that they, too, might pass away."

The duke stopped in his tracks, mulling her words. "I had not thought of that." He raked a hand through his hair. "But how do I tell them?"

"With love and honesty, Your Grace. It may be painful, but the truth is what is important."

"Would you . . . would you be with me when I tell them?" he pleaded.

"I will."

"Good. Then I shall tell them today when we are out and about."

He crossed the room and took her hands in his, his touch causing shivers to run through her.

"I am glad you came to Spring Ridge, Miss Fennimore. I am beginning to think I need you as much as the girls do."

CHAPTER NINE

X ANDER MEANT WHAT he said. He believed Willa Fennimore not only was the correct choice to be his nieces' governess, but she also might be the person he had been looking for his entire life. He had not known he was searching for anyone. He had lived a life of privilege and even though he was a fourth son who, once he graduated from university, lived on a limited income, he had pursued a life of pleasure. Xander lived for himself alone, beholden to no one, never admitting how shallow he was and how bored he grew as time passed.

Now that he was the Duke of Brockbank, however, his life's purpose and priorities were quickly shifting. He had never thought to wed and knew now he must do so in order to provide an heir.

Why not a beautiful, intelligent, capable woman such as Willa Fennimore?

Of course, she would be all wrong in the eyes of Polite Society. A governess who had been orphaned as a girl. Yet Xander had never been one to play by the rules, much less the unwritten rules of Polite Society. He had thought when he became the duke that he would not be bound by them. That he would continue to live his life as he saw fit, only finding a duchess to provide him an heir years down the line.

He did not know what had shifted in him but realized that Cecily and Lucy played a part in it. Despite their troublemaking ways, Xander was growing fonder of them as each day went by. Miss Fennimore was also showing him how wrong his perceptions of his nieces had been.

Would this woman be willing to take a leap of faith and start a new kind of life with him?

It remained to be seen. Miss Fennimore was strong-willed, opinionated, and seemingly set in her ways for one so young, devoted to her pupils though she barely knew this pair. Would she be willing to go on the adventure of a lifetime and show that same kind of devotion to him? Xander had been liked by many over the years but never loved. Did he even want to see if he could make this woman love him? Even better, would he be open if she gave him her love in return?

The thought of love was foreign to him and in many ways, frightened him. Yet the jumble of emotions he was feeling toward Miss Fennimore let him know that he might very well be capable of love.

With the right woman . . .

He went down the stairs and out the door to check on the weather, seeing the morning was cool and crisp but had no wind.

Coming back inside, Xander waited impatiently for the others. His heart skipped a beat when the three appeared on the landing above him. As they came down the stairs, he was drawn in by Miss Fennimore's beauty and knew if anyone could conquer the *ton* and convince them of her worth as the Duchess of Brockbank, it would be Willa Fennimore.

He opened the door himself, and they all filed out. Surprisingly, Lucy took his hand and then Miss Fennimore's, leaving Cecily to think a moment about what she wanted to do. She moved to the other side of the governess and slipped her hand into Miss Fennimore's.

They started off, and Miss Fennimore asked, "Where shall we go first on this fine day? Perhaps to your favorite place on the estate?"

"We haven't been outside the house once since we got here," Cecily complained. "That is why I wanted our first lesson to be outdoors."

Miss Fennimore looked at him questioningly, and Xander

shrugged.

"I did not know you had been cooped up inside the house since your arrival. I apologize for that."

"Fresh air and exercise are very important," the governess told her charges. "We will be certain to have outdoor time each day unless it is raining."

"I think I want us to go to the gardens," Lucy suggested. "Miss Fennimore said she likes gardening. I like pretty flowers. Maybe I would like gardening, too."

"Then the gardens shall be our first stop," he declared, leading them the length of the house and turning to go toward the gardens in the rear.

"The Spring Ridge gardens were one of my favorite places when I was growing up here," he told his nieces.

"Did you and Papa play in the gardens?" Cecily asked.

"No, I did not play with any of my brothers. Your papa was twelve years of age when I was born. Your Uncle Peter would have been eleven and Uncle Stanley ten at that time. They did not want to have anything to do with a newborn. Boys that age think they know everything."

"Then who did you play with, Uncle Xander?" Lucy wanted to know. "I always play with Cecily."

"I learned to entertain myself," he told them. "I was on my own quite a bit. My father liked to remain in town most of the year. With all my brothers away at school, I was left mostly to myself."

"Did no one live nearby for you to play with?" Cecily asked.

Xander thought of Linfield, the adjoining estate to Spring Ridge. Henry Vaughn, Viscount North, had visited there a few times each year and was close to Xander's age. They had only played together a couple of times when Henry came to visit his grandfather, the Duke of Linberry. Henry was a dutiful, well-behaved young man and after being in Xander's company, he had told Xander that he did not wish to play with him because Xander misbehaved all the time. He had thought Henry priggish and had nothing to do with him once they wound up attending the same school.

Henry had become Duke of Linberry the previous year and wed an interesting young woman, Lady Fia Sawyer. Gossip had arisen because Lady Fia had never made her come-out into society. Instead, she taught music lessons to children of the *ton*. Xander recalled seeing her as a member of the orchestra on last year's opening night ball, thinking it highly unusual for a woman to play in a group composed strictly of men. He did not know many of the particulars but did know that Linberry had wed the woman rather quickly.

He supposed it would be the neighborly thing to do and visit the Duke and Duchess of Linberry soon or even invite them to tea.

"To answer your question, Cecily, there were no other children of my class in the neighborhood to play with, only the Duke of Linberry's grandson who visited him two or three times a year. This boy was my age, but I was known for misbehaving and not considered a good influence on my peers."

"You were naughty like we are?" Cecily studied him, waiting for his reply.

"I will admit that I spent a good deal of my childhood not behaving properly. My father ignored me, and I thought I could gain his attention by being bad."

"Did it work?" Lucy pressed.

"No, it did not. It was a bad idea from the start."

"That is what I have been doing," Cecily admitted quietly. "Papa didn't like Lucy or me because we weren't boys. I heard him talking to Mama, and he said that girls were worthless."

Miss Fennimore spoke up. "That was wrong of him, Cecily. Girls have as much worth as boys do, though many men in Polite Society do not recognize this. I am not saying your father was a bad man. I am only saying that I am sorry he did not recognize your value."

"Why did he act like that, Miss Fennimore?" Cecily asked. "Papa hardly ever talked to us or paid us any attention. I am like Uncle Xander and tried to see if I could make him pay attention to me. Lucy just went along with whatever I told her to do, but Papa never did like us. He was mean."

"I am sorry to hear that," Miss Fennimore said quietly. "You have a loving uncle now, however. One who is committed to spending time with you and your sister."

"I like seeing you every day, Uncle Xander. We go see him after tea," Lucy said brightly. "He likes us. He didn't even have to tell us. We just know he does."

Xander's heart warmed at the small girl's words, and he squeezed her hand. "I do, indeed, like you a great deal, Lucy. I even like Cecily, troublemaker that she is."

Cecily laughed. "I will try to be better, Uncle Xander."

"I don't expect you to be perfect, Cecily," he said to her. "Neither does Miss Fennimore. Everyone makes mistakes sometimes. But it is important to learn from those mistakes. I have not always behaved my best, but I strive to do so, especially now that I am the Duke of Brockbank."

"Is a duke an important person?" Lucy wanted to know.

He pondered her question a moment. "Dukes have a very high rank in Polite Society. Many look to them to be leaders. I also have several estates beyond Spring Ridge and am responsible for a great number of tenants. I will strike a bargain with the two of you. I will strive to be the best man and duke I can be—and you will be the best girls you can be. Not only for Miss Fennimore and me, but everyone in the household. Do you agree?"

"Yes, Uncle Xander," Lucy said brightly.

He turned to Cecily. "Yes, Uncle," she said, more quietly than her sister.

Xander supposed her habitually poor behavior was more ingrained in her and would take longer to weed out. Still, she was very young and had Miss Fennimore to influence her now.

They reached the gardens and entered them. Immediately, Miss Fennimore began pointing out various plants and a couple of early-blooming flowers.

The girls seemed quite interested and had their governess repeat the names of various plants and flowers they passed. Lucy talked about the flowers she would draw. When they reached the rose bushes, Miss Fennimore stopped and gave them a lesson on how to care for roses each year. She explained how they grew and what pruning meant and why it was done each spring.

"I wish I had my pruning shears to demonstrate for you," she said.

"Are there flowers that should be planted now?" Cecily asked.

"Some flowers can be planted annually—each year—and they only last that one year. Others are called perennials. If you care for them well, as roses, they grow back."

She explained the difference and gave examples of each kind. The girls decided they would meet with the Spring Ridge gardener and see if they could participate in some of the spring planting and pruning. It gave Xander a sense of pride in the two, seeing them interested in a subject and wanting to learn about it enough to put in the work.

"I am certain that your cook also has an herb garden," Miss Fennimore told them. "Herbs are used especially in cooking, but sometimes for medicinal purposes."

"I don't understand," Lucy said.

"Let us go and see if we can find the herb garden, and I will show you," the governess said.

They found it within ten minutes, Xander guiding them, and Miss Fennimore pointed out various herbs and their uses.

"Cook most likely uses dill, oregano, sage, and chives as she cooks. They are popular herbs to place in foods. Over here, though, I see such things as mint. While it can flavor items such as tea, mint is used to soothe your belly if you have indigestion or vomiting."

Xander listened as she taught the girls how to recognize some of the different herbs planted in this garden and the variety of ways they could be used. He found himself asking questions and learning as much as his nieces did.

"We probably can work in this garden, as well. I will speak to Cook about it. Most likely, a gardener or even one of the scullery maids picks the herbs used in the kitchen. We might decide to take on that job ourselves and help out Cook."

Cecily frowned. "Why would we help Cook? She works here."

"Helping others is something you should not only strive to do— but *want* to do," Miss Fennimore said gently. "Helping other people will not only assist them, but it will make you feel good about yourself."

"I would like to help Cook," Lucy said.

"Then Lucy and I may be the ones who choose to pick the herbs," the governess said.

Xander saw the frown on Cecily's face, and the girl quickly said, "I want to help, too."

"Good girl," he praised, squeezing her shoulder lightly.

"What about cooking?" Cecily asked.

"What about it?" Miss Fennimore countered.

He liked that she nudged the girls to express their thoughts. It was a clever way to help them learn to think and articulate what they wished to say.

"Well, I wonder how it is done. I like biscuits and cake. Do you think we might watch Cook make them sometime?

"That would be an excellent lesson, Lady Cecily," Miss Fennimore said. "We could watch Cook because baking is as much an art as it is a science. You must measure your ingredients precisely, but I do believe a little love goes into everything a cook makes for others."

"You mean we might get to make biscuits and eat them?" Lucy

asked eagerly.

"Is that something you might be interested in, my lady?"

"Yes!" both girls cried.

"I like that idea. I will speak with Cook. Both about the herb garden and us coming to the kitchens for some lessons. Perhaps we might even prepare tea for your uncle one day soon." She glanced to him and smiled. "Would you enjoy that, Your Grace?"

He nodded. "I cannot imagine a better tasting tea than one done for me by my nieces. And you, Miss Fennimore," he added, smiling warmly at her.

Xander saw her cheeks flush with color. That let him know that she was not totally immune to his charms. He would have to think of a way to approach her. Although he said he would never take advantage of her, he was aching to kiss her. He believed if he had the opportunity to kiss Willa Fennimore, he would take it.

It would be the first step in his campaign to win her as his duchess.

CHAPTER TEN

W ILLA HAD ENJOYED walking through the gardens with her new
charges and promised them they would have all kinds of
lessons outside every day. For now, though, she had them return to
the house.

The duke bid them a good day and said he needed to spend time
with Key, the Spring Ridge steward. He told her to make certain the
girls were brought to the drawing room at five o'clock.

She fully intended to honor his request—but would not accompany her pupils.

Willa danced a fine line now. She realized she was far too interested in the Duke of Brockbank and needed to tamp down the feelings
she was rapidly developing for him. He did not seem to be the rogue
that Ralph had claimed. Rather, he was polite, interested in his nieces,
and wonderful company. Perhaps the change had come when
Brockbank assumed his title. The multiple deaths within his family
may have caused him to finally mature, knowing so many others
counted on him.

She could not imagine being a fourth son, a man who would not
have been prepared to assume any kind of leadership position, either
within his family or Polite Society. It was hard to imagine how quickly
the duke's life had changed with the death of his father, followed
closely by the sudden deaths of his three elder brothers. Willa knew

the kind of man the duke must have been previously. Spoiled. Entitled. Yet living on a limited income, due to his position in the family. As a gentleman of the *ton* with no set responsibilities, he would have visited the gaming hells with regularity. Been invited to *ton* events and flirted with pretty girls making their come-outs. His life would have not counted for much.

Now, however, he had heavy burdens placed on his shoulders, the most important being the welfare of his nieces. At least he seemed truly interested in the girls and comfortable in their presence despite having no children of his own. It was obvious that they, too, enjoyed being in his company. She would have to draw a line, though, to keep herself outside their little group. It would be important to encourage Brockbank's interaction with them and yet absent herself from any activities if the duke chose to be present. Already, she worried about the daily breakfasts they would share. It had been difficult enough going about the gardens with him in tow. Her heart had beat too rapidly, and she had found herself losing her focus, merely wishing to gaze upon his handsome visage.

She shrugged off all thoughts of the duke as she led her charges up the stairs, telling them it was time to assess their reading and writing skills. She spoke several words aloud and had them record these words on the slates she found in a cabinet, wanting to see how well they spelled. She had both girls read aloud to her to listen to their cadence and pronunciation. She asked each to write a short passage in which they described their favorite food and favorite time of the year, wanting to see not only their penmanship and the way they put sentences together but also wishing to see how far their imaginations stretched. It was also important that she take into account their ages, thinking Lady Cecily should be more advanced in her learning than Lady Lucy.

After Willa reviewed their work, she realized they were close to-gether in all areas, despite Lady Cecily being two years older than her sister. It would take hard work on both their parts to bring the older girl to the level she should be.

"I wish to read a story to you now, and I want you to listen to it carefully," she explained. "I will ask questions about the story—the characters and the plot—after I finish reading. It will test what you comprehend and your ability to predict events."

Both girls did much better in this exercise. They were also articulate for their ages, much better at expressing themselves orally than on paper. They would need to work on silently reading and also writing to arrive at an equal level as their listening skills. Overall, though, she was pleased by what she had discovered about them and happy to see both girls excited by the prospect of studying what they wished to learn more about.

"I think we have done enough for today," she told the pair.

"We are stopping?" Lady Lucy asked, clearly puzzled.

"Our governesses never did that," Lady Cecily informed her. "We worked all the time." She grinned mischievously. "Or at least they tried to make us work."

"I think every child should have a bit of free time on their hands," Willa explained. "Sometimes, it is nice to do simply nothing. Sit. Let your thoughts drift. Find something to entertain yourself. Go downstairs to the library and choose a book. I do not believe every minute of your day should be filled. You should have some control over time given exclusively to you."

They looked at her as if she had grown two extra heads.

"What do you want to do?" she asked.

"Draw," the younger girl said.

"You can use your slate if you wish to. Or I have some extra paper I can give you, and you may use your pencil. Tomorrow, we shall go to the closest village and obtain drawing paper and paints for you. I think you will find you will enjoy having extra time to draw and paint."

"What about the pianoforte?" Lady Cecily asked. "I want to start lessons on it tomorrow."

"Then why don't you go to the drawing room and investigate the instrument now?" she suggested. "Count the keys. Touch them. Listen to the tones. See which notes draw your attention and if there are any you might prefer."

A maid arrived with a tray. "Tea for you and the ladies, Miss Fennimore."

"But I was going to the drawing room," Lady Cecily pouted.

Willa laughed. "No one passes up tea. Look at all the scrumptious items here. Stay for tea, my lady, and then you can go to the drawing room."

They spent a lively teatime together, with the girls telling her about the house they had lived in before they came to Spring Ridge. She thought it interesting they did not really speak of their parents and remembered her promise to be with the duke when he spoke to them about their mother's death. Willa also talked about the house she had grown up in, telling about her time with Felton and her favorite flowers to grow.

"May I be excused?" Lady Cecily asked. "I want to go see the pianoforte."

"I want to go, too," Lady Lucy declared. "I don't think I want to learn to play, but I want to go with Cecily. And Uncle Xander will be there having his tea."

She had not thought about interrupting the duke. "Will he mind you showing up early?"

"No. He likes us," Lady Cecily said with confidence. "I think he likes you, too, Miss Fennimore."

"It is nice to be liked," she said lightly. "While you spend time with your uncle, I shall go to the kitchens and talk over things with Cook."

She accompanied the girls downstairs. They parted ways, and she headed to the kitchens, finding Cook sitting at a small table with a cup of tea.

"May I join you, Cook?" she asked.

The older woman began to rise, and Willa placed her hand on Cook's arm. "No, stay. I don't need a thing, other than your ear."

She took a seat. "I am a different governess from most."

"Let's hope so," Cook said. "Pardon me if I'm speaking out of turn, Miss Fennimore, but those two young ladies are hellions. They've had this household upside down ever since they arrived. Of course, they're sweet as pie when His Grace is around."

Laughing, she said, "I am hoping they will be much better behaved now that I am here, Cook. I am all for book learning, but I believe there is so much to be taught beyond the world of books."

Briefly, Willa shared with the older woman some of the ideas she wished to implement, including harvesting herbs from the herb garden.

Cook looked doubtful. "It would be nice if you could get them to do so, but I must have herbs when I need them."

"I can guarantee you that you will. Both Lady Lucy and Lady Cecily are interested in the herb garden. They will also be helping in the flower gardens, as well."

Cook whistled low. "If you can accomplish that, Miss Fennimore, then you are a miracle worker. I can write out what I need and have it sent to you each day so you will know which herbs to pluck." She paused. "Are you sure you don't want a cup of tea?"

"I will take one."

They talked for half an hour, Cook sharing a few recipes and Willa doing the same.

"How did you learn to cook?"

She sighed. "The house I grew up in was turbulent. Oftentimes, we were with few servants and no cook. I had to learn to provide for myself."

"Well, your recipe for huckleberry pie sounds delicious. I can't wait to try it."

"I have another favor to ask of you. My pupils would like to learn some cooking themselves. Lady Cecily mentioned biscuits and cake, in particular. They would like to prepare tea for their uncle someday."

"Well, I never," Cook proclaimed. "Ladies in the kitchen?"

"I believe it is important that they see the hard work which goes into preparing meals," Willa said. "It will make them appreciate your efforts more. And they do love pleasing their uncle."

"He's a one himself. That Lady Cecily is just like him at that age. His Grace was a troubled lad. Poor thing. Didn't get a bit of attention from his father or those older brothers. He misbehaved left and right."

"Children often do so to gain attention from adults, especially ones they wish to please."

Cook sighed. "Thank goodness His Grace has changed. He has been most pleasant since his return to Spring Ridge, according to the servants who deal with him. Maybe his nieces can do the same."

"If they do anything they are not supposed to, simply let me know. I will handle things," Willa promised.

"All right, Miss Fennimore. I'll let you and those girls in my kitchen. Come first thing tomorrow morning. They can help make something sweet for tea tomorrow."

"We will come down after breakfast. Then once we have finished, I would like to go to the nearest village to see if I can find paints for Lady Lucy. She is interested in art."

"Sherfield is only two miles from here."

"Oh, we could walk that easily. There would be so much to see along the way. Can you give me directions?"

Cook did so, encouraging her to go to Mrs. Salt's store, which housed a variety of merchandise. Willa even promised to pick up some honey for Cook while they were there.

Lorry appeared. "Miss Fennimore, His Grace is asking for you. He is in the drawing room."

"Thank you," she told the butler. Rising, she added, "And thank you for your time, Cook. I look forward to having you share what you know with my pupils."

Willa left and went upstairs, finding the girls with the duke. They were gathered about the pianoforte.

"Ah, here is your governess," Brockbank said. "We are exploring this instrument, Miss Fennimore, per your instructions. We have counted the keys. Opened the lid and seen what is inside."

"I like this note," Lady Lucy proclaimed, tapping a key several times.

"That is Middle C," she informed the girl. "Everything is built from that place on the keyboard."

"I like when you strike two keys at the same time," Lady Cecily said, demonstrating.

Willa sat on the bench and showed Lady Cecily what a chord was, and they talked about flats and sharps. Then she asked, "Are you ready to have a lesson tomorrow on this instrument?"

"Yes," Lady Cecily said, her enthusiasm bubbling over.

"No. I would rather draw than learn music," Lady Lucy said.

"Then Lady Cecily and I will have our first lesson once we return from Sherfield."

"Where is that?" the younger girl asked.

"It is the local village," the duke supplied, looking to Willa. "What is in Sherfield?"

"Paints, I hope. Lady Lucy is keen on art. We are going to look for different types of paints and other art supplies."

"We may have to go farther afield than Sherfield," he said. "But it would be good to check there first. What time are you leaving?"

"Directly after our lesson with Cook, which starts as soon as the girls finish their breakfasts."

"Then I shall have the carriage brought around."

"No, Your Grace. We will walk. Who knows what lessons we can learn along the way?"

"Have you had tea, Miss Fennimore?" he asked.

"I drank a cup with Cook a few minutes ago. And my pupils and I had tea together before that."

"Did you have any scones?"

"No," she replied.

"Then you must try one of the scones. They are delicious, especially with a bit of the clotted cream."

They left the girls at the pianoforte, and the duke himself placed a scone on a plate for Willa.

"I thought you would have joined us," he said, his tone conveying his disappointment.

"I want my charges to feel some independence. They did not need me to explore an instrument. I want their curiosity to go beyond when they are with me."

"I think perhaps we should have tea together each day, and then I can spend time with them afterward."

"That is a lovely idea, Your Grace. I will send them to the drawing room each day in time to do so."

"No, I think we should *all* have tea together." He gazed at her intently.

She realized he meant for her to come with the girls. "That is not necessary."

"I see how my nieces light up when you are near. I believe it would be good for them to have you present when they talk to me about their day. You have a way about you. You know when to nudge them and when to pull back."

"Surely, that is something you can do, Your Grace."

He smiled, his white teeth gleaming. "You yourself have pointed out I have no experience with children, Miss Fennimore."

"You are learning, though."

"I will learn more if you are with us. I insist."

She had no way to refuse a duke and simply said, "Of course, Your Grace."

"What lessons do you have planned tomorrow?"

"Besides going to the village and Lady Cecily's introduction to the pianoforte, we will be working on spelling, handwriting, and a cooking lesson. Cook has agreed to not only letting us harvest the herbs she needs, but she is also letting us enter her domain for a cooking lesson. You may be getting that tea prepared by your nieces sooner than you might think."

He shook his head. "You are changing things very quickly, Miss Fennimore. I am simply amazed."

"I think the old saying that the devil makes work for idle hands is true. I hope to keep your nieces busy, entertained and learning, so that they won't have the time, energy, or inclination to act out."

"It will make for exhausting work," he pointed out.

"That is what a governess' job entails, Your Grace."

He smiled, causing her pulse to quicken. "I think I have it easy, being a duke. I thought I was busy, but you are much more engaged than I am."

"Then I suppose it is good thing that you are the duke, and I am the governess," she quipped, her heart beating against her ribcage as she spoke.

The girls joined them, and Lucy asked what she thought of the scone.

"I quite like it. Did you know you will be baking something tomorrow with Cook?"

As the girls chattered happily about the possibilities of what they might make tomorrow for their uncle's tea, Willa listened, hearing how the duke teased with his nieces and how naturally they behaved together. If an outsider observed them, he would think these girls were Brockbank's daughters. She knew this relationship was a good one for the girls.

On the other hand, all this time spent in the duke's presence gave her something to worry about. Already, she was fighting her attraction to this man. Spending more time in his company would make it harder and harder for her to keep her feelings to herself.

And the last thing she wished for the Duke of Brockbank to know is just how much she wanted to kiss him.

CHAPTER ELEVEN

X ANDER ARRIVED IN the dining room meant for a dozen people and felt forlorn. Since he had become Duke of Brockbank, he usually ate quickly, not lingering over his meal, typically returning to his study to either deal with estate business or to read a book from his vast library.

Tonight, though, he wanted more—and knew he could have a companion in Willa Fennimore.

"Have my dinner brought to the winter parlor," he informed Lorry. "I will eat there in the future. It's ridiculous to have so many footmen on duty, attending to one person's needs." Pausing, he added, "And send for Miss Fennimore. I am in need of adult company."

Lorry's raised brows conveyed his displeasure at Xander's request. "I believe Miss Fennimore has already received her tray in her room, Your Grace."

"Then have it—and her—brought to the winter parlor," he said, his voice icy, not liking the longtime butler questioning him or his motives.

What *were* his motives?

He was afraid to voice them, even to himself.

Xander retreated to the winter parlor and seated himself. Lorry arrived with a bottle of wine and several covered dishes on a cart. He decanted the wine and removed the covers from the dishes, placing each in front of Xander.

"Did you send for Miss Fennimore?"

"Yes, Your Grace."

"Where is her wine glass?"

The butler hesitated. "I will bring it at once, Your Grace."

"See that you do."

By the time Lorry returned and poured a glass of wine for the governess, she still had yet to appear. Angry, Xander picked up his knife and fork and began to eat. He was halfway through his meal when he heard the knock at the door and called out, "Come."

Willa Fennimore entered, in the same gown she had worn all day. She crossed the room.

"Sit," he commanded.

She did so.

"What took you so long to answer my summons?" he asked, before shoving a bite of roasted chicken into his mouth.

"I had to finish eating my meal, Your Grace. I did not know how long our conversation might go on, and I thought to eat before I left my bedchamber."

Furious, he said, "I asked that your tray be brought down and you to dine with me."

She frowned. "That was not conveyed clearly to me, Your Grace. I was already halfway through my meal as it was and did not want the food to go to waste."

"Have some wine," he said, indicating the glass.

"Very well."

She picked it up and sipped it. He noted her long, thin fingers holding the stem and decided she must play the pianoforte extremely well because of them.

"I would like you to join me each evening for dinner," he said.

"No. That will not do," she said evenly.

He placed his fork on his plate very deliberately. "I do not believe I gave you a choice in the matter, Miss Fennimore."

He saw anger visibly sizzle through her. "You are saying this is not a request. Rather, it is a command. An order to be obeyed."

"Yes."

The governess picked up her wine glass and took a sip. Xander did the same. The wine was smooth and rich, a hearty red. He doubted she ever had the opportunity to drink so fine a wine because of her occupation. He continued watching her, thinking how delightful it would be to have her sitting across from him at the end of each day.

She gazed at him a long moment, and then said, "I am going to be most frank with you, Your Grace."

He smiled. "I would expect nothing less from you, Miss Fennimore."

"Actually, I will be more than frank. I will address things never said aloud." She paused, drawing in a deep breath and releasing it slowly. "Sitting across from you each evening would be difficult for me. I find I am far too interested in you, Your Grace, and I shouldn't be. My body seems to come to life in your presence. I have deep longings rippling through me. Things I have never thought of. Things that make me wish to behave recklessly and lose my head."

He felt triumphant hearing her words, knowing she was attracted to him. Before he could speak, she raised a hand.

"Let me finish, Your Grace. I am your nieces' governess. Period. I refuse to become your mistress. I will not give in to the temptations I now feel." Setting down her wine glass, she added, "You can force me to sit at your table—but you cannot make me converse with you."

Sitting back in her seat, she pursed her lips. Xander felt the anger building in him. How dare she defy him! And yet, he respected her for being so blunt. He managed to tamp down the anger and deliberately relaxed his limbs.

"You are exactly right, Miss Fennimore. I cannot make you talk with me." He picked up his own wine glass, studying her a long moment before taking a long swallow and placing it on the table again. "I suppose I can simply talk to you and not expect any reply."

She stubbornly sat, her gaze locked with his, a battle of wills being silently fought between them.

"I suppose you wonder why I requested your presence at my table. It is because . . . I am lonely."

Sympathy sprang within her. She had always had the ability to see things from someone else's point of view and empathize with their situation. She thought about the duke's current situation. He was a rogue, a man about town, likely to have been surrounded by friends. He drank. He gambled. He visited his mistresses. He attended *ton* affairs. Even though it sounded like an empty life to her, it had been his entire world. One which had been ripped from him. Suddenly, he was a titled duke with untold wealth. A man who had lost a family he never truly had. He was isolated in the country, far from any friends or support, and had been tasked to be the guardian of two small girls. Responsibilities he had never dreamed of piled high before him.

And Brockbank had no one to guide him. No one to offer friendship or support.

No one to talk to.

Willa never had been one to hold a grudge and she, unlike many others, could admit when she was wrong.

"I apologize, Your Grace," she said simply. "I behaved churlishly. I thought you had ulterior motives asking me here this evening—and the evenings to come. I can understand your situation and see how you might very well be lonely. You are without the companions you trusted and no longer frequent the places you are familiar with. A tremendous burden has been placed upon your shoulders. I misinterpreted the situation and ask for your forgiveness. If you wish for me to dine with you, I will. If you have things to talk over, I am open to listening. If you seek advice, I will offer what I can."

He reached for her hand and brought it to his sensual lips, placing a tender kiss upon her fingers. The gesture was sweet and romantic and almost undid her.

"Thank you," he said, his voice low and rough with emotion. "I feel as if I were a passenger on a large ship which sank and was fortunate to find myself in the only lifeboat. The only survivor of a terrible catastrophe, washed up on a desert island. The island is full of food and items I can use to build a shelter. The fish practically jump into my arms. The sun is warm and turns my skin to bronze. Yet I am alone. Utterly alone. I have everything I need—and nothing at all."

The duke released her hand. "I have immense wealth now, Miss Fennimore. I am learning each day more and more about my responsibilities. Yet it is if I am stuck on that island, with no way off."

She placed her hand over his; the rush of warmth occurring made her breath hitch. "You will not always feel this way. You will grow in your role here at Spring Ridge. You will eventually return to town, to your friends and Polite Society. Being a duke, you will naturally be accepted everywhere. You will have your friends and even make new ones. You will find a woman to make your duchess and wed. You will start a family and get your heir."

Willa patted his hand. "It will take time, however. You must be patient." She withdrew her hand.

"Not exactly my strong suit," he quipped and then sighed. "I miss my old life, and yet I see how empty it was. I know I am doing some good here at Spring Ridge. I like being in charge and helping others. I am eager to visit my other estates and see how they fare." Brockbank paused. "I suppose I am missing a friend. Someone to talk over my day."

"And you wish for us to dine together each evening so you can do so."

"Yes," he said softly. "You are an intelligent woman. One who seems more than willing to give me her opinion."

"I will help you," she promised. "I will sup with you if you wish."

"Thank you."

He picked up his fork again and began telling her about his day. Willa asked a few questions to clarify things he mentioned. He asked her questions, and she answered as best she could. When the clock chimed, she was aware of it for the first time—and heard it ring ten times.

"Oh, dear. It is so late," she said, quickly rising.

The duke also came to his feet. He captured her hands in his and brought them to his lips, gently kissing them and quickly releasing them.

"Thank you. It was good to have someone to talk over things. May I see you to your room?"

She had to draw some kind of line between them, before she flung herself into his arms and made a fool of herself.

"No, Your Grace. That is not necessary. After all, I am merely the governess."

Willa bowed her head briefly and exited the room, returning to her own at the top of the house.

It took her a long time to fall asleep.

﹥﹥﹥﹤﹤﹤

WILLA TOOK THE girls down to the kitchens after breakfasting with the duke. She had tossed and turned last night, regretting being so open with him, embarrassed by the fact she had told him she would not consider becoming his mistress. Well, Brockbank hadn't asked her to do so. Instead, he had asked for her friendship.

Yet the tender way he had kissed her hands had Willa thoroughly confused. Nothing was easy about her relationship with this man. She shouldn't even have one, other than employer and governess, yet she had acknowledged his plea for a friend. They had talked for hours the night before, both comfortable in one another's company. She would have to try and remain friendly with him, giving him advice and listening to his problems without becoming overly friendly.

Without wanting to climb into his lap and kiss him until she turned breathless.

Pushing that wayward thought aside, she entered the kitchens, seeing the looks she and the daughters of the house received from various scullery maids.

Cook waved them over, giving her a hearty welcome, and then said, "I hear you ladies wish to do something special for your uncle and his tea today."

"Today?" Lady Lucy asked, her eyes round with wonder. "I thought we would just watch you."

"Hmm," Cook said. "And here I thought Miss Fennimore said you were interested in learning to bake something."

"*I* want to bake," Lady Cecily declared. "Your sweets are really good, Cook.

"Miss Fennimore tells me that you are partial to cake and biscuits. I think, though, that everyone should start with learning how to bake a delicious scone."

"What kind?" Lady Lucy asked, jumping up and down.

"One which is fluffy and soft," Cook quipped, laughing. "I have everything out that we need over here."

They accompanied the servant to a large table, and Willa saw flour, baking powder, and sugar, along with butter.

"Let's get you into some aprons so you don't get flour on your pretty gowns," the old woman said.

Soon, she had the girls adding ingredients and mixing them together, advising them to add the softened butter only after the dry ingredients were well-blended.

"See, it has a sandy texture," Cook said. "Feel it."

Both girls did.

The servant had one girl pour in milk and taught them how to crack an egg, saving a bit of yolk for the egg wash later. The girls took turns mixing things, and then Cook dumped the contents of the bowl onto the table.

"See here, my ladies? The mixture is wet, but you mustn't add too much flour. That dries out your scones. Instead, lightly flour your dough and then you knead it, smoothing it out just a bit."

As she kneaded under Cook's watchful eye, Lady Cecily said, "This is sticky."

"Yes, some does stick to the table. That's all right. You must have a wet dough and soft texture to get a good rise from it, my lady. Enough kneading, Lady Lucy. Too much and your scones grow tough, and they won't rise as high and be fluffy."

"What's next?" Willa asked.

"We'll roll the dough about an inch thick," Cook explained. She reached for something and said, "This is a cutter which will make circles of our dough. Let me warn you now—don't twist it ever. Push straight down. That way, your scones will rise nice and tall."

The servant demonstrated, and then had both girls try. Willa was pleased with how well they did, and soon the entire dough had become a group of circles. Cook showed them how to do an egg wash, and then they placed them in the oven, telling them how long a scone usually took to bake but that they needed to keep a watchful eye on them.

"Never walk away when you are baking," Cook warned. "You want a scone that's high and puffed up, golden brown in color."

When they came out of the oven, the girls clapped, marveling at how they had made scones.

"Next time you come to the kitchens, I'll show you how to make jam for them. I know Miss Fennimore wants to take you into the village this morning, so we'll save that for another time."

"Are these the scones we'll eat with Uncle Xander today?" Lady Lucy asked hopefully.

"They are," Cook assured the girl. "Not everyone has a good first effort, much less one suitable for serving to a duke. You two did quite well, though. I'll heat them slightly and have the jam and clotted cream ready for you this afternoon."

Before Willa could prompt them, Lady Cecily said, "Thank you, Cook. We liked learning to bake from you. Will you teach us how to make a lemon cake?"

"And macaroons," Lady Lucy prompted. "They are my favorites."

The old woman smiled indulgently. "I would be happy to have you in my kitchens any day, my ladies. Miss Fennimore and I will arrange another time for you to come and learn."

"Thank you, Cook," Lady Lucy said. "I hope you liked our help. And we'll pick herbs for you today, too. Miss Fennimore showed us your list at breakfast this morning. I couldn't read all the words, but I promise I will learn."

"I thank you for your help, my ladies."

Willa also thanked Cook, and they returned upstairs. They changed into boots in order to walk into the village and slipped into spencers to keep warm as they went.

Though she had not given the duke a specific time, he was waiting for them in the foyer.

"I am here to accompany you three ladies into Sherfield," he said.

"Miss Fennimore isn't a lady," Lady Cecily said. "She is just a miss."

"I am still here to escort you," Brockbank said, slipping his hand around hers. "I learned so much in the gardens yesterday that I simply had to go with you to the village and see what Miss Fennimore teaches you along the way."

Lady Lucy joined hands with her sister and then offered Willa her free one. She took it and they set out, arriving at Sherfield an hour later. They could have walked it more quickly, but they paused every now and then as she pointed out various things to them and took the opportunity to teach small lessons as they went.

"We are to go to Mrs. Salt's," she told the duke.

"Yes, I remember her from years ago," he said. "If there are art supplies to be found, Mrs. Salt's shop will have them."

He pointed out which door they should enter and opened it for them. The girls went in first, and Willa followed them. A tall, handsome man just over six feet and with deep brown hair and chocolate brown eyes was on his way out. He tipped his hat to them just as the duke entered the shop.

Brockbank halted and said, "Linberry. I was thinking of you and your wife. Wanting to be neighborly, I wish to invite you to tea at Spring Ridge."

She saw the gentleman frown. "That is not necessary, Your Grace."

Recalling the name, Willa surmised this man had been the grandson Brockbank had mentioned playing with a few times. The one who thought the duke too naughty to be around. Hurt for the duke filled her.

"I am not the incorrigible boy I once was," the duke said softly. "Nor the man I was in town only a few months ago."

She saw a shift occur in the man's posture. "I suppose I am not, either. I was a bit prudish as a child. I remember telling you I wanted nothing to do with you. I apologize for hurting your feelings for I know I must have done so."

"You were a dutiful son with loving parents," the duke replied. "I constantly misbehaved, trying to gain my father's attention." He smiled wryly. "I would not have wanted to be around me. I certainly do not blame you for being mature enough to recognize what I was then."

"Everyone deserves a second chance, Brockbank. As for tea, my duchess and I cannot come to you. She is due to give birth in the next week or so and cannot possibly ride in a carriage." He held up a sack.

"She is made for peppermints, which is why I came into Sherfield this morning. But I know she would be happy to host you for tea."

"Might I bring my nieces?" He indicated the girls. "This is Cecily and Lucy and their governess, Miss Fennimore."

Linberry nodded. "It is a pleasure to meet the three of you. Fia would like that very much if you came to tea. Why not this afternoon?"

"Oh, we can't," Lady Cecily piped up. "Lucy and I made scones for Uncle Xander this morning. He has to eat them for his tea today."

"You made scones, my lady? How delightful. I am sure my duchess would be eager to sample one of them. Do you think your cook might box them up so you could bring them to tea today and share them with us?"

Lady Lucy frowned. "Do you have jam? Or clotted cream? We were going to serve that to Uncle Xander with the scones."

Linberry smiled indulgently. "I believe we do, my lady."

"Then it is settled," Brockbank said. "We shall bring the scones, and you may provide the rest of tea."

"We look forward to seeing you this afternoon."

"And Miss Fennimore," the duke added. "She accompanies my nieces wherever they go."

Willa sucked in a quick breath, horrified that her employer was trying to include her in the outing. "Your Grace, my presence is not necessary. You can easily escort the girls to tea without my help."

"I believe His Grace's wife is something of a musician, Miss Fennimore. Since you are about to start lessons on the pianoforte with Cecily, Her Grace might have some suggestions for you. I insist."

She felt her face burning as the Duke of Linberry said, "Yes, my wife gave lessons to children for many years. Please come, Miss Fennimore. You would be most welcomed. I know the two of you will have much to discuss."

"Thank you, Your Grace," Willa managed to say, her eyes downcast.

Linberry departed and the girls asked, "Can we look about the store, Miss Fennimore?"

"May we look," she prompted. "It is better to ask in that manner. *May* indicates you are asking permission."

"Then *may* we?" Lady Cecily asked, her exasperation obvious.

"You may."

They scurried off, and Willa turned to the duke. "Why did you insist I be included in this outing?"

"You heard my reason, Miss Fennimore. Her Grace has a wealth of experience teaching children on the pianoforte and might be able to give you some advice."

Not satisfied with his reasoning, Willa added, "It is highly irregular, Your Grace. Even inappropriate, my taking tea with a duke and duchess."

"No more inappropriate than a duke wedding a musician," he quickly responded.

The duke looked blandly at her, but she sensed more was going on. She also knew this was not a battle she would win.

"Very well, Your Grace. Now, we must find Lady Lucy's art supplies."

Willa turned away, her face still full of heat. Thankfully, the girls distracted her, pointing out several items and finding things they both wanted. Their uncle indulged them and allowed them to choose whatever they wished as she stood apart, questioning the duke's motives in insisting that she be allowed to accompany him and his nieces to tea with a duke and duchess.

Even more, Willa questioned if she should even remain at Spring Ridge.

CHAPTER TWELVE

X ANDER KNEW HE had taken a risk asking Linberry to include Willa Fennimore in the invitation to come to tea today at Linfield. He thought about it as he purchased the items his nieces wished to buy, asking Mrs. Salt if they could be delivered to Spring Ridge since the four of them had walked into Sherfield.

"I can do so, Your Grace," the shop owner told him. "My boy will be making deliveries this afternoon. I'll be sure Spring Ridge is his first stop."

"But I want to paint when I get home," Lucy complained.

"Then I will carry the charcoals for you," Miss Fennimore said. "We can use some of the paper in the schoolroom for you to start on."

"What about the paints?" Lucy whined.

"I think it best for you to start with pencil and charcoal," the governess said firmly. "We will work our way up to the paints. We will have to have a few lessons about paints. How you can mix different ones together to form new colors."

"Really?" Lucy said, curiosity filling her face. "Like what?"

"Oh, if you put a little red onto the page and mix in a bit of blue, you get purple. The more red you mix in, the more the purple becomes a reddish-violet color, while the more blue you add to your mix, it deepens into darker shades of purple, such as aubergine."

"I want to make pink," Lucy declared. "Pink is my favorite color."

"What might you mix together to get pink?" Miss Fennimore asked, and Xander bit back a smile, thinking she turned every conversation into a lesson.

Lucy's face scrunched up in thought. Finally, she said, "Red. But red is too dark. You have to make it lighter so it will look like pink."

"I know," Cecily said excitedly. "White! White is very light."

"Well done, my lady," Miss Fennimore praised. "Red and white do indeed combine to make pink. And what did we just learn, my ladies, that could apply now?"

Lucy jumped up and down. "I know. The more red we put in, the darker the pink will be. The more white we add, the lighter the red will get."

"You are mastering the basics of colors in painting, and we have yet to open a pot or tube," the governess proclaimed. She turned to Mrs. Salt. "I will take the charcoals, and you can have the rest of the supplies sent to Spring Ridge, Mrs. Salt."

"I will do that, Miss Fennimore. And tell Cook hello for me."

"I shall do so," the governess promised.

They left the shop and took a quick turn about the village. It had not changed much in the ten years in which Xander had been gone. He pointed out a bakery, an inn, and a blacksmith. When Cecily asked if they could stop in the bakery for a treat, he reminded them they were going to tea at Linfield this afternoon and would get their fill of sweets there.

"Perhaps we can walk into the village once a week," Miss Fennimore suggested. "I myself have a fondness for sticky buns. I would be happy to buy one for each of us on our next trip to Sherfield."

Both girls clapped their hands and begin skipping ahead of them, holding hands.

He turned to Miss Fennimore and said, "I think I should speak to them on the way home about their mother's death. It would be wise to do so away from the house."

"Whatever you think best, Your Grace. But let them frolic a moment longer since they are finally enjoying time outside the house."

"I regret that. What I mean to say is that I regret not knowing they had been cooped up for so long. Now that you are here, though, Miss Fennimore, I hope to be better informed about everything regarding my nieces."

After half a mile, his nieces began to slow, and he and the governess caught up with them.

"I want to talk with the two of you about something," he began. "Something serious. Give me your hands as we walk."

Each girl took one of his hands and as they walked, he said, "I know that you were told that your father and Uncle Stanley drowned in the lake nearby."

"It was dark and rained a lot." Cecily shivered. "I remember the lightning and being afraid of it."

"You understand that your mother died the next day, don't you?" He glanced down at Lucy and saw her frowning.

"I heard some servants say she was in the boat, too."

"That is not the truth, Lucy. Remember, I told you your mama was sick and sad, and then she died."

Cecily tugged on his hand, looking up at him. "I remember you saying that, Uncle Xander. Mama wasn't ever sick, though. But I know she was so sad that Papa and Uncle Stanley died. I am glad I didn't like Papa very much because I'm not sad he's gone. And we hardly ever saw Uncle Stanley. I told Lucy we can't be sad because we don't want to die like Mama did."

He turned, his gaze meeting Miss Fennimore's. The governess had been right.

"Your mama was very sad, but you are right. She was not sick."

"Then why did you say she was?" Lucy asked him, looking confused.

"When you are older, you might be able to understand it better.

What I will say now is that yes, your mama was very sad when your papa and uncle died. So sad that the doctor came and gave her some medicine. Your mama accidentally drank all the medicine. It was very strong and killed her."

"Mama said medicine makes you feel better," Lucy wailed, her bottom lip quivering.

"That is the purpose of medicine," he agreed quietly. "But only when it is taken in the right amount."

"Did the doctor not tell Mama how much she should take?" Cecily asked.

"I am certain he must have, but your mama was grieving over those two deaths. She might not have been listening to what the doctor said and only remembered that the doctor told her if she took the medicine, it would make her feel better. Medicine can be good for you unless you take too much of it. Sometimes, it can make you grow even sicker. In this case, it made your mama so sick that she died."

Cecily burst into tears and Xander stopped, kneeling and enfolding her in his arms. Lucy flung her arms about both of them and also began crying. He looked up, and Miss Fennimore nodded encouragingly. She mouthed, *"You are doing fine,"* bolstering his confidence.

He rubbed each girl's back, trying to comfort them as best he could. When they stopped crying, Xander took out his handkerchief and dried the tears from their cheeks.

"I did not want you to think that being sad would kill you. It is perfectly all right to be sad. Why, there are all kinds of reasons to be sad. It may be something big that happens, such as a family member or friend dying. You would naturally be sad because you would not see them anymore."

"I believe our loved ones watch over us," Miss Fennimore said. "Even after they are gone and we can no longer see them."

"Do you think your mama and papa watch over you, Miss Fennimore?" Lucy asked.

"I do—and I try to make them proud of me every day."

"There are also other times you might be sad. You might be sad if you say something to hurt someone's feelings. You might fall down and skin your knee and be sad because it hurts. I just want you to understand that it is perfectly normal to *be* sad sometimes. No one can be happy all the time."

Lucy studied him solemnly. "Are you ever sad, Uncle Xander?"

"I have been known to be sad sometimes. I don't always like to talk about it with others, though. I think it is best if you do tell others you are sad, however. They might be able to cheer you up."

He looked from Lucy to Cecily. "So, do you understand now that it is a part of life to be sad? Just as it is a part of life to be happy—and everything in-between. People have all kinds of emotions. They might be angry. They might be frightened. They might be joyful. Never hide your emotions, girls. And if you wish to talk about something bothering you, you can do so with Miss Fennimore or me."

Cecily flung her arms about him and buried her face against his neck, while Lucy gave him a timid smile. He said, "Come, we need to continue on our way. Once we return to Spring Ridge, Lucy can test out her charcoals with Miss Fennimore."

"What will I do?" Cecily wanted to know.

"Cecily, you can do one of two things," he continued. "You might watch Lucy and be supportive of her as she draws. Ask her to draw certain things and even draw something yourself because I know Lucy would be willing to share her charcoals with you."

When Lucy gave Xander a belligerent look, Miss Fennimore stepped in. "Although they are Lady Lucy's charcoals, I know she has a generous nature and will share if Lady Cecily asks her to do so. Or we can do another lesson, my lady. It will be up to you."

The girl smiled brightly. "That's because *we* choose what we study."

"You certainly do," Xander agreed.

They set off in the direction of Spring Ridge again.

XANDER SENT WORD to the schoolroom that it was time to come down in order to leave for Linfield. He had told the girls that he would arrange with Cook to have the scones they had baked wrapped up, and so he went to retrieve them now.

Cook passed him a hamper, and he opened the lid, seeing cloth wrapped around what had to be the scones.

"I put a jar of my raspberry jam in there, Your Grace. Your nieces were so happy to have made these scones for you. Why, they were bursting with pride."

"I must thank you for allowing them to invade the kitchens, Cook. I know it is not the habit of family members to do so."

"It's quite all right, Your Grace. That Miss Fennimore is lovely, isn't she? She explained how the little ladies wanted to do something special for you." Cook smiled broadly. "There isn't anything more special than a scone baked with love. I hope Their Graces also enjoy them."

"I will have to think twice on whether or not I will share *my* scones with them," he said, laughing.

The old woman cackled with glee and at that moment, Xander felt like a very different man than the one who had arrived at Spring Ridge more than two months ago. Part of the change in him had been due to the title he had taken on—but another part of the change was because of Miss Fennimore's influence. It seemed he wanted to be a better man, not only for himself, but for the beautiful, kind governess.

The one he was still desperate to kiss.

He returned to the foyer and found his party waiting for him.

Lucy ran to him. "Are those our scones?"

Opening the lid, Xander said, "I would say see for yourself, but

Cook has wrapped them thoroughly. She did include a bit of her raspberry jam to share along with the scones."

Cecily came and peeked inside the hamper. "I hope you like them, Uncle Xander," she said worriedly.

"Cook praised your baking skills and said that you had baked them with love. I think I will enjoy these scones just fine. In fact," he said, closing the hamper, "I may eat all of them myself."

Lucy's jaw dropped. "You mean you wouldn't share with us?"

"Oh, I suppose I should let each of you have at least one so you may taste the results of your lesson in the kitchens."

"Miss Fennimore needs to eat one, too, Uncle Xander," Cecily pointed out. "After all, she is the one who helped get us to make them." She thought a moment. "And it would be rude if we went calling on the duke and duchess and didn't share with them."

Pride filled Xander, and his gaze met that of Miss Fennimore. The governess, too, beamed.

"You are exactly right, Cecily. It is better to share with others. Besides, I hope to make friends with the duke. I didn't do a very good job of it years ago. I hope I am a better man than boy and that His Grace will accept my offer of friendship."

"He'll like you now, Uncle Xander," Lucy assured him. "And maybe Miss Fennimore and the duchess can become friends. You could all be friends together."

He smiled and turned to the governess. "Yes, that would be rather lovely, wouldn't it?" He watched a blush tinge her cheeks.

"We should be leaving now," Miss Fennimore said brusquely, taking charge of the situation. "We do not wish to be late for tea."

Xander escorted them outside to the waiting carriage and handed up his nieces first before offering his hand to Miss Fennimore.

"Thank you," he said. "For being there while I spoke with them. I know that the day will come in the future when they will have more questions than they did today. I promise I will not hide anything from them."

"Trust your instincts," she said to him. "You did an excellent job, talking it over with them. When that time does come, you will know what to say—and how to do so."

Cecily appeared in the door. "Aren't you coming?"

"Yes, of course," Miss Fennimore said, stepping into the carriage.

Xander followed her and saw his nieces on one side and their governess opposite them.

"Sit with us, Uncle Xander," Lucy begged.

Although he would have preferred sitting next to Miss Fennimore, sitting across from her was the next best thing because as he looked straight ahead, she was directly in his line of view. He would be able to stare at her all he liked without having to apologize.

The girls chattered nonstop on the short ride to Linfield, which was only two miles away. The entire time, Xander drank in Willa Fennimore's beauty. He longed to unpin her sable hair and have it spill past her shoulders and down her back. He knew he wanted her in his bed, wearing nothing but a smile. And at some point, his wedding ring.

Xander couldn't believe how much he had changed in so short a time and once more hoped this beautiful, intelligent woman would find him worthy to spend the rest of her life with.

CHAPTER THIRTEEN

THEY ARRIVED AT Linfield, and Xander was surprised to see none other than the Duke of Linberry standing outside to greet them. It was not a practice of dukes to do so, and he felt honored Linberry was putting aside their past differences and behaving in such a gentlemanly fashion.

They left the carriage, and the duke smiled warmly. Xander noted that his nieces curtseyed to the duke this time, and he knew their governess had prepared them for this social meeting.

"Come inside if you would," Linberry invited. "My duchess is waiting in the drawing room for you."

Ascending the stairs, they reached the drawing room. He saw the duchess seated in a grouping of furniture close to the fireplace. Going toward her, Xander recognized her from when he had seen her playing in the orchestra last Season. She was heavy with child but glowed with vitality.

"Pardon me for not rising, Your Grace," she said, "but it is lovely to meet you."

"Dearest, may I introduce to you the Duke of Brockbank and his nieces, Lady Cecily and Lady Lucy?"

Xander took her offered hand and kissed it, while his nieces curtseyed.

"And this is Miss Fennimore, the girls' governess," Linberry continued.

Miss Fennimore also curtseyed to their hostess. Then Cecily said, "You are very pretty, but you are so big."

Horror filled him at his niece's untoward remark, and Xander said, "You are a better girl than that, Cecily Hughes," his tone terse.

She looked at him. "But Uncle Xander, she *is* pretty."

"The best rule is if you have good things to say to someone, express them. Other than compliments, keep your opinions to yourself."

"I shouldn't say Her Grace is large?"

"That is exactly right," he said firmly. "Remember what Miss Fennimore has taught you—that others have feelings—and you do not wish to hurt them. That you want to help others always. Your unkind words to Her Grace made her feel bad."

Cecily's eyes filled with tears, and she turned back to the Duchess of Linberry. "I'm sorry, Your Grace."

"Thank you for your apology, my lady," the duchess said graciously. "I am rather large because I am going to have a baby any day now."

"I like babies," Lucy said. "At least I think I do. I haven't really been around them before."

"Then you will be welcome to come and visit me once my babe is born," the duchess told her, smiling. "Please have a seat if you would. The teacart should be here shortly. I hear you girls are providing part of our tea today."

"Miss Fennimore talked to Cook, and we got to go to the kitchens this morning," Cecily said brightly. "We made scones for Uncle Xander. And Cook sent some jam, too."

"I told our cook she did not need to make scones because our guests were bringing some along," Linberry said affably as they sat. "However, she also makes excellent jam so I believe the teacart might have both it and some clotted cream which we might use on your scones, my ladies."

Servants rolled in two teacarts, and the duchess poured out for them.

"I also had some milk brought in case your nieces preferred it," Her Grace said.

"I like milk with scones," Lucy declared.

"Me, too," Cecily chimed in.

As the duchess made certain everyone had something to drink, Xander opened the hamper Cook had provided and unwrapped the cloth, seeing the scones were still warm. Everyone helped themselves to a scone, as well as other delicacies provided by the Linfield cook. Xander made certain he used the raspberry jam his own cook had sent along but also placed a dollop of the clotted cream upon his plate.

As he bit into his scone, he saw his nieces eyeing him. He chewed slowly, making the appropriate sounds of someone thoroughly enjoying his food.

"So, you like it, Uncle Xander?" Cecily asked.

"This may be the best scone I have ever had," he declared. "Don't tell Cook, though. We would not want to hurt her feelings."

As they ate, Her Grace apologized to Xander. "I am sorry my husband and I did not attend the funerals of your family. We both had dreadful colds at the time and were in bed for days."

"It looks as if you have recovered your good health, Your Grace," he said. "I am sorry it has taken us this long to meet. I do recall seeing you last Season, however. I spied you in an orchestra, playing the night of the opening ball."

Linberry smiled with pride. "My duchess plays several instruments, as well as composing her own music. She has been hard at work, finishing numerous pieces while we have been in the country. Once we return to town, I plan to host a musicale so Polite Society might hear her compositions."

The duchess looked to Miss Fennimore. "I understand that you will be giving music lessons to His Grace's nieces. Will you start them on the pianoforte?"

"It is the only instrument I know how to play," the governess said. "Only Lady Cecily will be learning how to play it, however. Lady Lucy has an affinity for art and will be concentrating on it instead."

Lucy said, "Miss Fennimore lets us study what we want to learn."

The duchess nodded, studying Miss Fennimore with interest. "That is a most unusual philosophy."

"I was given quite a bit of liberty as a child to pursue what interested me most. No topic was forbidden. Because of that, I found that I became interested in many areas. I would study one thing, and then it would lead to another. I would follow different threads. Overall, I received a well-rounded education."

"What were you most passionate about?" asked the Duke of Linberry.

"Languages fascinated me, Your Grace. I speak three fluently and have more than a smattering of German. I, too, have written a few pieces for the pianoforte though it was long ago."

"My, how interesting," Her Grace said. "Perhaps you might perform one for us once tea concludes."

Miss Fennimore laughed, and Xander was drawn in by it.

"I have not practiced in a good while, Your Grace," the governess said. "Besides, you are such an accomplished musician. I do not think I should play in front of you."

The duchess gave the governess a conspiratorial smile. "Then when tea concludes, we shall retreat to my music room with the girls. You can play in private for me, and I can show Lady Cecily and Lady Lucy some of my other instruments."

"My wife plays the violin, viola, and cello, as well as the pianoforte," Linberry bragged. "What I most enjoy hearing her play, however, is the harp. The angels in heaven have nothing on my Fia when it comes to the harp."

What Xander now witnessed unfold was exactly what he read of in the gossip columns. That the Duke and Duchess of Linberry were a love match. He watched as Linberry took his wife's hand and laced their fingers together, and brought their joined hands to his lips for a tender kiss.

A deep longing overwhelmed him as he wished he could do the same with the woman sitting beside him. Determination filled him, and he vowed to himself by the end of today, he would kiss Willa Fennimore.

The teatime was most pleasant, and Xander found himself liking the duke and duchess quite a bit. They were open and honest, no pretension about them. All the scones were consumed, and the duchess had Cecily and Lucy promise her that they would bake a new batch and come and visit her with them once her babe was born.

"I can send word to Spring Ridge once our new addition arrives," Linberry said.

Innocently, Lucy looked at Linberry and asked, "Are you going to be friends with Uncle Xander now? He told us you weren't friends before."

The duke chuckled as Xander said, "Forgive my nieces, Your Graces. Miss Fennimore and I are still working on what is acceptable conversation."

"You have no work to be done, Brockbank," the duke proclaimed. "I find your nieces delightful." Linberry turned his attention to Lucy. "So, your uncle mentioned we were not friends before?"

"Yes," Cecily said quickly, eager to share what she had learned. "Uncle Xander was naughty as a boy, and he said you didn't like him because of it. That you were a good boy and did what your parents asked." She frowned. "I am sometimes naughty, too, but I'm trying to be better now."

Lucy spoke up. "Miss Fennimore says it's important for people to have a second chance. Will you give Uncle Xander a chance to be your friend now?"

Linberry's gaze met Xander's, and the duke nodded. "Something tells me that I will become very good friends with your uncle, girls."

"Why don't we ladies adjourn to the music room now?" Her Grace said. "Even though Lady Lucy is not drawn to the pianoforte, she might want to see my other instruments. I think she will find the harp's tones soothing."

Linberry quickly stood and helped ease his wife from her seat. Xander could see now how rounded her belly was and couldn't help but picture Willa Fennimore in the same condition, his babe resting within her.

Miss Fennimore stood and asked, "May I take your arm, Your Grace?"

"Oh, thank you, Miss Fennimore. That would be so very helpful."

The four left the drawing room, and Xander and Linberry seated themselves again.

"You have changed, Brockbank," the duke pointed out.

"I hope so. I was incorrigible as a child. No wonder you did not want to be around me."

"Why were you so ill-behaved?"

"I sought attention from my father," Xander admitted. "My mother died giving birth to me, and my father called me a murderer."

Sympathy filled the duke's eyes. "No child should be told something so awful."

"Well, you didn't know my father. My three brothers weren't much better. They were all born closely together and were many years my senior. They all seemed to be of the opinion that I, the afterthought, killed their mother, and they were cruel to me. It made sense to me—at least back then—that if I got my father's attention, things might change. The only way I knew how to do so was to act out constantly, hoping he would finally take notice of me."

Xander paused. "I was jealous of you, you know. I saw how your parents doted upon you. I had never experienced that kind of attention, much less love."

"Love is a marvelous, powerful thing," the duke said quietly. "I have found lasting love with my Fia. Yes, Polite Society did not deem her suitable to be a duchess." He grinned. "When has a duke ever listened to what Polite Society thought?"

Both men laughed, and Xander said, "This being a duke is very new business to me. As a fourth son, I had no hopes of ever gaining a title."

"I know two of your brothers drowned. You did have a third, I believe."

"Yes, Peter. He attained the rank of major-general and was recently killed in battle." Xander shrugged. "That is how I became the Duke of Brockbank. I must apologize to you, Linberry. When you rejected me as a playmate, I turned quite bitter against you. I don't recall ever saying a single word to you during our time at school, much less acknowledging you once we became grown men. I realize that I have been living a hedonistic life and doing no good to anyone. Becoming a duke has been a sobering experience for me, but I am taking my responsibilities seriously."

"I, too, suddenly became a duke," Linberry told him. "My father and grandfather both died on the same day, and I found myself in a position which I did not think I would fill for many years. I will admit it has been a struggle at times, but I have made some good friends, some being dukes themselves."

Linberry offered Xander his hand. "Shall we shake to our new friendship, Your Grace?"

He took the proffered hand and grasped it firmly. "You are a good man to overlook my past transgressions, Linberry."

"I can see the change in you, you know. The way you are with your nieces. The way you speak to them and try to teach them. Becoming their guardian, you have become an instant parent and authority figure to them. I believe you are doing a remarkable job."

"It is all thinks to Miss Fennimore," he said. "I must give her the credit."

"Speaking of Miss Fennimore, how long have you been in love with her?"

Xander froze. "What?"

The duke laughed easily. "Come now, Brockbank. You are speaking to a man who is besotted with his wife. Let me tell you that I can recognize the signs in other men."

"Am I that obvious? I thought I had more finesse than that."

Linberry laughed again. "Oh, I think it would take another man who is madly in love to recognize that in you. Does Miss Fennimore share your feelings?"

Xander raked a hand through his hair. "No. She hasn't a clue. You see how very beautiful she is. When I hired her, she was most blunt. I assume she had . . . difficulties with previous employers, thanks to her looks. Because of it—and because I was so desperate to find a governess since Cecily and Lucy kept chasing them off—I gave her my word that I would never take advantage of her."

Linberry nodded thoughtfully. "You think if you spoke of your feelings to her that she would reject you?"

"I haven't a clue," he said honestly. "All I think about night and day is kissing her. She is a brilliant woman, Linberry. Smart and kind. Different from any woman I have ever known."

"I think you need to share your feelings with her, Brockbank. They may very well be reciprocated." He smiled. "And I would kiss her, as well. If your words do not convince her of your feelings, perhaps your kiss will."

"Your words have encouraged me to take action, Linberry," Xander declared. "If this backfires, though, I will expect you to find a new governess for my girls."

His new friend laughed heartily, and Xander joined in. He knew if he did kiss Willa and share his feelings for her, she might very well up and vacate her position at once. Was he willing to risk the progress she had made with his nieces simply to selfishly make himself happy? Cecily and Lucy had been through so much. Despite his feelings, he must think of his nieces first.

Xander decided he must wait, after all, before he could tell Miss Fennimore what he had in mind for their future.

Chapter Fourteen

THREE AFTERNOONS LATER, Willa was out walking the estate with the girls. They had gone to the stables after breakfast with the duke and visited each stall with his head groom since Lady Cecily was still interested in learning how to ride. Lady Lucy was still deciding whether or not she would take lessons with her sister. The groom recommended which horses the girls might use during their lessons, and they had gone to the pasture where the horses had been let out to stretch their legs.

"They're awfully big," Lady Lucy said.

"They are," she agreed. "But riding is a good thing for a lady to know how to do. In the country, it is an easy way to get around and visit others. In London, you may have gentlemen ask you to ride in Hyde Park once you make your come-outs. Besides, animals are soothing to be around."

"I think it would be fun to sit up so high and see the world on top of a horse," Lady Cecily said dreamily.

"I'll think about it," Lady Lucy finally said.

"You can always change your mind about anything," she told the girls. "While Lady Lucy isn't interested in the pianoforte now, she might be in a few years. The same is true for learning how to ride a horse. They may seem large and frightening now since you are only six years old, but in a few years when you are your sister's age, you may want to learn how to do so. It is the same with anything you choose to study. As you mature, your interests might change and you'll want to explore new areas."

A horse came up to the fence where they stood, and Willa stroked his long nose and then scratched the area between his ears.

"He likes that," Lady Cecily said. "Would you like to learn to ride with me, Miss Fennimore?"

"No, my lady. I have no need to learn."

"What if I want to ride about the country? I need someone with me, don't I?"

"In that case, you may take a groom with you or your uncle would accompany you. Come, we should head back to the house. It will be teatime soon."

The duke had asked they share tea with him each day, and Willa did not wish for them to be late. She was growing fond of being in Brockbank's company. Too fond. She worried that if she could not curb her attraction that she might have to leave Spring Ridge for good. It would break her heart to walk away from these two, wonderful, curious, loving girls. Of all her charges, Lady Cecily and Lady Lucy were by far her favorites, even after so short a time in their company.

Perhaps she should try to reason with the duke again. She already saw him at breakfast each morning. Then at tea. Once again at dinner when they supped together in the winter parlor, an intimate room that lent itself to shared confidences. If she cut back on her contact with him, she might be able to get over the incredible rush of feelings that poured through her each time she was in his presence. The giddiness that made her belly flip and flop. The shortness of breath and quickened pulse. The awareness of him as a man.

Why, after all these years, did she have to want this man? A duke. Someone so far removed from her realm as to be laughable. She had spent years in the company of actors, notoriously handsome men, and yet not one of them had made her breath catch and her senses soar the way the Duke of Brockbank did.

They left the pasture, with Willa telling the girls the next time they visited they would bring carrots or apples to feed the horses and make friends with them. Lady Lucy seemed entranced by that idea, befriending such a large beast. As they crossed into the meadow, they saw a carriage coming up the road.

"Who could that be?" Lucy asked.

"Let's find out," Cecily cried and began running toward the main road.

Lucy took off after her sister, and Willa hiked her skirts, wanting to keep up with her charges. Not knowing if anyone was expected at Spring Ridge, she did not want the girls to speak to a stranger without her being present.

Both girls waved at the coachman, and he waved back. A man appeared in the window and waved as well, as if he knew the girls, and she wondered if this might be a relative from their mother's side coming to call to see how the girls fared after losing their parents so recently.

The vehicle came to a halt, and the man who had waved hopped from it. He called up to the driver, who nodded and took up the reins again, starting the carriage back up again.

The girls had reached the road and came to a stop. Willa hurried to them, placing her hands on their shoulders as a well-dressed gentleman with wavy, blond hair stepped toward them.

"I say, you must be His Grace's nieces. Lady Cecily and Lady Lucy." He bowed. "I am Viscount Swanson and used to share rooms with your uncle in London."

The girls curtseyed. "Pleased to meet you, my lord," Lady Cecily said, echoed by her sister.

"And you must be the new governess," Lord Swanson said, eyeing her up and down in appreciation. "The last I saw Brockbank, he was in town to hire a new one."

"Yes, my lord," Willa said stiffly. "I am Miss Fennimore."

"Delighted to meet you, Miss Fennimore," Swanson said, awarding her with a flirtatious smile.

She knew his type—and knew to stay far away from him.

"Shall we walk together to the main house?" the viscount asked.

"Have you come to visit Uncle Xander?" Lady Lucy asked.

"I have. Without an invitation, in fact. I told your uncle to send for me if he got bored in the country. He did not send for me and I was bored in town, so I decided to come see him at Spring Ridge." Again, Lord Swanson looked at Willa. "I understand now why he is not bored."

"Oh, Uncle Xander is always busy," Lady Cecily said, the undercurrent between Willa and this lord going over the young girl's head. "He works very hard to be a duke."

"I am certain he does."

"Let us return to the house, girls," she said abruptly, nudging them along.

Unfortunately, the girls ran ahead. Cecily called over her shoulder that she would tell Lorry they had a guest.

That left Willa to walk with Lord Swanson. She wished she could run after the girls but maintained her dignity as he fell into step alongside her.

"You look a bit familiar to me, Miss Fennimore. I wonder if we have possibly met before."

Having looked into her mirror each morning, she knew her resemblance to her mother had grown over the years. Still, how would this man have seen Theodosia? Her mother had been dead for years, long before this man would have attended the theater.

"We have not met previously, my lord. I am very good with names and faces and know we have never been introduced."

"Hmm. Well, how are you adjusting to life in the country, Miss Fennimore?" asked the viscount.

"My posts have all been in the country, my lord. I find the country more to my taste than town."

"Pity."

She stopped in her tracks and confronted him. "Why would you say that?"

He flushed at her directness. "I believe town has a lot to offer. Of course, if you are enjoying your sojourn in the country with His Grace, I –"

"Let me stop you right there, Lord Swanson. His Grace hired me as governess to his nieces, not as a nursemaid or mistress to him." She paused. "Or his friends. I will expect you to keep your hands to yourself and leave me in peace."

With that, Willa strode off, not glancing back.

She arrived at the house just as the viscount's carriage was pulling away and assumed Lorry had instructed its coachman to take the vehicle to the stables. Entering the foyer, she saw two footmen carrying a trunk up the stairs, following Mrs. Dylan. The housekeeper must be directing the footmen to a guest bedchamber for the duke's unexpected guest.

"It's time for tea, Miss Fennimore," Lady Lucy said. "We should go wash our hands."

Accompanying the girls upstairs, she saw that they cleaned their hands and faces.

"Go to the drawing room," she instructed them. "I will see you upstairs in the schoolroom after tea."

"You aren't coming with us?" Lady Cecily asked, clearly puzzled by the change in routine.

"No. Your uncle has company. I would merely be in the way. I will remain in the schoolroom and work on lessons for the next few days."

Reluctance shone in the girls' eyes, but they obeyed Willa and left the schoolroom. She busied herself for the next several minutes, refusing to think about the flirtatious viscount, telling herself she should be glad he arrived. He would occupy some of His Grace's time and allow her to put some distance between her and the duke.

"Why did you not come to tea?" a familiar voice demanded.

Turning, she saw Brockbank in the doorway. Rising, she said, "You need time to visit with your old friend, Your Grace. My presence was not necessary. Neither will it be at dinner while you are entertaining your guest. You should eat in the dining room during his visit."

"His visit was entirely unexpected," grumbled the duke. "And I am asking you to accompany me to the drawing room now to pour out for us."

She sniffed. "You cannot be bothered to pick up a teapot and pour tea into a cup?"

He gave her a beguiling smile. "But you do it so much better than I, Miss Fennimore. Please?"

"Oh, all right," she said gruffly, pushing in her chair and accompanying him back to the drawing room.

They arrived, and Lord Swanson looked a bit overwhelmed as the girls both stood before him, jabbering away. He glanced up as they entered and smiled.

"Ah, I see your uncle and Miss Fennimore have arrived. What a relief that is. Now, tea can begin."

Willa seated herself behind the teapot and placed a cup on a saucer. As she poured tea into the cup, she asked, "How would you like your tea, my lord?"

"Just as it is," he replied. "I do not require anything in it."

She handed over the saucer and prepared tea for the duke as he liked it, making sure her pupils had their usual cups of milk.

"We were telling Lord Swanson about making scones," Lady Lucy shared. "We told him everything that goes in them and how long to bake them and why you can't knead the dough too much."

The viscount took a sip of tea. "Yes, the entire process sounds a bit confounding. I was curious as to why young ladies of the house would even be in the kitchens, though."

"Because we *want* to be in them," Lady Cecily said emphatically. "Miss Fennimore lets us learn about whatever we wish. Sometimes, we do spelling and reading and writing."

"We also get to draw and paint," Lady Lucy interjected. "And Cecily is going to learn how to ride a horse. And we planted flowers in the gardens yesterday." She giggled. "My hands were so muddy. I had to scrub and scrub before all the dirt came off."

"You were . . . gardening?" Lord Swanson asked, clearly looking uncomfortable with the idea.

"Yes!" Lady Cecily said. "Miss Fennimore is right. It is so fun to dig in the dirt. Why, even Uncle Xander helped us."

The viscount looked at his friend in shock. "You . . . were digging . . . in the dirt."

The duke smiled evenly. "You might try it sometime, Swanson. I did not think I would enjoy it but found it most satisfying."

"You have changed," the viscount said, giving Willa pause. "You are not the man I spent all those years with."

"I am changing," Brockbank agreed pleasantly. "Hopefully, for the better. I have numerous duties and obligations here at Spring Ridge, including being the guardian for my nieces."

"Will you even return for the Season this year?" Lord Swanson pressed. "You know I intend to look for a wife. I could use your advice in the matter."

The duke turned to her. "I think it would be stimulating for my nieces to come to town. What is your opinion, Miss Fennimore?"

"There are a number of activities to take part in while in London," she said. "We could visit several of the fine museums. We might walk along the Serpentine in Hyde Park each morning."

"I think we will go," the duke said decisively. "Would you like that, girls? To go to London?"

"Yes!" they cried in unison, Cecily adding, "We have never been there before. It will be fun, Uncle Xander."

"Your uncle will be quite busy attending events," Lord Swanson said dismissively. "You would spend a majority of your time in your governess' company."

"We like Miss Fennimore," Lady Lucy said. "She's nice to us."

"She's nice to everyone," Lady Cecily added. "And it will be fun to see London, won't it, Miss Fennimore?"

"Yes," she agreed. "We might even take a picnic to the park one day. I used to do that sometimes when I was growing up there."

"A picnic sounds lovely," Brockbank agreed. "I would like that very much."

Lord Swanson looked skeptical. "When did you decide you enjoyed picnics, Brockbank?"

The duke gazed evenly at his friend. "When I became the guardian to two lively nieces. I am finding there are more things to life than what I once thought."

A chill ran through Willa at those words. Yes, she had supposed the duke to be a rake from Ralph's reaction to him, but she hadn't truly thought about the kind of life he had led in town. And he was so involved with his nieces and tenants here at Spring Ridge, it was hard to see him as anything but a responsible, titled duke. This friend, Lord Swanson, was a reminder to Brockbank of what he had once been.

Would he revert to his old ways in his friend's company?

And if he did, what would it mean for his nieces—and her?

CHAPTER FIFTEEN

W HEN MISS FENNIMORE left with his nieces after tea ended, Xander stared at Gil.

"Why did you come?"

His friend shrugged. "I was bored in town without you. I miss you, Xan." He raised his brows. "But I do see what has kept you buried in the country. Miss Fennimore is a delicious tidbit for you to devour on a nightly basis. Even if she did deny it."

He shot to his feet, grabbing Gil's lapels and yanking him to his feet. "You are wrong," he said, gritting his teeth.

They stared at one another a long moment before Xander shoved Gil back into his chair. He began pacing about the room, agitated, saying, "Miss Fennimore is my nieces' governess. She is not some trollop for you or anyone else to dine upon. You are to stay away from her."

Gil shook his head. "What is going on, Xan? Talk to me. We have known each other since we were boys. I have never seen you this upset, much less over a mere servant."

He stopped pacing and took his seat again. "You do not know what it is like, Gil. How my life has changed." He sighed. "There is so much for me to learn. So many obligations and things and people to care for. Bloody hell, I have *children* now!"

His friend snorted. "They really aren't *your* children, Xan. They're from a brother you never liked and rarely saw. Yes, do your duty to them. Feed, clothe, and educate them. You owe them nothing of you."

Xander shook his head. "That is where you are wrong," he said softly. "They are everything to me now. In a short time, those two girls have stolen my heart. I do not think I ever spoke to a child before I returned to Spring Ridge in January. They are my flesh and blood, Gil. They worship me. Me! They talk to me, about all kinds of little things. I know their favorite colors and foods. Their likes and dislikes. I have gone on walks with them and yes, even dug up weeds in the gardens and planted new flowers in their place."

Gil whistled. "It is as if you have become a stranger before my eyes, Xan."

He shook his head. "I think the same thing each day when I look into the mirror. The thing is, I really like who I am becoming, Gil. My life never really had any meaning."

"We had fun together, Xan. You know we did."

Nodding, he agreed. "We did. But I doubt I would have ever grown up if my brothers had not perished in that storm and on the battlefield. I would have been utterly content, chasing lightskirts and drinking and gaming each night away. You have said yourself that you wish to wed this Season. I would have lost you to a wife, Gil, not to mention when you come into your title. You would have left me behind, and I would have wallowed in drink and misery."

He shook his head. "These deaths have greatly impacted me. I find I am responsible for so many others. Cecily and Lucy are charming little girls, ones who were sadly neglected by Rollo. I have showered them with attention, trying to make up to them all the times their father pushed them aside, merely because they were born females and deemed useless by him. They are my blood, Gil. The two I am most responsible for. I am, in every way, now their father. And I plan to be a good one to them, as well as the children I sire."

Looking at his longtime friend, he added, "You are to leave Miss

149

Fennimore alone. My nieces were little hellions before she arrived, chasing off governesses left and right. They have taken to her, and I will not have you dallying with her, causing her to flee. If she left, I might very well lose my sanity. She has worked a miracle with the girls."

"If you simply want her for yourself, Xan, I understand. I will keep my hands to myself." Gil chuckled. "But I am afraid my eyes will feast on her all the same. She is an incredibly beautiful woman, despite the shapeless gown she wears."

"Dammit, Gil! You are to treat her with respect. She is under my roof. Under my protection. I won't have you ogling her like she's some London lady-bird."

His friend studied him a long moment. "Are you warning me to stay away from this woman because you fear I might scare her off? Or do you want her for yourself?"

Xander wanted to scream. Gil was his oldest, dearest friend. And yet suddenly he no longer trusted this man. Gil had been a loyal friend to him but was too careless and carefree in his attitude toward women. Xander had been the same until he had returned to Spring Ridge. He felt as if he had never pushed himself in any way. Never challenged himself. He had led a life of ease, undisciplined and reckless, not caring about much of anything and certainly not being respectful of women.

Yet as Duke of Brockbank he had enormous responsibilities. Ones he wanted to live up to. He wanted to be a good example to his people. To his nieces. To his peers. More than anything, he wanted Willa Fennimore's respect.

And love.

Frankly, he wasn't even certain what love was. He only knew he felt starved for it—and that he might find it with this woman.

Calmly, his gaze met that of his best friend. "I am going to have to ask you to leave, Gil. I will see you back in town."

"I knew it," Gil said. "That governess has turned your head."

Trying to contain his temper, Xander said, "I have not even kissed Miss Fennimore."

"What?" Gil's jaw dropped. "It is unlike you, Xan. I was certain you had already bedded the tart."

"She is not a witless tart, Gil. She is an extremely intelligent woman. One I am not fit to even look at. I will tell you this. I plan to marry her."

"*Marry* her? Are you mad, Xan? Dukes don't go about wedding governesses."

His lips thinned. "Dukes can bloody well do as they please, Gil. I need you to go before I pummel you so badly you would not be recognized for a month of Sundays. Your chances of finding a bride with a fat dowry this Season would be gone."

Gil shot to his feet. "You are choosing a bloody governess over me?"

Xander also stood. Placing his hand on his friend's shoulder, he said, "You are my oldest friend, Gil. I want nothing to come between us and our friendship, least of all a woman. What I am telling you is that I am a different man from the one you have known for so long. I am not the carefree bachelor who has been your bosom friend all these years. I have had the weight of the world thrust upon my shoulders these past few months. I must think about what is best for my family's name and estates. I need an heir. I—"

"You can do better than a governess, Xan. As a duke, you can have your pick of the litter. Granted, your Miss Fennimore is quite striking, but you need someone of your own class. If you are so worried about your reputation and your nieces and those children you have yet to sire, you know you need to wed a woman of substance. One who comes from the highest echelon of the *ton*. A woman who has family connections. Whose father has political influence. I don't see your Miss Fennimore being any of those things."

"She will be my duchess," Xander said stubbornly. "Polite Society will accept her—or else."

Gil frowned. "Have you even said anything to this chit? You said you hadn't kissed her. Does she know she is destined to be the Duchess of Brockbank?"

"No," he admitted quietly, causing Gil to chuckle.

"You are in over your head, Xan. You should stick with learning about your estates. Come to town for the Season and hunt for an acceptable bride with me. If you are so taken with your Miss Fennimore, then simply buy her a house and make her your mistress."

Xander acted before he thought, slamming his fist into Gil's nose. He heard the crunch. Saw the blood spurt. Listened to Gil curse as he pulled out a handkerchief and held it to his face.

Anger filled Gil's eyes. "You have chosen someone who is inconsequential over our longstanding friendship, Xan. You are dead to me. Have my things sent to town."

Gil stormed from the drawing room. Xander did not bother to follow him. He had stayed friends with Gil over the years out of habit, overlooking things that displeased him. Gil could be selfish and cruel. Xander had always laughed it off. Now, though, he decided he neither needed nor wanted Viscount Swanson in his life. The new life he wished to build with Willa Fennimore.

He had to find her now. They must talk.

Ringing for Lorry, he told the butler to see that Viscount Swanson's things were packed up and returned to him in London, giving the butler the address and no explanation why his guest had vacated the premises so abruptly.

"Lord Swanson's carriage is being readied now, Your Grace," Lorry said. "I could have things . . . delayed. In order to give enough time to have his trunk packed and placed aboard it."

"I like your suggestion, Lorry. Please see to it."

Xander climbed the stairs two at a time, heading straight to the schoolroom. He found Lucy sketching, a maid sitting with her. Cecily poured over an atlas.

"Where is Miss Fennimore?"

"She said she needed digging time, Uncle Xander," Lucy said, not looking up from her drawing. "That we were to have our milk and bread, and she would be in later to tuck us in."

Wheeling, he hurried down the stairs and cut through the kitchens, heading out to the gardens. He and Miss Fennimore had helped the girls plant some flowers yesterday, and Xander thought she might be at that patch of the gardens, checking on them.

She wasn't.

It was about an hour before sunset. Where might she be?

He decided to continue further into the gardens. Perhaps she was digging somewhere else in the dirt. She had told the three of them how much pleasure gardening gave her. How satisfying it felt to plant something and tend to it throughout the year.

Hurrying along the path, he looked from left to right. Then he spied her when he reached the center of the gardens. She was seated in the gazebo, her eyes closed. He had loved this gazebo as a boy. No one came to it but him. He had spent hours playing here.

This would be the place he would kiss Willa. It would become *their* place.

Silently, he moved toward her, afraid if he spoke it would frighten her away. Instead, he seated himself beside her and waited for her to acknowledge his presence.

"You left your friend to entertain himself?" she asked, her tone low and quiet.

"Lord Swanson decided to return to London, nursing his broken nose."

That got her attention. Her eyes opened and fixed on his. Xander thought he could lose himself in those pools of amethyst and never wish to leave.

"You struck your friend?"

"Yes. He deserved it. And I doubt we will be friends anymore."

"Was it because of me?" she asked softly.

"Yes."

She turned to face him. "I have known men such as your viscount. They think women are playthings, especially ones in a subservient position such as me." She paused. "You did not have to make him leave, Your Grace. I would not wish to come between you and your friend."

"I did not want him to come between us."

She drew in a quick breath. Her cheeks flushed with color.

Taking her hands in his, Xander said, "I have known Gil for many years. We were friends because we shared many things in common. We no longer do, however. I am a duke, with duties to uphold. Gil is the kind of man who will wed for position and go from his bride's bed to that of his mistress without giving it a thought."

He paused. "I was once like that. Seeking nothing but my own pleasure. Reveling in sin. Not thinking of tomorrow because I did not have a future."

He brought her hands up to his lips and kissed them. "I find I am changing every day. Being a duke is part of it. Being in your company has made all the difference, though."

He watched the pulse in her throat throb quickly. Desire flooded him.

"I asked Gil to leave because I did not want him to touch you. I do not want any man to touch you but me, Willa."

She swallowed. "What are you saying?"

"I told you I would not take advantage of you. If I were your employer and kissed you, I would be doing so. But I want to make you my wife, Willa."

"Your *wife*?"

She shook her head, trying to withdraw her hands from his. Xander only held on to them more tightly.

"Yes, Willa. I find that you are the woman I want to call my duchess. My friend. My lover. My wife. The mother of my children."

"But . . . you are a duke. A duke! I am a no one. What would Polite Society think?"

He laughed. "They might possibly think that I have gone mad. That as a fourth son, I am unsuited for the role of duke. But a duke I am, the Duke of Brockbank. And I choose you as my duchess, Willa. No other will do."

"You know very little about me, Your Grace. You should know that I am unfit to be a duchess. For goodness' sake, I am a governess."

"Xander."

"What?"

"Call me Xander," he said, knowing his tone was low and seductive. The Duke of Linberry had suggested that Xander tell this woman how he felt about her. And if she needed more convincing, to kiss her.

He decided Linberry was right.

Releasing Willa's hands, he brought them to frame her face. "I have done some terrible things in my life, Willa. Things I am not proud of in the least. I can live with all I have done wrong and look to the future if you are by my side."

"But I . . . I . . . ." Her voice faded.

And Xander lowered his lips to hers.

CHAPTER SIXTEEN

WILLA HAD SENSED that the kiss was coming, but she was so overwhelmed by the duke's declaration that she was powerless to stop it. No, she lied to herself. She would never have stopped this kiss. She wanted it.

Desperately.

His mouth touched hers, and a shiver raced through her. His hands still framed her face and his thumbs began to stroke her cheeks softly as his lips moved gently over hers. She had no idea how to respond and clutched his coat's lapels to steady herself.

He brushed his lips softly against hers, letting her get used to the contact between them. Then shock rippled through her as his tongue slowly outlined the shape of her mouth. The sensations running through her were unlike any she had ever experienced.

He broke the kiss and gazed at her with such intensity she should have been frightened. She wasn't, though. Willa felt safe with this man.

"I am going to kiss you for a very long time, Willa," he promised.

Xander bent again, and his mouth fused to hers. The gentle kiss from before became harder. More demanding. Her hands slipped from his coat and wound around his neck so she could be closer to him. His hands caught her waist, and he pulled her to her feet, enveloping her in his arms, their bodies pressed against one another. His was hard, solid muscles everywhere, so different from her own body. Then he teased her mouth open and suddenly, his tongue was inside. Sweeping. Searching. Tasting. Taking. She had had no idea that a kiss could be like this. Fierce. Drugging. Empowering.

His hands roamed her back as he kissed her, causing delicious sensations to run through her. She found her fingers plunging into his thick hair, tightening. He let out a low rumble and for the first time in her life, Willa felt her feminine power.

Xander tilted her head, giving him better access. The kiss deepened and became all-consuming, like a fire lit on a cold winter's night that blazed out of control. Need ran through her, and she wanted him. She did not know exactly what that meant or how it would occur, but she was flush with desire.

Suddenly, he swept her up into his arms, never breaking the kiss, and she sensed him sitting again on the bench in the gazebo. He ravished her mouth as she clung to him, her breasts growing heavy and the place between her legs coming to life.

"I want you so much, Willa," he murmured against her lips.

His hand moved to her breast and kneaded it, causing a wealth of new sensations to pour through her. She pressed against him as he broke the kiss, trailing kisses along her jaw and touching his lips to her neck, nibbling where her pulse beat out of control. Her breathing grew rapid and shallow, her fingers still tangled in his hair, as his tongue trailed down her throat and ran over the swell of her breast. He slipped his hand inside her gown and lifted out one breast, his mouth going to it. As he ran his tongue across her nipple, the fire within her blazed higher. His tongue teased the swollen bud, his teeth grazing against it, causing her to gasp aloud.

Xander lifted his head, a satisfied smile on his lips. "I want to make you gasp. Sigh. Scream my name. I want you more than any other woman I have ever known."

A small voice warned her. This man had been with many women

before her. Ralph had called Xander a rogue. Her body was willing to give itself to him without question—but doubt began to fill her.

She let her fingers fall from his hair and said, "This was a poor idea, Your Grace."

Willa struggled to push herself from his lap and found his arms like steel bands tightening about her.

"I told you that I had done things I was ashamed of. Yes, Willa, I have had many women in my life. None have meant anything to me. My life was a wasted one, until I met you. Until I became the Duke of Brockbank. I have purpose in my life now because I have so many others depending upon me. I find myself growing and changing every single day. Most of the changes have been wrought because of you."

"Me?" she squeaked.

"You." He gazed intently at her. "You are the most fascinating creature I have come across. You have a great sensibility and confidence about you. You are the woman I want by my side, Willa. Without even realizing it, you have convinced me that not only can I be a better man, but that I *am* a better man when I am with you."

She started to speak, but he touched a finger to her lips, silencing her.

"I know you will think this is sudden because we have not known one another for very long and still have so much to discover about each other. But almost from the first moment I spoke with you, I have felt in my bones that you were the one for me. You have such focus and determination. You think differently from others. You are fierce and possessive when it comes to Cecily and Lucy. I can tell how they, too, are becoming the best versions of themselves under your steady hand."

Xander looked tenderly at her, and she saw more than yearning in his eyes.

"I told you before that I wish to make you my duchess. What I really want is to make us a family. I had never been around children before and I am still learning much about them, but I feel like a father to Cecily and Lucy. Are you willing to marry me, Willa? Become not only my wife but these orphaned girls' mother, too?"

Willa tried to separate her emotions and look at the situation critically. She had never been one to let her heart rule her head. She had thought like an adult from an extremely early age.

"I am overwhelmed by your offer, Your Grace," she began.

"Xander," he prompted, a wry smile teasing his sensual lips.

"Xander," she repeated. "You must understand that this is all new to me. It is a decision which I cannot make lightly."

He grew solemn. "I understand. I know I am asking a lot of you. Becoming a duchess will not be an easy thing to do. You will constantly have the eyes of the *ton* upon you. Yes, some of them might disapprove of a duke wedding a governess. Then again, I am slowly learning that dukes make their own rules. As a fourth son and dedicated bachelor, I have never adhered to Polite Society's rules, though."

He gave her a disarming smile. "Why would I start now?"

She couldn't help but laugh, being taken in by his immense charm and looks.

He sobered. "As I said, I realize how life-altering this could be for you. It is a decision that should require some thought on your part. You would not only be taking on me. You would also become an instant mother to my girls."

She liked that he called them his girls. Even she, not having known him prior to his becoming the Duke of Brockbank, could see the growth in him each day. He was taking his responsibilities seriously and nurturing a close relationship with his nieces. Since the girls were both so young and their memories of their own father would fade as time passed, the duke would be the only father they knew.

Would she like to be a mother to them?

Willa found her heart would like that very much.

Still, she did not want to rush into such a decision. She knew nothing of the glittering world of the *ton*. She doubted she would be accepted by its members, duchess or not. Even people such as the Duchess of Linberry, who had been quite kind to her when meeting Willa as a governess, might not like to think of her as their equal.

"Will you give me some time?" she asked.

"I will give you all the time you need, Willa. I want no other but you. If you wish for us to wait, I am willing to do so." He brushed his knuckles against her cheek. "I hope you won't keep me waiting too long with your answer."

Xander bent and gave her a slow, sweet kiss. He broke it and smiled. "We should return to the house. It is growing dark. My belly will be growling at any moment."

She laughed as he helped her to her feet and slipped her hand through the crook of his arm. They strolled through the gardens until they came close to the entrance, where he removed her hand and said, "We cannot be seen together like this."

His words caused doubt to surge through her once more. It was quickly replaced by anger and she puffed up, afraid everything he had said to her in the gardens was only meant to seduce her.

Her anger subsided when he said, "I do not wish the servants to think anything improper has occurred between us. As it is, you are living under my roof. That will not cause questions now but when we return to town, I will need to deposit you at your former guardian's house. When you become my duchess—and I have faith that you will—I want everything to be proper."

"When do you wish to return to London?"

"Another week here at Spring Ridge should be enough time. We can then stop at another of my properties which is on the way to town and spend another day or two there. I would like to meet its steward and ride the land to get an idea of the estate. It is one I have never seen before. Actually, I have never visited any of the other ducal estates and only saw my London residence the one day I went to town and hired you."

He cupped her cheek. "Go inside now and freshen up. I will meet you in the winter parlor for dinner as usual."

Willa stepped from the gardens and hurried toward the house, overcome by emotion. She entered the kitchens and went up the back staircase to the top floor. Entering her bedchamber, she went to the small hand mirror she had brought with her and raised it, gazing at her reflection. Her cheeks were flushed with color, and her lips swollen from Xander's kisses.

She realized that she needed to put the girls to bed and quickly entered the schoolroom and then their bedchamber. They were both sitting on Lady Lucy's bed.

"Hello, Miss Fennimore," Lady Cecily said. "I am making up a story for our bedtime."

"I am so glad to hear that," she said brightly, perching on the edge of the bed. "I will want to hear this story myself. For now, however, it is time to go to sleep."

Lady Cecily returned to her bed as her sister slipped under the bedclothes, and Willa tucked them around the small child.

"It is a very good story, Miss Fennimore. You will like it."

For the first time, Willa kissed Lady Lucy's brow. "I am certain I will."

Moving to the other bed, she brushed her lips against Lady Cecily's forehead and said, "I shall listen to your story first thing in the morning."

"May I tell it to you over breakfast? I think Uncle Xander will like it, too."

"We shall hear it then," she promised.

Willa left the girls' bedchamber and went downstairs to the winter parlor where Xander awaited her. They had a lovely meal together, with him telling her stories from his school days. He had her laughing so hard that at one point, snot bubbled from her nose. Horrified, she wiped it away with her napkin, only to hear his peals of laughter.

He came to his feet and took her hands in his. They gazed at one another for a long moment.

"Tell me you will not make me wait, Willa," he whispered. "Tell me now that you will do me the honor of becoming my wife."

She knew they might be rushing into things, but Willa could not imagine a future without this man in it.

"Yes, I wish to marry you."

"Yes?" he asked, joy filling his face. "Yes?" he asked again, rich laughter coming from him. "Yes!" he cried.

His mouth came down on hers, hard and demanding. She gave over to the kiss, all doubts fleeing.

Willa would build a life with this good man and his girls.

Their girls . . .

CHAPTER SEVENTEEN

WILLA AWOKE WITH a smile on her face and stretched lazily. *She was in love.*

She didn't know how she had become so fortunate. Xander not only was attracted to her but actually wanted to marry her. And more importantly, he loved her. He had told her so numerous times last night after she had agreed to wed him. They had sat in the winter parlor for hours, kissing and talking, and she knew her betrothed would open an entire new world to her. A world of physical sensations, made all the richer because of the love between them. They talked until the wee hours of the morning about the kind of life they would build together, a life with Cecily and Lucy.

Xander was grateful that she was willing to take on not only him, but the girls as well. Never thinking she would be a mother, Willa now reveled in the fact that she would already have two daughters on the day she wed. She also looked forward to any children they might have together in the future. Xander admitted he had never thought to marry, much less be a father, but becoming the Duke of Brockbank had changed his outlook on a great deal of things.

That included not living in town year-round. He had spent all his years after university in London, simply because he had no country estate to go to. Now, he had seven. They had decided raising the girls in the country would be an ideal life, with them traveling as a family to town each year for the Season. Willa thought it would be the best of both worlds, but in truth, as long as Xander was by her side, she didn't care where they resided.

He talked about them embarking on a tour of his various estates scattered throughout England. She agreed it was a good idea for him to become familiar with each of them. They would make a start at it, as he had suggested, by visiting one of the smaller estates, which would be on their way when they traveled to London. Xander said that Spring Ridge would always be home since it was his ducal country seat, but he wanted to get to know his staff and tenants and the land itself at his various properties. He thought they should visit at least a few of his holdings after the Season ended, as part of a delayed honeymoon, taking the girls with them.

That had brought up the question of when they might wed. He had left the decision to her, whether she wanted the banns read or wished for him to purchase a special license. He had only a few distant relatives whom he had not seen in many years and had no intention of inviting them. Being estranged from Lord Swanson now, he did not want the viscount at their wedding.

Willa, on the other hand, had only Ralph. She told Xander that a small, quiet wedding would be best but asked that she be given time to talk things over with Ralph before Xander bought their license, and they arranged a date.

Ralph was a good man, and Willa knew she could bring him around, especially if Xander came and spent time with the director. Her new fiancé agreed and said they would keep things open, but he wished for them to wed before the Season began because he wanted them to be presented to Polite Society together, as a married couple. He warned her again that there would be talk. Not only about him, a fourth son unexpectedly becoming a duke, but of that duke wedding a governess. Some would look down upon her because she had been in service, but once they got to know her, they would love her as much as he did.

The fact that Xander loved her still shocked Willa. She had thought her feelings for him would go unrequited and eventually, she would have to leave Spring Ridge and the girls because it would be too painful to be around him all the time. She supposed Viscount Swanson's unexpected visit had set into motion what had occurred. She might not like the man, but she was grateful for what his visit had accomplished.

Rising, Willa readied herself for the day in one of her shapeless, practical gowns. Xander had teased her about them last night, saying he knew of the beautiful curves that lay beneath them. He promised once they reached town that he would set up an appointment for her with one of London's top modistes because he wanted an entire new wardrobe prepared for her. He was excited to show off his duchess and for once, Willa was ready to take the spotlight, Xander having given her the confidence to do so. She wondered what her mother would have thought, Willa wedding a duke and taking her place at the head of Polite Society. Knowing Theodosia, she would have been jealous.

A small warning sounded to her. Yes, she was a governess—but she was also a child of theater people. That worried her. Those associated with the theater were viewed by the masses as some of the most wicked, sinful people in society. She wondered if she should tell Xander of her background and who her parents had been. She did not think it would make a difference to him and yet she still hesitated to do so. She herself had never set foot on the stage and had been away from the theater world for a decade now. She decided to keep to herself the family she had come from. Just as Xander had changed from the carefree rogue he had been for many years, Willa was far removed from her origins.

She finished dressing and then went into the schoolroom, waiting for her charges to appear. In her two previous posts as a governess, she had been expected to ready her pupils for the day, helping them to wash and dress each morning. Here at Spring Ridge, however, that had not been a part of her assigned duties, most likely because the girls had arrived without a governess in tow. She could hear movement in the next room, though, and her heart beat quickly, knowing Xander intended to tell his nieces this morning of their wedding plans.

She moved to the window and looked out over the gardens, thinking of how she had shared her first kiss with Xander in them. He had told her how he had used to play in the gazebo and thought it an appropriate place for their first kiss, saying it would be their special place to steal away to and spend time together in the future.

An arm snaked about her waist, and her betrothed nuzzled her neck, causing her pulse to leap. He held her flush against him, and that giddiness which filled her whenever he was near erupted.

Xander turned her to face him and framed her face with his large hands. His lips touched hers for a sweet kiss.

He broke the kiss. "I suppose I shouldn't be doing this in the schoolroom, of all places, especially since we might be caught by the girls. *Our* girls."

"How do you think they will take our news?" she asked, worried.

"They already adore you as it is. I think they will be quite happy to have you as their aunt by marriage."

He released her, and they went to the table and took a seat. The girls came into the schoolroom, talking and laughing, as two maids appeared with trays holding their breakfasts. Willa decided to follow Xander's lead regarding their news. Since he said nothing, she supposed he would wait until they finished their meal.

"Cecily needs to tell her story to you," Lucy said.

"I haven't thought of an ending for it yet," her sister said. "Maybe you can help me."

"Tell it from the beginning," Lucy urged as they began to eat.

The tale was a bit outlandish but rather clever. Cecily spoke of a girl who could perform magic. She loved animals and took on one of the mousers in the stables as her pet, bewitching it so that it could speak with her. In turn, the cat returned to the stables and began teaching his fellow mousers how to talk, as well. The cats wound up teaching the mice they chased how to speak and also the horses in the stables. The horses, when let out to pasture, then helped the sheep in the next field learn how to talk. It spread until every animal on the estate could talk—but only the little girl who worked the magic could understand what they were saying.

"That's as far as I got," Cecily shared. "I don't know how it should end."

"I am amazed at your imagination," Xander told his niece. "Do you think the animals should talk to others at the next estate?"

"Or perhaps they could teach the birds who landed on the estate how to talk," Willa suggested. "Why, the birds could spread this secret all across England."

Cecily's brow furrowed in thought, and then she said, "I wish the little girl had enough magic in her so that she could get other people to understand the animals. I will have to think about it."

Lorry appeared at the door, bearing a silver tray. "A message has come from Linfield, Your Grace."

Xander accepted it and thanked the butler. He broke the seal and opened it, a smile appearing on his face.

"It seems Her Grace has given birth to a healthy boy," he told them. "The birth occurred yesterday morning, and mother and babe are doing well today. In fact, Her Grace says in this missive that she is ravenous and would like scones from the two of you."

Both girls clapped in glee and looked to Willa. "Can we go to the kitchens now, Miss Fennimore, and bake some for Her Grace?" Lucy asked.

"I don't see why not. We should finish our breakfasts first, though, and then go down and ask Cook if we can do so."

Xander turned to Lorry and said, "Tell the messenger we shall come calling at Linfield this afternoon. We will arrive at teatime if that is convenient."

"Very well, Your Grace," the butler said, and departed the schoolroom.

As the girls chatted about what kind of scones they wished to make, Willa turned to Xander. "Why don't we wait a bit before we share our news with them?"

"I agree."

She took her charges to the kitchens, where they told Cook all about the duchess having a baby boy and how the new mother wanted scones baked by them. Cook agreed and winked at Willa.

"Now, my ladies, what kind of scones shall we make for Her Grace?" Cook asked.

They debated for several minutes, finally deciding upon blueberry scones. As usual, Willa turned the baking into a lesson, testing the girls' memories of the ingredients to be used and then letting Cook walk them through the process again. They mixed the scones, kneading the dough and adding the fresh blueberries to it before placing them in the oven. The four then sat at the table, and they told Cook about the flowers they had planted previously. She handed over her daily list of herbs for them to gather and they did so after the scones came out of the oven.

Once the herbs had been delivered to the kitchens, Willa told them it was time to return to their lessons. They went to the schoolroom and worked on spelling and handwriting and then Willa gave them a lesson about English history. She had been doing so for the last several days and was delighted how entranced the girls became listening to how history unveiled.

"I think I like history best of all," Cecily declared. "It's like a story, the way you tell it to us, Miss Fennimore."

She smiled. "I am sorry there were no talking cats at the Battle of Hastings."

Her remark caused the girls to giggle, warming her heart. Oh, how she had grown to love not only Xander but these special little girls, too. She hoped they would accept her in her new role as aunt to them and wondered when the best time might be to tell them. Of course, once the girls knew their news, it would be hard to keep it from the rest of the household. Perhaps on the way home from Linfield today might be the ideal time to discuss matters. She would suggest this to Xander, as well as gathering the Spring Ridge servants and sharing the news with them.

The day flew by, and Xander arrived in the schoolroom, telling them it was time to leave for Linfield. They went downstairs, where Lorry held the wicker basket containing the scones baked this morning.

Once inside the carriage, they talked about the babe and what he might look like.

"He might have brown hair like His Grace," Lucy said.

"Or he might have blond hair like Her Grace," Cecily added.

"Remember that you must be gentle and quiet around him," Willa reminded them.

"Do you think I can hold him?" Cecily asked.

"Probably not," Xander told her. "He is very new, just a day old today. As he grows, you might be able to ask Her Grace if you could hold him. For now, he will want to be in his mother's arms."

They arrived at Linfield, and the butler greeted them, taking them not to the drawing room, but upstairs to the duchess' rooms instead. The duke met them at the door, inviting them in. The duchess sat in bed, holding the babe in her arms.

"Congratulations from all of us, Your Grace," Xander said.

The duchess smiled. "Come closer, girls. I am sure you would like to see Harry."

"Is that his name?" Lucy asked.

"It is. Actually, we have named him Henry, after his father, but it would be too difficult having two Henrys in the household. We will call him Harry, which is a nickname for Henry."

Cecily and Lucy went to stand next to the bed, and Willa and Xander stepped behind them. She looked down at the sleeping newborn, and a wealth of emotions rushed through her. While Willa was happy to mother Cecily and Lucy, she realized she wanted a child of her own. Xander's child.

"I thought we might have tea in here," the Duke of Linfield said. "The staff is bringing up trays. I know we don't have as many seats, so I hope Lady Lucy and Lady Cecily will not mind sitting in the window seat with their tea." He raised his eyebrows, looking at the hamper Xander held. "I do hope those are your scones, my ladies."

"Blueberry!" cried the girls in unison.

"Oh, just what I wanted," the duchess said, sighing.

Servants arrived with trays of tea, along with small sandwiches and macaroons. Willa was asked to pour out since the duchess held her sleeping infant in her arms.

She set the saucer and cup for Her Grace on a table beside the bed, and the new mother looked at her.

"Would you mind holding Harry while I help myself to a scone and some tea, Miss Fennimore?"

"Of course, Your Grace."

Rising, Willa bent and accepted the small bundle from the duchess. She instinctively began swaying back and forth with the babe, feeling a powerful contentment roll through her.

"He is so small," she said. "I was an only child, so I have never been around an infant before."

"I hope you will be around Harry quite a bit," the duchess declared, then biting into a scone and saying, "Mmm." Looking to the girls, she said, "These are even better than the previous scones you made for us."

"Cook says you bake with love," Lucy piped up.

Her Grace smiled warmly. "Then much love went into these scones. I can taste it."

Willa continued to stand and rock the babe in her arms as tea progressed. The duke offered to take his son, but she shook her head.

"He is sleeping and shouldn't be disturbed. Go ahead with your tea, Your Grace."

As Cecily started asking questions about the newborn, Xander turned to her and said, "You look at home with a babe in your arms."

Quietly, she said, "I am experiencing emotions I never have. It is a powerful thing, this tiny babe."

"I hope by this time next year that you hold our child in your arms," he said, his eyes so full of love that she almost burst out in tears.

"I think it is time to tell the girls—and these new friends—about our future."

She nodded, hoping the Linfields would not reject her outright.

"Miss Fennimore and I have something to say," Xander began.

The room quietened and then Lucy asked, "Have you figured out the end to Cecily's story, Uncle Xander?"

He chuckled. "No, but I have discovered the end to my own story." He stood and came to Willa, placing his arm around her waist. "Miss Fennimore has done me the honor of accepting my marriage proposal. We are to wed soon."

Willa first glanced to the girls to see their reactions. Both looked puzzled and then smiles crossed their faces. Lucy jumped up and ran to them, wrapping an arm about Xander's leg. Cecily hurried over, as well, and stood by Willa, touching and stroking her arm.

"I hope you will be happy about this," she said to the girls.

"We will be a family of four," Xander proclaimed.

"We can't call you Miss Fennimore," Cecily said matter-of-factly. "You will be our aunt."

"My given name is Willa," she told the girl.

"Aunt Willa," Lucy said, testing it out. "I like it!"

Harry woke and started to squirm, so she said, "Let me return him to his mother."

She handed the newborn to the duchess, who beamed at her as she accepted the bundle. "Oh, Miss Fennimore, I am delighted for you and His Grace. And just think—we will live next door to one another. I knew we would be fast friends." She paused. "I hope you will do me the honor of addressing me as Fia."

Tears sprang to her eyes. "I would be happy to do so. Only if you will call me Willa, in return."

Relief poured through her as they remained for another half-hour. Xander mentioned they would be heading to town soon because he wanted the *ton* to meet his wife at the start of the Season. Fia apologized that they would not be in town at the beginning of the Season, waiting until June to arrive.

"Henry wishes for me to regain my strength, but we will let you know as soon as we reach town. We are to host a musicale. The musicians will play nothing but pieces which I have composed."

"And Fia will join in, playing her violin or harp on some of the numbers," Linfield said, beaming with pride at his wife.

"You will be invited, of course," Fia added. "Will you wed in town by special license?"

"Yes, that is our plan," Xander said.

"We want to come," Cecily said.

"You are our family," Xander told her. "Of course, you will come. I know oftentimes children do not attend weddings, but your Aunt Willa and I expect you to be there."

"Where will we stand?" Lucy fretted.

"Right next to us," Willa assured the girl. "We will also explore London together. I grew up in the city and have many favorite places to show you."

"Is there a piano?" asked Cecily.

"Yes, there is a piano," Xander said. "You can continue your lessons with Aunt Willa."

"But . . . if she is our aunt, then who will be our governess?" Lucy asked.

"I can remain your governess for now," she said. "We can also look for one while we are in London."

"What if she is mean to us?" Lucy wanted to know.

"Or what if she makes us study things we don't wish to learn about?" Cecily added, her bottom lip in a pout.

"We will make certain your new governess knows you are to pursue what interests you," Xander informed them. "Things won't change in that regard."

Lucy looked at Willa. "Will you still tuck us in at night?"

"I will do so every night until you leave our household and go to a new one," Willa promised. "That will be many years down the line, after you have made your come-out and fallen in love and agreed to marry."

Cecily studied her. "Do you love Uncle Xander?"

"She does," Xander replied. "And I love her. Very much. And we both love the two of you."

"Love is a wonderful thing," proclaimed the Duke of Linberry, smiling at Willa. He held up his teacup. "To love—and to good friends."

Willa, Xander, and Fia raised their teacups and echoed his words.

The first hurdles had been cleared. They had told Lucy and Cecily of their plans and received no objections. As far as the Duke and Duchess of Linfield, it seemed they also were supportive of the match, the couple welcoming her without hesitation. Though she knew not all of Polite Society would feel the same way, for now, contentment spread through Willa.

Perhaps with Xander being a duke, her acceptance by the *ton* would be easier than she had supposed—but only their time in London would tell.

CHAPTER EIGHTEEN

A TAP SOUNDED at Willa's door, and she answered it, finding Mrs. Dylan standing there, along with two footmen.

"The carriage is waiting for you, Miss Fennimore," the housekeeper said.

"Thank you, Mrs. Dylan." She stepped aside and indicated her packed valises. "These are all I have."

One footman lifted both and the pair left her room as Mrs. Dylan said, "I hope you will have a safe journey to London. If you think of anything you wish to be done here at Spring Ridge, please write me so it will be done by the time you and His Grace return."

Knowing the girls could not keep quiet about the upcoming wedding, Xander had gathered his entire staff in the foyer and announced that he and Willa would marry in London within the next few weeks. She had thought to see disapproving faces but instead was pleased to see smiles instead. Several servants, including Mrs. Dylan and Cook, stole private time with her, telling Willa of their delight and how if she wanted any changes made, she had only to ask them.

"I cannot think of a thing I would change," she said to the housekeeper now.

"Not even to the duchess' rooms?" Mrs. Dylan pressed. "We could always freshen them with paint and hang new curtains. Have new rugs brought in."

Willa realized the housekeeper wanted to do something and said, "All those things would be lovely, Mrs. Dylan. We will be gone several months, so you will have plenty of time to make those changes. You have impeccable taste. Please feel free to change out anything you see fit. I know I will be happy with the results."

What she didn't say to the servant was that Xander had already informed Willa that she would not be spending much time in those rooms. To bathe and dress, yes. But he had made it abundantly clear that she would never sleep in the duchess' bed. That she was to share his bed.

And make love—and babies. Lots and lots of babies.

She smiled at the thought. For a man who had been a confirmed bachelor with no thoughts of marriage or children, Xander Hughes had changed quite a bit in the last few months. Then again, Willa herself had also changed. She, too, had never thought marriage and children would be a choice given to her once she had chosen the path of companion and then governess. Now, it was the only future she wished for herself. As long as Xander was a part of it.

"Shall we go downstairs?" she asked, accompanying Mrs. Dylan to the ground floor, where Xander and the girls awaited her.

In the past week, she had grown even closer to all three of them. The girls were so accepting and in need of love and a woman's touch. Willa herself already thought of the two as her own.

"There you are," her fiancé said, coming to her and giving her a chaste kiss on the cheek, unlike the hundreds of kisses they had already exchanged. In the gazebo. The library. The stables. It seemed her betrothed had a hard time keeping his mouth off her.

And Willa reveled in that fact—and his kisses.

Xander led them to the waiting carriage and handed them up. This time, both girls wished to sit on either side of Willa as Xander sat opposite them. She didn't mind in the least because she was able to drink him in for the next hour and a quarter, the time it took to arrive at Stanridge. The estate was a minor holding belonging to the Duke of Brockbank. It consisted of a small manor house and a much smaller hunting lodge. They met the gamekeeper who managed the property, along with his wife, who cleaned both places and would be cooking for them during their short stay. They would spend all of today and tonight at Stanridge and a portion of tomorrow before leaving and making their way to Xander's townhouse in Mayfair.

When they arrived, the gamekeeper and his wife met them since Xander had sent a messenger ahead alerting the couple of their arrival. The manor house had no suite of rooms for the duke or duchess, only a large bedchamber for the duke and three other bedchambers, two of which had been prepared for Willa and the girls. Cecily and Lucy were used to sharing a room and were placed next to the one assigned to Willa.

Since there were no tenants on this property, Xander had none to meet. The gamekeeper took the coachman to the stable to care for the horses and returned to walk the property with Xander. Willa took the girls upstairs and helped them settle in and then they, too, went outside to traipse about the small estate. They came across the hunting lodge and entered it, finding one large room on the ground floor and a single bedchamber upstairs.

"This is so tiny," Lucy said.

"So is the main house," Cecily pointed out.

"Well, your uncle did say that this was a small holding," she said, doubting Xander had known exactly what size the property was. He would be able to see all he needed to today, and she believed they would be well on their way to London by this time tomorrow morning.

They came across a lake, which surprised her.

"I have an idea," she said. "Come down to the water's edge and gather as many flat, smooth stones as you can find." She bent and retrieved one, holding it up. "Similar to this one."

"Why?" Cecily wanted to know.

"Perhaps I simply like flat rocks and wish to collect some," Willa teased.

After a few minutes, they had assembled a nice pile. She took one and made sure each girl had one.

"We are going to learn how to skip stones across the water's surface. We are fortunate that the day has little wind because it is easier for a stone to skip with water that is flat and calm. The best rocks that will get a good bounce fit into the palm of your hand. The thinner they are, the more they will bounce along the surface."

She held up her stone. "You will hold it between your thumb and your middle finger. Start first by making a partial fist like this. See, I am clenching my middle and ring fingers, along with my pinkie."

Both girls imitated her.

"Good. Now, I want you to place the rock on top of your middle finger and then use your thumb to hold it firmly in place."

Lucy stepped closer and studied Willa's hand for a moment and then did so. Willa nodded and then inspected Cecily's before saying, "What you will do next is wrap your index finger around the stone."

"Why?" Cecily wanted to know again, always the one to ask questions.

"It will add spin to your stone once you toss it. The spin will help it to skip along the surface."

Willa turned toward the water and demonstrated how they should stand, keeping their feet shoulder-width apart and slightly bending their knees.

"You should hold the rock parallel to the ground. Take your arm and wrist and move it so they are behind your body. Try it."

She corrected Lucy's hold. "Try and keep your stone parallel to the ground when you do this. Watch again. See how my shoulders and chest still face the water? Do that. Let's practice our backswing."

The three of them moved their arms back and forth and the girls became comfortable with the motion.

"Now, you will throw your arm in front of you. Let go of the rock when it reaches the front of your body. It should spin off your index finger."

Willa swung her arm and released her stone, getting three hops from it as the girls laughed and clapped in glee. She had them try a few times.

"No, you are both throwing hard. You want to throw your arm quickly."

She demonstrated again for them and then had them both practice shifting their weight to their back foot as they swung their arm back and then pushing their weight to their front foot as they brought their arm around. That did the trick, and both girls had successful skips. They ran out of stones and scoured the shoreline for more, continued to practice.

"What's this?"

Willa's heart beat faster as Xander emerged from the woods. As he strode toward them, she couldn't help but feel possessive. This strong, powerful, handsome man was to be her husband. They would share decades together. It amazed her how her life had changed in so short a time—and would continue to change after they reached London. Truth be told, she was apprehensive about all that lay ahead but knew with Xander by her side, all would be well.

"We're skipping stones, Uncle Xander!" Lucy cried.

"Come join us," Cecily encouraged.

"I have not done this since I was a boy," he said. "I may not remember how to do so."

"Oh, we can teach you," Lucy said sweetly, handing him a rock and telling him how to hold it.

Cecily joined in, giving her uncle more advice, until they thought him prepared enough to make an attempt. When he did, his stone skipped six times, causing his nieces to erupt with laughter.

"Let me see you do it now," he said.

The girls ran through their stack of rocks, and Willa said they should explore the rest of the forested area. She walked alongside Xander, who took her hand and laced his fingers through hers.

"Should you do so?" she asked.

"I want them to see that we are not afraid to hide our affection for one another. That it is natural." He paused, gazing deeply into her eyes. "If I could wish one thing for them, Willa, it would be that they find love. As we have."

Joy soared within her. "I love you," she said quietly.

He grinned. "I love you more."

Xander remained with them, taking them about the land and pointing out things. They finally returned to the manor house, where tea awaited them. Once they finished it, Cecily asked if she could play a song on the pianoforte she had recently learned, a simple tune. She played the piece without a single error, and Xander praised her efforts. Then he asked Willa to play some for them. She had actually been doing a little practice and did so, playing two of the pieces she had composed years ago and a third one by Haydn.

"I liked the second one best," he told her after she rejoined them. "Did you write it?"

"I did. I actually played it for Fia. She liked it, too. It was a great compliment because she composes her own music."

"I remember Linberry saying so. That we are invited to a musical evening where Her Grace will play her own pieces, accompanied by others."

He took her hand and kissed it. "We will attend that event as husband and wife. I cannot wait for that day."

"When are you getting married?" Cecily asked her uncle.

"Soon." He kissed Willa's hand again and lowered it but kept his fingers wrapped about hers. "Once we reach town, I will need to purchase the special license which will enable us to wed."

"And Aunt Willa will be at a different house," Lucy said.

She nodded, having explained it to them before. "Yes, I will go and stay with the man who acted as my guardian after my parents' deaths. I would like you to meet him. His name is Mr. Baldwin, but I think he will wish for you to call him Ralph."

"We will see about that," Xander said. "Since tea is over, I need to meet with my gamekeeper for another hour and go over a few things. I trust the three of you will find something to do."

Willa kept the girls occupied until she gave them their supper and readied them for bed. Xander came in as she was finishing up and helped tuck them into the bed they were sharing.

"We will leave in the morning," he told them. "I have seen all that I need to."

"Will we like London, Uncle Xander? Cecily said we would, but I don't know."

"You can make up your mind about it, Lucy. Some people enjoy being in the city. Others prefer the quiet and solitude of the country," he replied. "I plan for us to go to town each Season and then spend the majority of our time either at Spring Ridge or another of my country estates."

"It is time to close your eyes and sleep," Willa said. "We can continue this conversation tomorrow."

The girls snuggled beneath the bedclothes, and she left a candle burning on a bureau since they were in an unfamiliar place and she didn't want them to be frightened.

They left the room, Xander closing the door behind them, and then he slipped his arms about her and gave her a slow, delicious kiss.

"I finally have you all to myself, Miss Fennimore," he said, his voice husky. "Whatever will I do with you?"

Willa said, "I have been giving that some thought. I think tonight is the night you should make love to your fiancée, Your Grace."

His brows shot up. "What?"

"Let us move away from the girls' door."

He released her, and they walked down the corridor and stopped. His hands settled on her waist. "Do you mean it?"

"I do. We will most likely be wed by this time next week. This place is rustic, but it gives us privacy since no servants are here." She cupped his cheek. "I think I would like to get to know you better. Much better."

This time Willa kissed him.

She broke the kiss. "I know dinner should be waiting downstairs for us."

"It will be a quick dinner," he said, smiling, a hint of mischief in his ice-blue eyes.

Xander accompanied her to where dinner awaited them. He looked over the table and thanked the gamekeeper's wife and dismissed her, telling her she could return to the house tomorrow morning after they left and clear the table and wash the dishes.

Once the servant had left, he sat and pulled her into his lap, and they fed one another, doing more kissing than eating.

"Are you ready to go to my bed?" he asked.

"I will always be ready to do so," she said honestly.

Laughing, Xander rose with her in his arms and carried her to his bedchamber.

CHAPTER NINETEEN

WILLA DID NOT know what to expect. She had been born and bred in the city and had never seen animals couple, much less people. Once, she had come across two actors kissing backstage and quietly hurried away before she was seen. Her mother had died before giving Willa any idea about what went on between a man and a woman. Not that Theodosia would have ever had that talk with her daughter. The last few years of her life, Theodosia Fennimore had been in denial of even having a daughter, much less one old enough to hear about such things.

She had never thought to ask anyone else about what went on between a man and a woman behind closed doors. While she had enjoyed spending time at the theater after her parents' deaths, she always knew she would need to support herself. Her pursuit of higher servant posts, such as a companion or governess, were positions an unmarried woman took. Very few in service ever wed, and Willa had thought she would be the same. That meant not caring or even being curious about the physical act of love.

What had worried her were the two employers who had tried to force themselves on her. Knowing as little as she did, she had not known what it would take to lose her virginity, and had been petrified that she would become with child and be unable to support herself or the resulting babe.

Xander had changed all that. With him, she had experienced an incredible yearning within her. His kisses had brought an indescribable rush of physical feelings, as well as emotions. She wanted more than his kiss.

Whatever more meant.

He brought her up the stairs, passing the girls' bedchamber and her own, taking her to his room. He paused at the door and shifted her so he could open it, bringing her inside and closing the door behind him. Carrying her to a chair, he gently placed her in it.

"Don't move," he said, his eyes twinkling.

She watched as he went to the bed and pulled back the bedclothes. He then fetched his banyan and spread it across the bed.

"Why did you do that?" she asked as he scooped her up and sat in the chair, settling her in his lap.

"How much do you know of lovemaking, Willa?"

While she had heard various actresses gossiping about coupling with a lover as she grew up, Willa had very little interest in the topic and had usually left the room, finding scenery to paint or costumes to mend. It was the same at home. When her mother and father became boisterous behind closed doors—or her father's latest conquest began moaning loudly—she had fled the house and found Felton, who had always been her refuge and rock. Even now, she had little idea about the mechanics involved.

"Not much," she admitted. "I know somehow we are to join together and that sometimes a babe is made when you do so. I know when I kiss you that I feel as if I am on the top of the world." Hesitating a moment, she added, "And when we kiss, it stirs something within me. I feel restless. As if I want more. Need more." She shrugged. "That is what I know. That I want you—and have no idea how we are to go about this next step. I trust, though, that you *do* know what to do. I suppose you do it very well."

He smiled. "I do. At least I have had no complaints in the past." He framed her face with his hands. "I want to say to you that my past is in the past. Yes, I have been with other women. I will not make a secret of that. But those times all held no meaning for me, Willa. Tonight will. Tonight, I couple with the woman I love. The one I adore. The one I will be faithful to for the rest of my life."

Xander kissed her, a soft, sweet kiss.

Willa wanted more.

Her betrothed told her, "Things will heat up between us. I will go as slowly as I can and guide you this first time. Do whatever comes naturally to you. Kiss me. Touch me. Wherever you wish."

She swallowed. "All right."

"When the time comes for us to join together, there are many positions we can take. I must warn you the first time I enter you, you may feel a twinge of pain."

"Pain? Why?"

"Because I must break through your maidenhead. Thank goodness it never will bother you again. I just wanted you to understand before we go further."

Willa nodded. "You are the expert. I will follow your lead."

"We will become experts on one another," he said. "We will try things together. Some, you will like quite a bit. Others might drive you wild. Still others might seem tame or tedious. The most important thing is that we communicate with one another. Find what pleases the other and what pleases us as individuals."

She brushed her fingers against his cheek. "Have you always been so open with your lovers?"

"No. Not at all. I have had sex with a great many women, but the physical act did not have the intimacy that we will always share. I pleased the women I was with but never sought to speak to them about what they liked." He kissed her. "With you, it will be different, love. We will spend time getting to know our partner's body. How it responds to certain touches. Kisses. I want you to be vocal and tell me what you like and do not like. What you enjoy and what leaves you cold. I never really cared about all those women, Willa, and that is why I never had this kind of conversation with them.

"With you, I want to please you. I want to come to know you. Understand you. Yes, I am quite skilled in the art of lovemaking—but this is the first time I will truly be making love because I love you. Does that make sense?"

She cupped his cheek. "It does. When emotion is attached to the act, the very act itself takes on new meaning. We love one another. We are invested in this relationship and with making our partner feel the best we can."

Xander kissed her, long and deep. When he broke the kiss, he smiled at her. "You, Willa Fennimore, are very wise for claiming not to know anything about this."

"I know you excite me," she said honestly. "That I have longed for more than kisses from you."

He smiled widely. "Then let the games begin."

He kissed her for a long time, kisses that were deep and draining. Ones which filled her with yearning and desire and excitement. Finally, he stood and took her to the bed, setting her gently upon it.

Then slowly, Xander untied his cravat, his gaze pinning hers. She watched him undress, piece by piece. When he stood stripped to the waist, her breath caught. Her eyes roamed the broad shoulders and muscular chest, covered in a fine matting of dark hair that trailed down his chest, disappearing into his trousers. His arms rippled with muscles and she longed to touch them before realizing she could.

Willa pushed off from the bed and went to stand in front of him.

"I want to touch you," she said, her heart hammering wildly.

"Go ahead. I want you to."

She placed her flat palms against his chest, and his breath hitched. Smiling, she began moving them, seeing the muscles ripple and contract at her touch.

"You are very strong," she said.

"I will be gentle with you," he promised.

Her hands halted. "What if I don't want gentle?"

He growled low, and she found herself in his arms, his kiss demanding, his tongue seeking hers. They kissed as if they were starved for days. Her hands moved up and down his back, feeling how hard he was to her softness. As they kissed, he unpinned her hair, dropping the pins to the floor, her hair spilling down her back. His fingers pushed into her hair, kneading her scalp, holding her against him, his lips bruising hers.

Breaking the kiss, Xander said, "Help me with my boots."

"Oh, shall I play valet to you?" Willa asked saucily. "I suppose I could."

She grasped his shoulders and turned him, stepping him back to the bed. Bending, she lifted his leg and pulled hard—and made no progress.

"Turn around," he suggested. "I know they are tight. I am a fashionable rake, you know. My boots are cut to show off my calves."

Laughing, she did as he asked, standing between his legs and grasping his boot with both hands. Pulling with all her might, she managed to get it off him.

"One down, one to go," she said cheerily, moving to the other leg and repeating her actions.

Once both boots had been removed, she stepped away from him and set them together in the corner. As she turned, she saw he had unbuttoned his breeches. Her mouth went dry as he pushed them from his narrow hips and discarded them. Xander now stood before her, so magnificent that she forgot to breathe.

"Do you approve?" he asked huskily.

"I more than approve." She paused. "I only hope I am enough woman for so much man."

Laughing, he came to her and wrapped his arms about her, kissing her until she was dizzy. She held on tightly, afraid to let go.

"I won't let you fall," he whispered against her lips. "I will always have you."

Xander bent and reached for the gown's hem. Slowly, he pulled it up her body, his hands brushing against it as he removed the gown. He took his time peeling the other layers away from her until she stood in only her boots and stockings. She could feel the heat in her cheeks as he nudged her against the mattress until she sat upon it.

Gently, he knelt and removed the last remnants and then rose again. Taking her hands, he pulled her to her feet. She wrapped her arms about his neck and kissed him as his arms went about her. His hands stroked her buttocks, kneading them, smoothing them, cupping them. A fire ignited inside her at the intimate touch. Neither of them seemed to be able to get enough of the other as their kisses and strokes grew harder.

He broke the kiss, his lips hot against her cheek, her jaw, her neck. His teeth grazed her pulse point, and the fire inside her blazed out of control. She could feel something pressing between them and realized it was his cock. That caused her mouth to grow dry.

"What is it?" he asked, concern on his face.

"Nothing. Well, just a little something." She glanced down at their joined bodies. "It is just that . . . well, I can feel . . ."

"My cock. It is longing to be inside you, love."

Willa swallowed hard. "I think I want it there, but I am a bit scared."

"Of the hurt?"

"Of the unknown."

Xander brushed his lips softly against hers. "It is unknown for me, too, love. I told you—I have never made love with a woman before. You are the first. The last. My always."

He kissed her again, and her confidence soared, knowing he meant what he told her. He may have performed this act with other women, but it had held no meaning for him. This time, it would.

He caught her under her knees and lifted her in his arms, placing her on the bed and joining her there. His hands skimmed her body, touching her in different places and with a variety of pressures. Xander spoke to her constantly, Willa telling him what felt good, and she touched and asked him the same, in turn. She found she liked when he tweaked her nipples and sucked on her breasts. He did so, causing the place between her legs to throb almost painfully.

His mouth returned to hers and even as he kissed her, his fingers stroked along the seam of her sex. It felt marvelous. Then he pushed a finger inside her, and Willa almost came off the bed. He moved it deeply within her and began stroking her. His hand cupped her, and he pushed another finger inside, his strokes deeper and bolder. She found herself beginning to writhe, soft moans escaping her lips.

"Oh!" she said, a funny tingling starting to build inside her.

"How does this feel?"

"Keep doing what you are doing," she commanded. "Do not stop, I tell you."

She heard the laughter in his voice as he said, "Oh, I won't."

He knew exactly what she needed before she asked for it. Suddenly, something erupted within her, something wonderful and marvelous and purely physical in nature. Willa bucked against his hand, crying out his name, devoured in waves of pure pleasure.

Gradually, she fell to earth, weak and unable to lift a limb.

"You are ready for me now," he said, his voice low and rough.

She tensed, anticipating what would come next.

"No, relax," he said, kissing her again, taking her mind off what was coming.

Willa felt a pressure and guessed he had started pushing his cock inside her. She had been afraid to look at it, knowing as large as he was that his cock would be, too, and might frighten her off if she saw it.

Xander's fingers found hers and held on as he pushed hard against her. Pain made everything go white for a brief moment, and she sucked in a breath. His fingers still held hers as she merely felt uncomfortable now, stretched wide by his member.

"Are you all right?"

She nodded.

"That was the worst of it, love. It will get better now."

"I hope so."

He chuckled.

"It will," he promised.

And it did.

Xander began withdrawing from her and then pushed inside again. Each thrust went deeper, and they began to feel good. No, better than good. Addictingly good. Willa's body caught his unspoken rhythm and began to move with him. She wrapped her arms about him as their dance quickened, reaching new heights. Those same tingles surfaced again, and soon Willa was holding on for dear life, crying out her fiancé's name.

He thrust into her a final time and collapsed atop her, driving her into the mattress. He stayed there, filling her, her hands stroking his back.

"I'm too heavy," he said.

"No," she protested. "I like having you on me."

"I refuse to crush you," he said, rolling gently, taking her with him until they lay on their sides, facing one another.

His beautiful face brought tears to her eyes, and they began to fall.

"Are you still hurting?"

"No," she assured him. "You are just so incredible. Your handsome face. Your magnificent, chiseled body. I don't feel as if I deserve you, Xander."

She pressed her face into his chest, weeping.

"There, there," he comforted. "You are so beautiful yourself, love. Every sweet curve. Your skin, smoother than satin. I look at you and I am speechless."

Willa lay in his arms and asked, "How did I get so lucky?"

He kissed the top of her head. "I am the lucky one, Miss Fennimore. I thought I had struck gold in finding the perfect governess. Instead, I found the absolute, perfect duchess. The only woman for me. One who loves me—and my nieces."

"I do love you, Xander. I am overwhelmed by my feelings for you. And I love those girls as if they were my own."

"They are your own, Willa. They are ours. They may not have been made by us, but we will do our best in raising them."

She rested her cheek against his beating heart. "Will we always feel this way, how we do in this moment?"

"I believe that this is just the start. That our love will grow over time. That we will get to know one another's bodies and be able to please each other with a single touch."

"Every day will be better than the one before," she told him.

"I agree. Now, sleep, love. You've earned it."

As Willa drifted off, she wondered if she might ever be more content than she was in this moment.

CHAPTER TWENTY

X ANDER'S CARRIAGE PULLED up to his London townhouse. Despite the fact that Willa enjoyed life in the country, she couldn't help but feel that London would always be home to her. She had pointed out a few of the sights to Cecily and Lucy as they entered the great city, and she would now go inside and see them settled.

Her betrothed exited the carriage and handed down the three of them, and they stepped into what had to be the grandest foyer she had ever seen. While Spring Ridge had been large and its furniture elegant, it had a homey feel about it. This foyer screamed opulence and was meant to impress members of Polite Society who came calling upon the Duke of Brockbank.

"Sewell, I would like to introduce to you my betrothed, Miss Fennimore. We will be marrying soon."

"It is an honor to meet you, Miss Fennimore," the butler said neutrally, taking in her nondescript gown. Turning, he indicated the woman next to him. "This is Mrs. Sewell, the housekeeper."

"It is wonderful to meet you, Miss Fennimore," the older woman said, her tone more friendly. "After I give you a tour of the house, the three of us should meet and see if there are any changes you wish to make here."

"Thank you," Willa responded. "I would enjoy seeing the place. For now, however, I wish to get Lady Cecily and Lady Lucy settled in their room. We will be engaging the services of a governess soon, but for now, they will need a reliable, trusted maid to help care for them. Do you have someone on staff who might watch them?"

Mrs. Sewell smiled. "I know exactly who would fit the bill, Miss Fennimore. Her name is Betsy, and she is young, but a hard worker and quite friendly. I think the girls would take to her. Let me show you to the room set aside for the little ladies, and I will have Betsy summoned and brought there."

"I will accompany you," Xander said.

Mrs. Sewell led them upstairs and first showed them the schoolroom where lessons would take place. The girls' bedchamber was located on the floor below, next door to the rooms designated for the Duchess of Brockbank.

As they entered the bedchamber, Mrs. Sewell said, "It is a rather large room. His Grace wrote that he wanted his nieces to share a room. I hope this will suffice."

"Yes, they will be in a strange place and are used to being together," Xander informed the housekeeper. "As they grow older, we can always separate them and give them a bedchamber of their own if they so desire. For now, I believe it best for the two of them to remain together."

The girls liked their room, and Cecily looked out the window. "Look! The gardens are right outside our window. You will have to go see them with us, Aunt Willa."

She noticed the housekeeper's brows rose at how Cecily addressed Willa and said, "The girls are already practicing their new name for me and getting used to it."

"I see," the housekeeper said, her lips pursed. "Ah, here is Betsy." She motioned the servant over.

Betsy smiled broadly. She was a plain-looking girl of about twenty, but her smile showed her to be kind, nonetheless.

"This is His Grace and Miss Fennimore," Mrs. Sewell said. "And here are Lady Cecily and Lady Lucy."

The maid bobbed a curtsey. "It is ever so nice to meet you. Sewell says that I will be looking after you." She looked to Willa. "What does that entail, Miss Fennimore?"

"You will need to make sure they wash and dress properly each morning and supervise their meals, which they will take in the schoolroom. I will try to be with them some of each day, as will their uncle. We will be hiring a governess soon. Until then, you will need to spend time in their company."

"And keep them out of mischief," Xander declared, smiling at his nieces.

"Oh, we aren't bad anymore, Uncle Xander," Cecily said. "We have attention from you and Aunt Willa now."

"We don't need to be bad," Lucy added.

Willa looked to Betsy and said, "If you will see the girls' things unpacked and then show them around the house, I would appreciate it."

"We want to see the library," Cecily said eagerly.

"And the gardens!" Lucy cried.

"We can do that and more, my ladies," Betsy told the girls.

Willa liked the friendliness of the servant and knew she would be good with the girls. She nodded to Xander, who said, "We will leave you for now. I need to see Miss Fennimore to where she will be staying."

"Will you be back today, Aunt Willa?" Lucy wanted to know.

"No, not today. I, too, need to settle in and visit with the household. I will be back tomorrow morning, however. We will decide what we will do then."

"I want to go to the park you talked about," Cecily told her.

"Then Hyde Park will be first on our list," she promised.

Willa kissed the girls goodbye, and she and Xander returned to the waiting carriage, where she gave the coachman Ralph's address.

Xander handed her up and sat beside her, immediately kissing her as soon as the vehicle started up. The kiss was slow and delicious, causing her toes to curl.

"You are a marvelous kisser," she told him, as he grinned unabashedly at the compliment.

He lifted her hand to his lips and kissed her fingers. "How are you feeling today? Are you sore?"

"A little—but nothing to stop me from coupling with you again."

"Why, you little hoyden!" he declared, kissing her again.

Xander broke the kiss and threaded his fingers through hers. "I must stop. We can't have you showing up with swollen lips. Ralph Baldwin already thinks me the worst of rogues. I do not want him to believe I was taking advantage of you in the carriage."

"I doubt Ralph will be at home," she told him. "Most likely, he is at the theater, deep into rehearsals."

Willa told him about the two plays Ralph had said would begin the Season.

"Perhaps we should attend one—if not both," Xander suggested.

"Thank you. It would mean a great deal to Ralph."

"Well, we will have to get you to a modiste soon so that you will be dressed for the theater." He cupped her cheek. "I want you to stop hiding your voluptuous figure, Willa. I want to show you off to all Polite Society."

"I did so for a good reason," she said quietly. "I told you that I had been a companion to two elderly women and had no problems in either household. It was when I became a governess to Lord Dearling and Lord Appleton and their children that I found them to be far too interested in me. I thought if I dressed unassumingly that they would leave me alone. I was wrong."

"I am committing those names to memory," he said. "I already know Appleton, and he is a true arse. We will have nothing to do with either Lord Dearling or Lord Appleton. In fact, I may punch both of them in the face for good measure."

"You will do no such thing, Xander," she chided. "That is in the past. I want to live in the present and look forward to our future together."

"I know you are still a bit worried about how the *ton* will receive you. Don't be. You will hold the rank of duchess. That alone will cause others to tremble in their shoes. The few gossips who don't are not worth our time. Besides, you also have made friends with the Duchess of Linberry."

Willa smiled. "I have. In fact, I played one of my original compositions for her, and she told me how much she enjoyed hearing it. She asked if she could play it at the musicale she will be hosting in June."

"Ah, the one where she is playing all her own music?"

"The very one. I told her I would be most honored for her to include my piece among her own selections."

"It is a night I look forward to," he said, "as well as all my nights spent with you."

They arrived at Ralph's, and Xander himself lifted her two valises from the carriage and escorted her to the door.

"I still do not know why you refused to send word that you would be arriving in town."

Willa had done so because she wanted to speak to Ralph in person about her upcoming nuptials.

"They are used to me arriving unannounced," she said.

A servant admitted them and greeted her warmly.

"We didn't know you would be coming to London, Miss Fennimore. Mr. Baldwin will be so pleased to see you. Let me take your luggage up to your room."

"Thank you, Tommy," she said.

Turning back to Xander, she said, "We do need to find a governess for the girls as soon as possible. Do not under any circumstances hire one from the Wainwright Agency," she cautioned.

He laughed. "I don't know. I actually had rather good luck when I last visited there."

"I do not want to see a farthing go into Mr. Wainwright's pockets," she declared.

He told her of the other employment agency that had sent numerous governesses, all failing to do the job.

"I know of another agency we could use," she said, providing the name to him.

"Then I will write to them today and ask for an appointment for tomorrow afternoon since you and the girls will be going to Hyde Park in the morning."

"Thank you for doing so, Xander."

"I will leave you to get settled in and visit with your Mr. Baldwin. I will send my carriage for you tomorrow morning. What time do you wish it to be here?"

"That is not necessary, Xander. I will simply take a hansom cab to Mayfair."

He took her hands in his and sternly said, "My future duchess will not be traveling in hansom cabs. She will ride in my ducal carriage. It will be here at half-past seven and wait as long as needed. Come out whenever you are ready."

"You are already bullying me into doing what you wish?" she teased.

He brought her hands to his lips and kissed them. "You are the one who will always tell me what to do, Willa. I want to please you in every way possible." He lowered his voice and added, "In—and out—of bed."

She felt her cheeks burn at his remark. "You better leave."

He grinned mischievously. "Before I kiss you—or you slap me?"

She laughed. "Both."

Willa walked Xander to his carriage, and he told her, "I will miss you today."

"I will miss you even more."

She watched him mount the steps and waved to him as his carriage pulled away. Returning into the house, Willa went to her room, where she unpacked her things and set the valises in a corner. She doubted she would wear any of the gowns she currently possessed once she became the Duchess of Brockbank. Not only would Xander expect her to dress as a duchess, but she believed if she were appropriately garbed, it would give her more confidence as she took her place among the *ton*. It occurred to her that she should keep them, wearing them when she gardened with the girls. Just because she was soon to be a duchess did not mean she would give up so pleasurable an activity, one that she, Cecily, and Lucy enjoyed so much.

Going downstairs, she went and said her hellos to Cook and then found Tommy again.

"I suppose Mr. Baldwin is at the theater."

"He is, Miss Fennimore. He will be delighted you have returned to town."

"I will go and see him now. I would like to see how rehearsals are coming along."

Willa set out on foot for the theater and arrived less than ten minutes later. She had prepared herself to see Jemima James while she was here. She had no reason to avoid the actress and actually wanted to see how Jemima had grown in her profession over the years. The actress was frequently featured in Ralph's plays. Idly, Willa wondered if Jemima was as talented as Theodosia had been.

Entering the theater, she saw rehearsal was in full swing and recognized the scene from the first act of *A Midsummer Night's Dream*. She slipped into the row behind Ralph and settled herself directly behind him, not wishing to distract him while he watched his actors rehearse. The scene was going well, and he let it continue for several minutes. It gave Willa time to study the cast in this scene, some who were familiar to her.

Especially Jemima James.

While the actress had the lead role in Ralph's other production, here she played the supporting role of Hermia. Though Helena had a larger role, Hermia was key to this production. She was the character who was to wed Demetrius and yet did not want to, instead having fallen in love with Lysander, who wooed Hermia without her father's permission. Willa listened as Hermia told Helena, her best friend, of her plans to run away with Lysander before her father could beg for the ancient privilege of Athens and have her put to death.

Ralph was right in saying how much Jemima had matured as an actress. She was not only physically beautiful, but an inner beauty shone from her as Hermia spoke of her love for Lysander. Willa guessed the actress to be close to thirty now and in full possession and awareness of her talent.

Ralph called a halt to the scene and gave them a few notes. She watched as Jemima listened intently as the director spoke to her and then he moved on to other actors who gathered on stage.

That was when Jemima caught sight of Willa. A stillness enveloped the other woman. Then Jemima gave a tentative smile and small wave. Willa returned the wave, knowing she would be able to speak to Jemima without problems.

Rehearsal continued for another hour before Ralph gave the actors a break. After he did so, Willa touched him on the shoulder.

"Rehearsals are going extremely well," she said.

He whipped about hearing her voice and beamed at her. Springing to his feet, she did the same, and they embraced.

"Why did you not tell me you were coming to town?" Then his brow furrowed. "It's that damned Brockbank. He was like the others, wasn't he? He tried to abuse you, and you quit and fled the country. I shall kill that scoundrel."

She placed a palm on his chest. "If you do so, you will make me a widow before I can even become a bride."

Confusion filled his face. "What are you saying, Willa?"

"I am saying that while Brockbank may have been a rake of the worst sort when you knew him, he is no longer that man. Becoming a duke has sobered him. He is fully aware of the obligations and responsibilities which lie at his door, including caring for his two nieces."

She paused. "He is a good man, Ralph. No longer a rogue. Brockbank is my betrothed. We will soon wed, most likely before the Season begins."

Willa had never seen her former guardian speechless, but Ralph was now. His stunned expression and slack jaw caused her to laugh aloud.

Finally, he recovered his senses and asked, "You are telling me that you are going to become the Duchess of Brockbank?"

"I am."

The director's laughter filled the theater. Smiling at her, he said, "I wonder what Ambrose and Theodosia would think of you now."

"Can you imagine Theodosia having to curtsey to me?" she asked.

He laughed again and then grew serious. "They never knew what to do with you, Willa. They never should have been parents. I am afraid if they were here, they would still be ignoring you." He captured her hands and touched his cheek against them. "You were always so strong and mature, even as a child. I suppose if any woman could tame the gallivanting Duke of Brockbank, it would be you."

"I think he tamed himself, Ralph. I do know some of what he was like before the deaths of his father and brothers. He has had a heavy burden placed upon him, one which he never expected to carry. He has most certainly risen to the challenge, including becoming a loving guardian to his two nieces." She smiled. "Yes, I will be a sort of mother to the girls I was once governess to."

"Do you like them?"

"Quite a bit."

Ralph gazed intently at her. "And the duke? You have to admit, this is a bit sudden."

"It is—but it is so very right. He loves me, Ralph, and I love him."

Frowning, he said, "Are you certain he didn't say this to get into your bed, Willa?"

A blush warmed her cheeks. "He is a different man than the one you knew from before, Ralph. That is all I will say. Our feelings—and commitment to one another—are mutual."

"I suppose he will purchase a special license if you are to wed so soon."

"He has said he would. I want you at the ceremony. He has no one on his side, only distant cousins he has not seen since he was a boy."

"You will require two witnesses, Willa."

"I know." She took a deep breath. "I believe I am going to ask Jemima James to be the second one."

CHAPTER TWENTY-ONE

XANDER LEFT WILLA and headed straight to Doctors' Commons in order to purchase a special license. The Season was fast approaching, and he wanted to make certain that they were husband and wife when they attended the opening ball together. He knew as a duke that he would receive an invitation to literally every social event held during the Season. It was simply the way of the *ton*. It didn't matter that he might not know the hosts or that they did not know him. As Duke of Brockbank, invitations would pile up on his desk. Most of the *ton* had secretaries which dealt with those matters. If his father had ever had one, Xander wasn't aware of it. He did know that for a duke to attend an event was a feather in the cap of the host and hostess. Because of that, dukes rarely responded to invitations. They merely let the spirit move them and attended the affairs they wished to.

He chuckled to himself, thinking of how surprised Polite Society would be when they saw him as the new Duke of Brockbank. His father's death notice had appeared in the newspapers, thanks to Rollo, but Xander hadn't bothered to submit news of the deaths of his three brothers to them. Rollo's and Stanley's had occurred at a time when few were in town anyway. As for Peter, the notification from his commanding officer expressed sympathy but gave no specific details as to where and when Peter's death occurred, only that it had happened during battle and that he had exhibited extraordinary bravery during his time as an officer in His Majesty's army. With as slow as the post was with the war going on, Peter could have been killed last summer or autumn, with the family only receiving news of his death this winter.

Xander supposed a few might know of his recent good fortune if they had spoken with Gil. He hated that he and his friend had parted on such ill terms but realized that Gil hadn't been as good a friend to him as Xander had supposed. They had been the merry bachelors together, cutting a wide swath through Polite Society, bedding women left and right. Gil would most likely continue to behave as a bachelor, even after his marriage. Xander vowed to be the exact opposite. His loyalties would lie with Willa, his duchess, and their family. All desire for a string of mistresses had vanished.

The one time they had made love, Willa had been tentative at first but had become exceedingly bold as things progressed. He had much to teach her about the art of love and knew she would be a willing student. His cock sprang to life just thinking about bedding her, even as a foolish grin seemed stuck on his face. Just the thought of his fiancée could stir desire within him.

He arrived at Doctors' Commons, a place he never thought to set foot inside. He left his coachman and entered, asking a few people he came across where he needed to go for a special license. Each one got him a step closer until he reached the office of the Archbishop of Canterbury, the clergyman who had the power to grant such a request. Xander doubted the archbishop kept regular hours at this London office and wondered what the process would entail.

After explaining his wishes, the clerk told him that he could speak with the authorized spokesman for the archbishop, who had the authority to grant such a request in the archbishop's absence. The clerk disappeared for a few minutes and then returned, escorting Xander down a hallway and to an office where he met with this representative.

"His Grace does not grant a special license lightly," the man explained. "Still, he would be happy to do so for a duke."

Once again, Xander couldn't help but think that dukes were men who lived by their own set of rules and that society treated them differently because of their noble titles.

After the paperwork was completed, the representative told him that posting banns would be unnecessary. The special license granted a couple the privilege to be wed at any time of day and in any place they chose. He liked having this freedom. He paid the exorbitant license fee, along with several pounds to cover the stamp duty for the paper, glad that he had availed himself of funds from the lockbox in his study at Spring Ridge before they had left for town.

"I wish Your Grace and Miss Fennimore every happiness," the archbishop's representative told him.

"Thank you," he replied, relived that this errand had been accomplished.

Returning to his carriage, he had the coachman drive home, where he sent for his nieces and then had the Sewells conduct a tour of the townhouse from top to bottom for the three of them. They shared tea together, and then the girls read to him for half an hour. Xander could already tell both of their reading skills had improved in the short time Willa had been instructing them.

That reminded him that he needed to write for an appointment with the Plowright Employment Agency. He did so and sent a footman to deliver the message, receiving a reply that he could call at two o'clock the next day to discuss the positions he wished to fill. Not only did he seek a governess for his nieces, but Xander also wanted to hire a valet. He had done for himself his entire life, but as a duke, he decided he could afford to spoil himself a bit. He had learned his father's valet had departed immediately after the duke's death, having been hired away by a neighboring earl. It was time for him to employ a trusted servant to make his life easier.

Xander ate alone, missing Willa's company. Already, his life was so tied to hers. It was as if part of him were missing with her being absent. Especially in his bed. He slipped beneath the bedclothes later that night, wishing she were beside him. Though they had only spent the one night together, he found it difficult to sleep, longing for her warmth and sweet, feminine curves to be pressed against him.

He rose early the next morning and went to the stables, taking a horse and riding for an hour in Rotten Row. A few others were taking an early morning ride, as well, and he nodded politely to them. He supposed they would be gossiping later at the change in the Duke of Brockbank. In his bachelor days, Xander had never arisen and gone riding at dawn. If anything, he was staggering in at that time from either the gaming hells or one of his mistresses' beds. He shook his head, thinking how truly different his life was now. He had his nieces' futures to consider and would soon have a wife, as well. He only hoped children of their own would follow soon after.

He cut through the kitchens, spying Sewell with a cup of tea in the servants' dining hall.

"Would you see that hot water is brought up so I may bathe?" he asked his butler.

"At once, Your Grace. I will assist you myself."

"That will not be necessary, Sewell. I have been bathing myself for many years now. However, you might wish to lay out my clothes for me. And do not fear—I plan to speak to an employment agency about hiring a valet this afternoon."

Going to his rooms, he stripped off his clothes and slipped into his banyan, catching a whiff of Willa's scent, bringing a sleeve to his nose and inhaling deeply. It had shocked him when she had been the one to approach him about lovemaking, especially when they weren't even wed yet. Xander had been more than willing to wait—until he had seen the hot desire blazing in her amethyst eyes. It had convinced him that she was right, and they should take advantage of the time they had together.

It had been joyful. Sensual. A time of exploration. It only affirmed his feelings for Willa. Oh, how he had matured in such a short time. He now knew there was only one woman for him.

That woman was Willa Fennimore.

A brigade of servants arrived, carrying in his bath water. Sewell supervised them, mixing the hot and cold together and keeping a few buckets in reserve to freshen the water and for rinsing. Again, Xander reiterated he could do these things himself and sent everyone away.

He shrugged out of the banyan and left it on the floor as he stepped into the tub. The rather large tub. He chuckled, thinking it was so huge that he could get lost in it. Then he laughed aloud, thinking it was the perfect size for him and his duchess. Sharing a bath with Willa—and everything that resulted from that—heated his blood. He decided to speak to her today about when they would wed, wanting to spend as few nights apart from her as possible.

After soaking a good while, he took up the bar of soap and thoroughly scrubbed the smell of horse from him. The bath sheet had been draped on a stool nearby, and he reached for it, standing and drying off. Emerging from his bathing chamber, he found Sewell awaited him.

"Your clothes are ready, Your Grace," the butler said. "I will assist you." The servant's tone left no room for Xander to protest.

He rather enjoyed Sewell ministering to him and even told the butler, "You tie a hell of a cravat."

"Thank you, Your Grace," the butler replied, a pleased smile turning up the corners of his mouth.

"Would you have my breakfast sent to the schoolroom? I usually have that meal with my nieces."

If Sewell thought this unusual for a duke to dine in a schoolroom, he did not show it.

"Certainly, Your Grace."

Xander left his rooms and headed upstairs, finding Lucy and Cecily already at the table, Betsy was seated with them.

The servant jumped to her feet and bobbed a curtsey. "Your Grace," she said, clearly surprised by his appearance.

"Uncle Xander always eats breakfast with us," Cecily explained.

"I do. You may be excused and eat some of your own, Betsy. Return in half an hour if you would."

"Yes, Your Grace." She left them just as servants arrived with their meals.

As they ate, he asked the girls a few questions, but he listened much more than he spoke. Xander had found that by doing so, his nieces revealed an incredible amount of information to him, and it didn't seem as if he were prying.

"Are you going to the park with us, Uncle Xander?" Lucy asked him.

"No, I have a few errands to run," thinking he would stop by a modiste the Duchess of Linberry had recommended to him when he had asked her for suggestions. He also wished to see Mr. Crockle and have the solicitor draw up the marriage settlements, wanting to present these to Ralph Baldwin so that the theater director would know how serious Xander was about Willa.

"Good morning."

He turned and spied his betrothed in the doorway. Both Cecily and Lucy jumped up and ran to her, hugging her tightly and jabbering away, telling her all about the house and what they had been doing. He let the girls talk for a few minutes as he gazed at Willa.

All mine . . .

As Cecily came up for air, Xander rose. "I have a few things to accomplish before Miss Fennimore and I go to see about finding you two a new governess."

He moved behind Willa, placing his hands on her shoulders and bending to kiss her cheek. He fought the urge to let his lips glide lower and quickly stood.

"Shall I meet you here after your sojourn in the park?" he asked.

"That would be lovely."

She looked too enticing, and he murmured, "To hell with it," bending again and kissing her briefly on the lips.

His nieces giggled and he laughed. "Take good care of Miss Fennimore for me."

"We will," Lucy solemnly promised.

"I suppose you will walk to Hyde Park because we are so close," he said to Willa.

"That was my plan. The carriage is still out front if you need it," she told him.

"Then I shall take the carriage on my errands. I will see you later."

Xander first gave his coachman the address of the modiste. He entered the dress shop and was immediately greeted.

"Ah, good morning, my lord."

The French accent was probably fake, but glancing about, he saw the gowns on display to be of quality.

"My good friend, the Duchess of Linberry, sent me to you, Madame Planche. I am the Duke of Brockbank."

Her eyes lit up. "Her Grace is a very good customer to me."

"I hope to be one, as well. I am to be married very shortly. My fiancée's wardrobe is . . . well, I should say . . ."

"Lacking?" the modiste offered.

He was thinking *abysmal*, but said, "Yes. The perfect word, Madame. She lacks in simply everything. Miss Fennimore is a quite beautiful woman, with a tremendous figure beneath her gowns. I wish to have her show off her figure." He decided to be frank. "She was a governess and sought to hide her assets from previous employers who . . . might try and take advantage of her."

A knowing light came into the dressmaker's eyes. "I understand, Your Grace. You are proud of her. I can see it."

"I am more than proud, Madame Planche. I love her with all my heart. I want the world to see her as I do."

The modiste beamed at him. "It is not every day I hear a fine gentleman talk of love. Yes, Your Grace, I will see that your duchess is superbly garbed and must thank Her Grace for sending you to me. Has she had her babe yet?"

"She has. A fine boy. They named him after the duke. They are calling him Harry."

"Is she still returning to town in June?"

"That is what I understand."

"I have sewn a blanket for her little one," the modiste shared. "Her Grace has been good to me."

Xander smiled. "She has also been good to me and my fiancée. When can we come in so Miss Fennimore might be measured?"

"As soon as possible, Your Grace. The Season is almost upon us, and we are very busy, as you can see. I will take your betrothed's measurements and then will start on her designs and gowns. It will take time to finish such an extensive wardrobe for Miss Fennimore. We will provide new gowns each week for her throughout the Season."

"She has taken my nieces to the park this morning, but I will bring her by once they return to the house, Madame Planche. Thank you for taking her on as a client."

The modiste smiled. "I do it for the Duchess of Linberry, Your Grace, but I also do it for you. It is the rare gentleman I see who has such love shining in his eyes for the woman he will marry."

"I will see you shortly then, Madame."

Xander left the dress shop and returned to his coach, giving instructions to drive to Mr. Crockle's offices. The solicitor saw him straightaway, promising Xander that he would draw up the marriage contracts and have them ready by tomorrow morning.

"While Miss Fennimore is of age to sign any legal documents, I wish for the settlements to be presented to her and a Mr. Baldwin, her former guardian, at the same time. I will send word to you regarding when we will meet. It will be in the next day or so, though, Crockle. I want this marriage to proceed with all due haste."

"I look forward to hearing from you, Your Grace,' the solicitor said.

Returning to his carriage, Xander saw a sweet shop next door and went inside, choosing a few items for Willa and the girls. He left the shop and told his coachman to return home now and keep the horses harnessed because he and Miss Fennimore would be running further errands soon. The vehicle stopped just outside his townhouse and as he disembarked, he saw Willa and his nieces only a stone's throw away.

"How was the park?" he called.

Lucy ran to him and hugged him, then eyed the box in his hands. "What is that, Uncle Xander?"

"These are treats for the three of you," he told her. "Shall we go to the schoolroom and try them?"

"Yes!" Cecily cried. "May I carry the box?"

"You may." He handed it over, and the girls went ahead, entering the house.

Xander tucked Willa's hand into the crook of his arm. "We have appointments at the modiste for you to be measured for a new wardrobe and then the employment agency."

She laughed. "Then I better not partake in any of those sweets you brought."

Xander leaned close and said into her ear, "You can always partake of me whenever you wish."

Willa laughed in delight.

CHAPTER TWENTY-TWO

THEY SPENT A few minutes with the girls, who consumed the sweets Xander had brought them. Betsy took charge, allowing Willa and Xander to leave the house for the modiste's dress shop.

"Madame Planche comes highly recommended," he told her. "I asked the Duchess of Linberry who she used, and Madame Planche was her reply. I stopped by her shop earlier today so that she knows we are coming."

"She must be quite busy, Xander. If Fia uses her, then I suppose many others of the *ton* do, as well. It is so close to the beginning of the Season. I do not see how she could possibly work me in and provide a complete wardrobe for me in such a limited amount of time."

Her fiancé smiled. "That is when being a duke comes in handy. No, Madame will not have an entire wardrobe ready for you by the beginning of the Season, but she assured me that you would have gowns to start it, and she and her seamstresses would provide new ones to you each week throughout the spring and summer."

"This is going to cost a great deal," she said worriedly.

Xander laughed and kissed her soundly. "I am good for the bills, love," he assured her. He cradled her cheek. "Besides, I would spend my last pound on you. My duchess will arrive wearing the height of fashion at every social event we attend."

They arrived at their destination, and Xander escorted her into the dress shop, where it buzzed with activity.

Suddenly, a tall, regal woman approached them and said, "It is good to see you again so soon, Your Grace." She turned to Willa. "And you must be Miss Fennimore."

The modiste's eyes swept up and down, looking Willa over. She clucked her tongue in disapproval.

"If you wore a sack, it might be more becoming, Miss Fennimore. Come with me. We must solve your problems first by measuring you."

Madame Planche led her to a back room, summoning an assistant along the way. Willa's measurements were taken by Madame herself and carefully recorded by the assistant.

The modiste said, "Bring the plum, sky blue, and daffodil gowns at once. You know which ones I speak of."

The assistant appeared confused. "But Madame, they are for—"

"They are for Miss Fennimore," Madame Planche said with authority.

The assistant left, and Willa said, "I cannot take gowns from another customer of yours."

"They will look much better on you than her," the modiste replied. "You have what we call an hourglass figure, Miss Fennimore. I can see why your betrothed wishes to show you off. I cannot let you leave this shop looking as you do. These gowns will be close to your size and may only new a few minor adjustments."

The assistant returned with the three gowns the modiste requested and Willa tried them on, one by one. She could tell by the fabric used and the cut of the gowns how clever a designer Madame Planche was. Gazing into the mirror, she did not even recognize the woman before her.

A few nips and tucks were made and Madame insisted that Willa wear the plum gown from the shop.

They rejoined Xander, whose eyes lit up the moment he saw her.

"You look incredible, love. I cannot wait to see you in Madame Planche's actual designs created for you."

The modiste said, "Miss Fennimore is going to leave wearing this gown, Your Grace. My assistant is placing two others in boxes for her. They will do for a few days. We will begin working on her wardrobe immediately. Expect several designs each week. If you would like, I can come to your townhouse for both fittings and final deliveries of these gowns."

"That is very thoughtful of you, Madame Planche," Willa said.

The older woman smiled at her. "I look forward to working with you, Miss Fennimore. You have the figure to do my designs justice. Please thank the Duchess of Linberry for her recommendation of me to you."

"I will do so," Willa promised.

Xander escorted her to his carriage, placing the boxes containing the other gowns on the seat opposite them.

Willa smoothed her new gown and said, "I have never worn something so fine, Xander. The quality and cut are exceptional."

He took her hand. "Only the best for my duchess. Speaking of that, we should set a wedding date. I would not mind seeing you wear the gown you now have on to the ceremony."

"You will need to purchase a special license," she reminded him, not knowing what the process involved.

Her fiancé tapped his chest. "I have already taken care of that important step and now bear the license in my pocket. We have a month in which we may wed on any day and at any location of our choosing."

"Then I suppose we must find a clergyman to perform the ceremony," she said.

"I will handle it. Tomorrow might be too soon. I shall aim for the day after it if that pleases you."

Willa squeezed his hand. "Everything you do pleases me," she said honestly, still in awe that this wonderful man would soon be her husband.

The carriage came to a halt, and they entered the employment agency. Willa recognized the block they were on since the Wainwright Agency, her former employer, was sitting catty-corner from the building they entered. A clerk greeted them and immediately led them to an office, where a plump, balding man stood and greeted them.

"Good afternoon, Your Graces. I am Mr. Plowright, owner of the Plowright Employment Agency. I hear you are in need of both a governess and valet."

Willa glanced to Xander to see if he would correct the man, who mistakenly believed her to be a duchess. Xander said nothing, however.

They took a seat, and Mr. Plowright asked, "What are the ages of your children and what are you most looking for in a governess?"

Xander looked to her and nodded, so Willa said, "Our girls are six and eight years of age. They are both bright and extremely curious about the world around them. We need a governess who will encourage their curiosity, one who is also flexible in the lessons she gives. Their last governess," she said, biting back a smile, "had a most unusual philosophy, in that she allowed Cecily and Lucy to pursue whatever interested them."

Mr. Plowright's eyes widened. "She did? That is something I have never heard. Was the method successful?"

Xander spoke up. "It was, indeed, Mr. Plowright. The girls have found the more they are interested in, the more they want to learn about a great many other things. Do you have any candidates in mind for us?"

The agency's owner told them of three women and then said, "I believe of these three that Miss Janus would be best suited for your children. She has about ten years of governessing experience and is openminded enough that she would be amenable to applying your unique philosophy in educating your girls. If you would like to meet her now, you may do so. She and another of the candidates I spoke of for this post were available this afternoon. I had them come in just in case you thought them suitable and wished to interview them."

"We would be happy to speak with Miss Janus now since it is convenient."

The potential governess was summoned, and Willa and Xander spent several minutes questioning her about her previous posts and her philosophy in general in educating children. When Willa spoke of how the girls had been recently learning, Miss Janus expressed delight with the method.

"I have never thought to employ something so clever," she said. "If your girls are as curious as you say they are, I can see where learning about one topic could lead to interest in many others, as well. Can you share some of their recent lessons with me?"

"I am happy to do so," Willa said. "Gardening has been something they have both taken to. They enjoy being out in the fresh air, and so botany has become a special interest. When you meet them, the girls will no doubt regale you with various varieties of plant life. They know which flowers are annuals and those which are perennials. They know the names of many of them and when they are to be planted. They have done weeding and planting themselves, delighting in digging in the dirt."

"They also have a great interest in herbs," Xander added. "They know which ones Cook uses in dishes she serves, and the girls have taken on the responsibility of collecting these herbs for the kitchen staff."

"My, that is most unique, Your Grace," Miss Janus said. "I have never heard of young ladies working in a garden."

"We still have stressed reading and writing with them," Willa shared. "Time is set aside each day for those things. We want the girls to have a good command of language and communication since reading and writing are the foundation of all learning. Still, oftentimes lessons take place outside the schoolroom."

She explained how the girls had had a few baking lessons, using mathematics, as well as their time spent working in the gardens.

"We believe learning is simply not strictly academic in nature," Willa continued. "Yes, there are many things to learn from books and sums to be figured on slates, but we wish for Cecily and Lucy to love learning so much that they will pursue it even after they leave the schoolroom behind."

"We think it important to breakfast with them each morning," Xander shared.

The governess looked puzzled. "Every morning, Your Grace?"

"Of course," he continued. "It is the right way to start our day as a family and also hear about what lessons and topics they will pursue."

"And we take tea with them each afternoon in order to discuss what they have learned," Willa said. "As their governess, Miss Janus, you would accompany them and take tea with us."

The woman's eyes widened in surprise. "I . . . would be expected at tea each day? I would . . . take tea . . . with a duke and duchess?"

"Absolutely, Miss Janus," Xander assured her. "You are a large part of their education, and we must include you in our discussions." He beamed and said, "Sometimes, the scones served at tea are baked by the girls. They are always so proud when we serve something they have created."

Willa knew they must be overwhelming the governess and said, "What we wish to convey to you, Miss Janus, is that there are no secrets in our household. His Grace and I will know everything about the girls' education and fully expect to take part in it, along with you, as you guide them in their lessons."

"They sound delightful," Miss Janus declared. "Moreover, this very unusual method of educating a child is one which intrigues me. I can assure you that I would be quite pleased teaching your girls in such an open atmosphere." The governess paused, looking confident. "I hope that you will give me serious consideration, Your Graces, for I would so enjoy working with Lady Cecily and Lady Lucy."

Willa glanced to Xander, and he nodded imperceptibly. She did the same, and he told the governess, "You are hired, Miss Janus. When would you be able to begin?"

"Why, I could do so at the beginning of next week," she told them. "I am finishing up my current assignment with a young man who will be going away to school next term. His parents are taking him for an extended visit with his grandparents in the country starting next week, and my services will no longer be required."

Xander asked Miss Janus for the address of her current employer and told her he would send a carriage for her. The governess looked taken aback but provided it. Xander said his coachman would arrive at eight o'clock next Monday morning if it suited her, and she agreed to the arrangement.

"Thank you again, Your Graces," Miss Janus said. "I promise you will get my best as I explore this unusual teaching method with your nieces."

Once Miss Janus left the room, Mr. Plowright said, "I think you will be most happy with her. Now, shall we discuss valets?"

Xander shared a few things he was looking for in a valet. Mr. Plowright said he had no candidates for them to interview at the moment but asked that they give him a few days.

"I believe I have the perfect valet in mind for you, Your Grace. If you trust me, I will send him to you within three days' time."

"That is acceptable," Xander said. "I will trust your judgment, Mr. Plowright."

"If he does not suit you, Your Grace, simply send a message to me, and I will try out a new candidate for the post."

They rose and thanked the agency's owner for his time and then returned to Xander's carriage.

"Shall you come home with me now?" he asked.

"Actually, I should return to Ralph's. He is having a few guests for dinner, and I have promised to act as his hostess."

In truth, only one guest was expected.

Jemima James.

Willa had spoken briefly with the actress at yesterday's rehearsal and invited her to come to dinner this evening since Jemima was already engaged for dinner that night. Jemima had thanked her profusely for the invitation, saying there were things she wished to discuss with Willa.

Xander instructed his coachman to take them to Ralph's, and they entered the carriage.

Once inside, he took her hand and said, "I know that Baldwin has been good to you over the years, Willa, but he *is* from the world of theater. While I am more than happy to escort you to the theater he owns to watch one of his plays, I do not wish to encourage you to spend more time with him than necessary. You may not realize this, but those who are involved with the theater are not looked upon favorably by Polite Society."

Anger bristled within her. "And when have you cared for what the *ton* thought?" she fired back. "You yourself have told me that you have never been much of a follower of rules."

"That is true," he said thoughtfully, "but I now have Lucy and Cecily to consider, as well as our future children. I am not saying you should ignore Baldwin, but I am asking you to put some distance between the two of you once we wed."

Doubt now flooded her, knowing she had kept from Xander her own connections to the world of the theater. Willa knew now would be the time to speak up and tell him of her parents, and yet she sat silently, staring at him.

What would he do if he learned of her origins?

She could speak now—and lose him—or continue to hide her past from him.

"You think my knowing Ralph would reflect on Cecily and Lucy?"

He nodded grimly. "I know it would. I want the best for my nieces and know you do as well, not to mention the children we will have. The sooner we get you out of Baldwin's house and my ring on your finger and title attached to your name, the better it will be."

His words paralyzed Willa, and she merely nodded as if she agreed with him. They rode in silence until they reached Ralph's, and Xander escorted her to the door. He cupped her cheek.

"I know Baldwin took you in when you had nowhere to go after your parents' deaths, love. I am asking that you make him part of your past, Willa. Our future is bright. For us. For our children—and that includes Cecily and Lucy. I would sacrifice anything for those girls."

She nodded, her eyes downcast.

"I do know you care for him. In fact, I would like him to meet with the two of us and my solicitor tomorrow morning. I have had Crockle draw up the marriage settlements for us. While you are of legal age, I know that you respect Baldwin and his opinions and would like the two of you to review these contracts together. Could Crockle and I come in the morning and meet with you?"

"Yes," she said quietly. "Make it nine o'clock. I will see that Ralph is there."

"I will see you tomorrow morning, Willa," Xander said, his thumb stroking her cheek.

He stepped away from her and returned to his carriage and drove off, giving her a jaunty wave.

Willa entered Ralph's house, sick to her belly, knowing that by not telling Xander of her background that she was lying to him by omission. She did not want to talk over the matter with Ralph, however. She needed someone else who might understand more the dilemma she faced.

She would discuss the matter tonight.

With Jemima James.

CHAPTER TWENTY-THREE

WILLA SAT AT dinner, carefully watching Ralph. While the director was as urbane as any gentleman of the *ton*, she did know he led a dissolute life outside of the hard work he put into the theater he owned and the productions he helmed. She thought of what his reputation must be. Xander had known who Ralph was, which meant that others in the *ton* would as well. Especially knowing how Xander himself had been a hedonistic bachelor, seeking pleasure at every turn, it did not surprise her that his path had crossed with that of her former guardian's.

Yet how was she to cut ties with this man?

Ralph had been there after the tragedy had occurred, the deaths of her parents. Even before that, actually. He had always spoken to her whenever Ambrose or Theodosia brought Willa to the theater with them. Ralph had been charming and polite and interested in her, apart from his relationship with her parents. When she had been orphaned, it was Ralph who had stepped up and made her his own, moving her into his house and comforting her in her time of sorrow.

He had encouraged her to go to the theater with him each day and not wallow in pity, thinking the distraction would do her good. It had, keeping Willa's mind from going to dark places. Ralph had also been supportive of her when she chose to walk away from the world of theater, though he reminded her every now and then that it still waited for her, and he would cast her if she decided to set foot on the stage.

Willa wanted to continue seeing him, and yet she understood how her association with the director might possibly taint Cecily and Lucy. Well, *possibly* was the wrong choice of word. Her closeness to Ralph would be noted and gossiped about viciously. She could not risk harm coming to those orphaned girls, much less children she and Xander might have.

"This meal has been outstanding," Jemima said, giving her host and hostess her signature smile. "I am positively stuffed. My compliments to your cook."

Ralph rose. "I have after-dinner plans, ladies, so I will excuse myself and leave you to entertain one another."

Most likely, Ralph would be gambling and drinking the rest of the night. She wondered how many of the *ton* would be at the same gaming hell and how much the director might win or lose at the tables.

"I will see you at rehearsals tomorrow," Jemima said, looking to Willa.

"Ralph, I need you to be home tomorrow morning at nine o'clock," she said. "Can you be here?"

He bent and kissed her check. "Anything for my Willa."

Though she had already shared news of her engagement with Ralph, she had not had time to discuss with him how Xander and his solicitor would arrive tomorrow morning with the marriage contracts in hand. She had planned to do so before Jemima arrived, but Ralph had rushed in from rehearsal and upstairs to change clothes, arriving only minutes before their guest did. Knowing Ralph would stay out until the wee hours of the morning, Willa supposed she would need to discuss why Xander and his solicitor were coming when she and Ralph breakfasted together tomorrow morning.

"Would you care to retire to the parlor?" she asked their guest.

"Only if I can stand," the actress said, chuckling.

They retreated from the dining room and settled themselves on a settee in the parlor, Willa's favorite room in the house. She had spent many hours reading in here and daydreaming of what life would bring her.

"Might I get you something to drink?" Willa asked.

"No, not a thing. Truly, I am full to the brim. I have not had a good meal like that in a long time."

"Your cook is a poor one?"

"I have no cook. I grab what I can from food vendors when I go and come from rehearsals or if a play is in season. My landlady does serve breakfast and dinner though I find often I am not awake for the first meal and rarely home for the second one."

"I would think you are earning a generous salary by this time, Jemima. Ralph is not stingy when it comes to paying his top talent."

"Oh, I totally agree," the actress said. "Ralph is only one of several directors who have cast me since my return to London." She paused. "It is I who am the frugal one, Willa. I put almost everything I earn into a bank account which Ralph helped me to set up. I know how fleeting fame can be. Yes, I still have my looks. I favor my father's side of the family and the women all hold their age well. Still, I know the day will come when directors will wish to cast someone younger in their leading roles. I will not be ashamed to take on supporting ones at that point. Sometimes, I find them more rewarding to play."

"I think you are perfectly cast as Hermia. She has always been my favorite character in *A Midsummer Night's Dream*. And I am looking forward to seeing what you do with Lady Brute in *The Provoked Wife*."

"Yes, Lady B has been quite the challenge for me. I dance a fine line in aiming to garner sympathy for having made such a loveless marriage with a hopeless drunk and yet convincing the audience that I must follow my heart when I become involved with the dashing Constant, despite my strict moral conscience."

"You will be successful. If what I saw in rehearsals is any indication, you have matured as an actress—even beyond Theodosia."

Jemima's cheeks pinkened. "That is a true compliment, Willa. Your mother was the best actress I ever saw perform." She paused. "And what I wished to speak to you about this evening."

She waited, letting the actress gather her thoughts.

"I owe you my life, Willa," Jemima began. "First of all, physically. I was wounded and had never been in such dreadful pain. You sent the doctor to me, however, and he tended to me beautifully. Why, I have but the smallest of scars now. I do apply a bit of makeup to it if the role I am playing calls for me to wear something off my shoulders, but I doubt anyone in the audience would ever guess that I had been shot, much less by the most famous actress on the London stage."

Jemima turned to face her. "I was foolish to be at your house that day. Naïve, actually. I realize now that Ambrose must have invited a countless number of women into his bed. I should have stayed at the theater that day and attended rehearsals. Learned from Theodosia. Then none of this would have happened—and you would not have been orphaned."

"You cannot know that, Jemima. Things between my parents had been escalating for some time. If not you, then something else would have triggered Theodosia's wrath. The situation was explosive long before you appeared upon the scene."

Jemima took Willa's hand. "You are too kind, Willa. I accept responsibility for what I did that day. And I give thanks that you, in your youth, had the maturity to send me away from the scene. I shudder to think what the authorities might have asked me. I have had nightmares of going to prison for Theodosia's death."

"It was an accident," she said gently. "I never thought it anything but that."

The actress' gaze pinned Willa's. "You saved my life professionally as well, Willa. If I had been discovered at the scene—if others throughout the theater world had connected me to the deaths of Ambrose and Theodosia—I would never have set foot on the stage again. Your courage gave *me* the courage to leave London and hone my acting skills. For too long, I had been trading on my looks. Yes, I had a bit of talent which surfaced every now and then in a particular role, but escaping London and working in plays throughout England really helped me to become the actress I am today.

"Thank you, Willa," Jemima said fervently. "My career is all because of you. I will act until I am no longer wanted by the audience, and then I will retire from the stage. As I said, I am miserly and put away as much of my salary as I can. I live in a humble boardinghouse instead of purchasing a house of my own. I dress modestly and walk or take hansom cabs to and from the theater. When London tires of me, I will leave it gracefully, with enough money to live out my days in the country."

"That is most commendable, Jemima. I cannot think of many who would think ahead as you have. Deny themselves so that they might save for the distant future."

"You gave me this chance. I will never forget it. I try to be the best person I can be. I know the reputation of actresses is little more than one of painted whores. I have taken no lovers since that day at your house. I even do charity work with the poor. All thanks to you, Willa. I hope that we can be friends and see one another whenever you are in London."

Jemima embraced her, moving Willa to tears.

"May I speak to you about something which has been troubling me?" she asked.

"Of course. I will help you in any way I can."

Willa took a deep breath and let it out. "It involves Ralph. And the Duke of Brockbank."

"Brockbank?" Jemima wrinkled her nose. "He is quite old. In fact, I have not seen him at any of the theaters I have played since my return to London."

"The man you knew has passed. The new Brockbank is Xander Hughes."

"I know something of Mr. Hughes," Jemima said. "He has a wicked reputation, Willa, much more than Ralph. You must know that Ralph is no angel. Even when he took you in, he was a wild one. Some things never change. The two must know each other for Xander Hughes has had numerous mistresses among my fellow actresses."

Even though Willa had known that was the case, Jemima's words still stung.

"Brockbank hired me as the governess for his two nieces. They were the daughters of the heir to the dukedom. Their parents died unexpectedly, making Xander Hughes the new duke."

"Well, isn't that interesting?" Jemima said.

"I am now betrothed to him," she revealed. "I will soon become the Duchess of Brockbank."

Jemima's jaw dropped. "What? Oh, Willa. I don't know what to say. Part of me wishes you the best of luck, having landed a duke. Another part of me thinks I should warn you about your new fiancé."

"We have discussed his reputation. He has changed, Jemima. He had to. Great responsibilities were thrust upon him, including becoming the guardian of his nieces." Her face softened. "Xander admits he is no longer interested in being the man about town he was. His carefree bachelor days are over. He has been attentive to his duties at his country estate and met with his tenants and steward. He also spends a great deal of each day with his nieces."

Jemima shook her head. "It sounds too good to be true. But I can see from your expression that you believe he has changed."

"I did not know him before, of course, but I know him quite well now. When he asked me to be his wife, he made certain I knew I was not only marrying him—but also his nieces. He is a family man now and puts their welfare above his own."

"Then Xander Hughes *has* changed. My congratulations to you, Willa. Oh, dear. I suppose I cannot address you in that manner any longer."

"Please do. I will hear *Your Grace* spoken by so many others." She hesitated. "But what I wish to obtain are two things from you. One, is a favor. I would like for you and Ralph to be witnesses to our marriage."

The actress' face showed her surprise. "You would invite me to your wedding?"

"It will be small. Only His Grace and me and his two young nieces, whom we will raise."

"I would be most honored to attend, Willa. What else do you wish from me?"

"It is your opinion. You see, Xander only knows me as a governess and companion, a woman orphaned and taken in by Ralph Baldwin. He does not know who my parents were."

Jemima sucked in a quick breath. "You have not told him you are the child of London's most famous actress and one of its best-known playwrights?"

She shook her head. "No. I fear . . . he will look at me differently if he learns of my background."

"Oh, Willa, you cannot keep hiding this from him. He will be angry when he learns you did so," warned Jemima.

Her eyes welled with tears. "I am afraid of that very thing. That he will cast me aside. Already, he wants me to limit my time with Ralph so that Polite Society will see no connection between us."

"The duke is right," Jemima said gently. "Your association with Ralph would cast a dark shadow upon you. You already have one hovering about you because you were in service. A duke wedding a governess is bad enough, but one marrying a child of prominent theater people who were involved in a huge scandal will cause an enormous stir among the *ton*. You must prepare him for it, Willa.

Now. Before you speak your vows together."

Tears flowed down her cheeks. "What if I lose him? I love him, Jemima, and he loves me."

"You will lose him if you do not tell him. If you go ahead and marry him and then he finds out?" Jemima shuddered. "It would not go well for you, Willa. Most likely he would cast you aside in order to protect his nieces. He might even sue for divorce."

No one ever divorced. Especially among the *ton*. It was a costly—and humiliating—public affair.

"I will tell him," Willa said, wiping away her tears. "It would be better to lose him before we wed than after."

Jemima took Willa's hands. "You can always count on me, Willa. I will be here no matter what happens with you and this duke."

"Thank you," she whispered.

Jemima left soon after, and Willa went to bed, knowing come tomorrow, she would have to share everything with Xander.

Even if it cost her his love.

CHAPTER TWENTY-FOUR

W ILLA SPENT A restless night, worried about what she must tell Xander, praying that it would not make a difference to him. Surely, he would see that she was the same person she had always been—the one he had fallen in love with.

But there was a world of difference between a governess and someone associated with the theater.

She finally rose and sat in the chair in her room, her mind drifting. She thought of memories from long ago. Her mother and father did not play prominently in these. They had both been far too busy to pay much attention to her. She hadn't been upset by that. In truth, she had relished their hands-off approach to parenting. It had left her free to pursue whatever interested her.

Yes, she did have many recollections of times spent in theaters. Talking with the crew. Painting backdrops. Arranging props. Running lines with actors. Those whose lives revolved around the world of theater may have dreadful reputations with the outside world, but they had been good to Willa, opening their hearts to her and taking her in as one of their own.

It was true that a good number of actresses became mistresses to men of the *ton*. She supposed her own mother might have done so if she had not attached herself to Ambrose. But Willa had never been on stage. She had never become an actress, even with Ralph's urging. She had left the life of the theater behind and gone into service.

Hopefully, Xander would see the distinction between the two. If he didn't, she did not know what she would do. How she would live without him.

"Don't go there, Willa," she cautioned herself, speaking aloud. "He loves you. He would not set you aside for something such as this."

Even as she tried to convince herself, Willa knew that possibility was quite real.

She dressed for the day in the sky-blue gown Madame Planche had sent home with her. The material was so soft, and the stitching impeccable. It was a treat to be garbed in something so eloquent. Willa unplaited her hair and brushed it until it shone before winding it into a simple chignon and slipping pins into it in order to hold the style in place.

She went to the dining room and was pleasantly surprised to find Ralph already seated at the table. He looked a little worse for the wear, and she wondered how long he had been out the previous night. Still, she was grateful that he was up and dressed and they could speak.

Their cook brought in plates of their breakfast as Willa seated herself and doctored her tea. Ralph asked for another cup of coffee, and the cook disappeared. Willa busied herself spreading marmalade on her toast points until the woman had come and gone again, wanting privacy for this discussion.

"I want to thank you for agreeing to be here this morning, Ralph," she began. "Xander is bringing by his solicitor, a Mr. Crockle."

Ralph's brows shot up. "Why is he doing so?"

"Mr. Crockle has prepared the marriage settlements and even though Xander knows I am of age and can sign them on my own, he understands how I want your opinion of them and suggested we review them together."

He took a bite of his eggs, a thoughtful expression on his face. "He really is serious about you, isn't he?"

"I told you that we love one another, Ralph. He wants to make his commitment to me by marrying me."

At least she hoped Xander would after she spoke with him.

Ralph shook his head. "It still is hard for me to believe the Xander Hughes I know is now a sober duke who wishes to wed you, Willa."

"I told you he has changed—and it is for the better."

He looked at her thoughtfully. "You have always had the best sense of anyone I have ever known, Willa, even when you were a child. I supposed it was being raised in the kind of household you were that made you that way."

Ralph took a bite of ham and chewed a moment. "I would be happy to serve as a surrogate father in this matter and help to look after your interests." He flashed her a familiar smile. "After all, we wouldn't want this duke taking advantage of you now, would we?"

The tension between them broke, and Willa laughed, Ralph joining in. They finished their meal, discussing how rehearsals were going, Ralph telling her just how incredible Jemima James was as Lady Brute.

"She has grown as an actress over the years and can take on more substantial roles now," he said. "I think she will have a long and illustrious career."

"I look forward to seeing Jemima as Lady Brute and Hermia, as well."

"I will have to give you tickets to both plays. You are welcome to sit in my box." He frowned. "I suppose His Grace might have other ideas, however."

"I know of no box which he holds," she said. "I doubt he did so before he gained his title."

"Oh, the Duke of Brockbank definitely has a box at every theater and opera house in London," Ralph assured her.

He set down his fork and took her hand, squeezing it gently. "Willa, you are to be a duchess soon. You will not want your association with me known."

Guilt filled her as she thought of Xander telling her the same thing.

"I would not abandon you, Ralph. You helped me at a time of great need. I refuse to desert you," she said stubbornly.

"It is all well and good for me to help a theater orphan, Willa. Being on friendly terms with a duchess is quite another matter. Already, there will be gossip about the both of you. His Grace because he was so far removed from the heir apparent and led such a debauched life. You, because of your humble origins. I doubt the *ton* will be receptive to a woman who has had to earn her living as a companion and governess for the last decade. I love you—and because of that love, I will keep my distance from you. I don't expect we will cut off all communication, but you must be careful, Willa. The *ton*'s gossips have sharp teeth. I would not see you wounded by them."

They finished breakfast and adjourned to the parlor, where Willa grew more and more tense, knowing she was about to tell Xander of her parents' occupations.

When she heard the knock on the door, she sprang to her feet. "I will get it," she said, hastily making her way to the door.

She opened it and found Xander with another man, the one who must be his solicitor. Willa invited them in and Xander made the introductions.

"Miss Fennimore, I would like you to meet Mr. Crockle, the family solicitor. As I told you, I asked him to draw up our marriage settlements. Is Baldwin here?"

"He is, Your Grace," she said, keeping things formal between them in front of this stranger to her. "Won't you please come to the parlor?"

They entered the room and once again, Xander made quick introductions.

"I want Mr. Crockle to share the marriage contracts with the two of you and see if you have any questions or wish for any additions to be made," Xander said.

Surprise filled Ralph's' face. "You would grant such a request, Your

Grace?"

"I want my fiancée to be totally comfortable with the arrangements," Xander said. "If she believes an addition should be made, then Crockle will do so. You may also choose to have your own solicitor look over the documents if you wish. For now, I am going to leave it to Mr. Crockle. I do not want to be hanging over you as you evaluate these papers. I will return in two hours' time. Good day."

Xander strode from the room, and Willa quickly excused herself, wanting to catch him before he left.

"Xander!" she cried.

He turned, his smile melting her heart. With trepidation, Willa stepped to him and said, "There is a matter of great importance that I must discuss with you now, Xander, before we review the settlements."

He captured her hands and brought them to his lips, kissing them tenderly.

"No, love. You are to analyze them without me hovering about. I am merely going to my club and will be back shortly. We can talk then about whatever you like."

He bent and gave her a soft kiss. All rational thought fled as he did so.

Breaking the kiss, he smiled at her. "I will see you shortly."

Then he was gone.

Willa hated that she had lost her chance to tell him what was on her mind. Reluctantly, she returned to the parlor, where Mr. Crockle waited patiently.

"What I would like to do is first give you a general overview as to what is in the marriage settlements," the solicitor told them. "Then I will allow you to read through the documents yourselves. Once you have done so and talked it over, I am happy to make any necessary changes you might require."

"You would change things on the spot?" Ralph asked. "Without speaking with His Grace?"

Crockle nodded. "His Grace told me what he wished, and I wrote it up as specified. He also said that Miss Fennimore is the one in charge of these proceedings and that I should alter the documents in whatever fashion she sees fit." He paused. "That gives Miss Fennimore great power. I hope she will exercise it with caution."

The solicitor withdrew a sheaf of papers from his satchel and then gave them an overview of the contracts.

When he finished, Willa was stunned.

Ralph said, "I have never heard of a marriage settlement such as this."

"Read for yourselves," the solicitor said, handing over copies to both of them to peruse. "I, too, have never drawn up anything such as this—and I have written my share of marriage contracts. His Grace has been most magnanimous with Miss Fennimore."

The solicitor smiled at her. "He told me it is because he loves you a great deal."

She burst into tears, worried that her secret might destroy the love between them.

Thankfully, Ralph handed her a handkerchief and said, "I know you are overcome with emotion, Willa. If I had any doubts as to Brockbank's intentions, they have been dispelled. Come, dry your eyes and let us look over Mr. Crockle's work."

She kept Ralph's handkerchief and dabbed the corners of her eyes repeatedly as she read through the document. When she finished, she waited for Ralph to be through. He finished a few minutes after she had.

"I cannot think of a single thing to add. Can you, Willa?"

"No," she said softly.

"Then if you are pleased with the wording, we can set up a time later today to come to my offices and sign the contracts. His Grace has instructed me that one copy will go to Miss Fennimore and another to you, Mr. Baldwin. I will maintain a third at my office and give His Grace the final copy. Miss Fennimore, you and His Grace will need to sign all four copies in front of witnesses, which I will provide. Would two o'clock suit you?"

"Yes, Mr. Crockle. Thank you for handling the matter."

Ralph saw the solicitor to the door and then told Willa that he was leaving for the theater and rehearsals.

She watched him leave and sat in the parlor, alone, fear filling her. She thought of how charitable Xander had been in the settlements, not only to her, but to their future children. Their daughters would be provided with extremely large dowries, while all sons beyond the heir apparent would be given estates of their own. While Xander could not hand over any of the seven entailed properties which accompanied the ducal title, apparently he was wealthy enough to purchase small country estates for any of their sons, as well as giving them monthly allowances. She thought of future children they might have, which brought a smile to her face. Already, she loved Cecily and Lucy as if they were her own and could not imagine the love she would feel for a child which sprang from her and Xander.

Willa began pacing the parlor, anxious for Xander's return. She was determined not to sign anything until she had been completely honest with him. If it cost her his love, so be it. She would not enter into holy matrimony with such an obstacle between them.

She only prayed that Xander was the man she thought he was and that he would still want her, warts and all.

CHAPTER TWENTY-FIVE

X ANDER ASKED HIS coachman to take him to White's. He had not been to his club since they had returned to London.

He would enter it as a duke.

Even though White's was a gentlemen's club, an obvious pecking order existed within it. Those of certain ranks reserved particular seats, and no one would think of sitting in them. He had eaten many a meal and drunk many a brandy at the club, oftentimes with Gil. The thought of his longtime friend saddened him. Or perhaps it was the thought of what he had believed they had together, a shared friendship over many years. He wondered if he might see Gil this morning and decided he wouldn't. His friend liked to stay out until the wee hours of the morning and then sleep until the afternoon.

He would have to see Gil sooner or later and would like to do so before the Season began. If they were no longer going to be friends, Xander at least wanted things to be civil between them when they met up at different events. Of course, the deciding factor would be how Gil treated Willa. He had called her a tart, forming his usual, low opinion of women. Only if Gil respected not only Xander's choice in his duchess—but Willa herself—would he be able to be on friendly terms with his old friend.

As he entered White's, he knew very few would be here at this time of day, usually the husbands who had escaped their breakfast tables and were sipping tea or coffee as they read over the morning newspapers.

He was greeted with a tone reserved for those who held the loftiest positions in Polite Society and almost found it amusing, biting back a smile as the staff fawned over him. He was settled in a prime spot and brought both coffee and tea, as well as various pastries. He was asked his preference in newspapers and those, too, appeared almost instantly, looking as if the sheets had been ironed before being given to him. They most likely had.

Thanking everyone, Xander settled in, turning the pages of his favorite newspaper and sipping on a blend of coffee that he would have to ask about because it was simply that good and he wouldn't mind being served it every morning at his townhouse.

He found it interesting that he was being left alone. Of course, those who knew him as Mr. Xander Hughes had known a man who was the very essence of a rake. Xander Hughes had discarded women left and right. He had gambled and drank and wenched his way through every week of every year. Yes, he was also acknowledged for being charming and a good conversationalist when called upon, but his reputation was that of a rogue, through and through. He understood why no one approached him. They didn't know if he was still the same or if his new title had changed him. Yes, members of the *ton* would view him with interest—and suspicion—until they figured him out.

"I see you have made yourself at home."

Glancing up, Xander saw Gil standing next to him, his eyes red and his face puffy from his late-night excursion. He was disheveled and in need of a good shave, as well.

Still, he put on a smile and greeted his old friend. "Ah, good morning, Lord Swanson. Would you care to join me? And have something to drink?"

He motioned and a cup and saucer appeared immediately.

"Coffee," Gil said, taking a seat next to Xander and accepting the coffee poured from a staff member, who quickly left them alone.

"You have quite the spot, Brockbank. Then again, you are a duke now. Have you been in town long?"

"No, just a couple of days." He folded his newspaper and set it aside. "I am actually glad to see you, Gil."

"Why? Are you ready to offer me an apology?"

Gil's tone was that of a petulant child, and Xander was not going to put up with it.

"I was hoping to speak to you regarding—"

"The way you threw me from your house?" Anger caused red splotches to appear on Gil's cheeks.

"Lower your tone," he warned.

Gil smiled benignly. "Oh, so the Duke of Brockbank does not wish to make it known that we are estranged."

"I am happy to be your friend, Gil. I have never stopped being it."

"As long as I treat that trollop of yours as a lady?"

Xander's hands fisted. Anger surged through him. He forced himself to relax, knowing the eyes of the room were upon them.

"It is apparent that we no longer see eye to eye," he said carefully. "Miss Fennimore is to be my wife. I have already purchased the special license. I was hoping we might patch things up, and you would attend the wedding ceremony."

"I don't think there will be one," Gil said airily, sipping his coffee.

He frowned. "What do you mean?"

"Your Miss Fennimore isn't suited to be a duchess, Xan. Oh, forgive me. *Your Grace.*"

"I know she was in service the last decade, Gil. It doesn't matter to me."

"True, many governesses are impoverished gentlewomen. Women who, because of extenuating circumstances, have had to go out in the world and earn a living for themselves." Gil paused, his gaze meeting Xander's. "That is not the case with Miss Fennimore, though, is it?"

"I don't understand."

Gil set down the saucer he held and leaned close. "You don't know, do you?"

"Know what?"

"Who she really is. What she comes from," Gil said. After a moment, he asked, "Do you recall how my mother adores going to the theater?"

The abrupt change of topic confused him. "What?"

"Yes, Mama has always fancied a good play. Comedies, in particular. She and my father even dragged me to enough of them over the years."

"What on earth does this have to do with Miss Fennimore?" he ground out.

"Everything," Gil said, his smile turning evil. "I thought I recognized Miss Fennimore when I came to Spring Ridge. She denied having made my acquaintance. I thought she was just another pretty face, but I kept thinking on it as I returned to town.

"And then I remembered why I thought she was familiar to me."

Xander felt his heart pounding rapidly, fearful of what his old friend was about to say. He should silence Gil—but his gut told him that he needed to hear what Gil would say.

"Your Miss Fennimore closely resembles her mother. Theodosia Fennimore."

He shook his head. "That name means nothing to me."

"It might not to you, Your Grace, but many in Polite Society would recognize it—and the scandal attached to it. Theodosia Fennimore was the leading stage actress in London more than a decade ago, with the same sable hair and amethyst eyes as your betrothed. I saw her in a good half-dozen productions. She was talented. Married to a playwright. Ambrose Fennimore. He wrote many of the productions his wife was in, calling her his muse."

If Gil had slammed his fist into Xander's face, he could not have been more shocked.

Willa was the child of *theater* people?

"I see your fiancée did not share her background with you." Gil laughed harshly. "And oh, it gets worse. Much worse."

Dread mixed with anxiety filled him. "Go on," he said tersely.

"Ambrose might have married Theodosia, but he always had a roving eye. In fact, he probably had more mistresses among actresses than you ever did, Your Grace. Theodosia finally had enough of being humiliated by her husband's infidelity. She killed him, Xan. *Shot him.* Murdered her own husband, naked in their bed. Supposedly, his latest light o' love had just left and missed being murdered herself. And then? Theodosia leaped to her death. Oh, it was in all the newspapers then. We were still in our first year of university. I recall Mama mentioning it to me when I arrived home, though. It was a scandal of the biggest sort."

Gil smiled triumphantly. "That is the woman you are thinking to wed, Your Grace. A woman raised by two of the biggest sinners in London, a serial philanderer and a murderer who died by suicide. Miss Fennimore is the spitting image of her mother at that same age. Every ballroom you take her into, every garden party you attend, every card party you partake in, she will be recognized and raked over the coals. You might be a duke—but you will *never* be able to fight the tide of gossip that will drown the both of you. And not only you. Your nieces, too, will suffer. No family in Polite Society would allow a son to offer for those girls. Or any children you have of your own."

Gil stood. "You are powerless to turn the tide of public opinion if you wed this woman."

He casually strolled away as Xander watched, horror filling him.

Why hadn't Willa told him of this? Why had she kept her origins secret?

Because he would not have offered for her otherwise.

He was already thinking like the parent he had become to Cecily and Lucy. Grief tore through him as he mourned the loss of Willa, knowing he must end things with her at once. Xander loved her—but realized he didn't know her at all. And he certainly couldn't risk Cecily and Lucy's futures. He may not have followed the rules set down by Polite Society, but he knew of them, all the same. His nieces would be tarred with the same brush that stained Willa when word got out about her parentage.

Xander could not risk that happening, much less seeing his own children ostracized by such scandal.

He would have to give Willa up. Now. Before he weakened and wed her and retreated to the country, thinking he could escape the infamy. He could not allow his selfishness to come into play. His feelings must be cast aside. He had the girls to think about.

He must go to her now and cut all ties.

He rose, his face a mask, and he left White's. Returning to his carriage, the coachman already knew they were to return to Ralph Baldwin's house. Xander's belly churned as the streets went by. He rapped on the roof of the vehicle with his cane and the carriage came to a halt. Throwing open the door, he puked into the street, shaking like a leaf.

"Go on!" he shouted, slamming the carriage door, wiping his mouth on his handkerchief, having no idea what he would say to Willa.

When he arrived, Xander steeled himself and knocked on the door. It opened almost immediately, Willa standing there, looking so lovely in one of her new gowns. Worry filled her face, though, as if she knew what he was about to say.

"Oh, Xander, come in. We must talk."

"We have very little to say to one another, Miss Fennimore," he said stiffly, stepping into the house because he didn't want to conduct his personal business on the pavement.

"What . . . what is wrong?" she stammered. Then horror filled her eyes. "You know." Her eyes shuttered and she said dully, "It is what I wanted to tell you earlier." Resignation filled her face. "How did you learn of . . . my background?"

He turned the anger within him on her. "That is neither here nor there, Miss Fennimore. When were you going to tell me who you really are? After we signed the marriage settlements? After we spoke our vows?"

She twisted her hands. "I did not mean to hide anything from you, Xander. I—"

"You will address me as *Your Grace*," he said.

Her eyes widened, filling with tears. "I never spoke of my parents because I was never close to them. It has been over a dozen years since they died—"

"They did not just *die*, Willa," he said derisively.

"One was murdered by the other. One died by suicide. They were of the theater world. How could you not think that pertinent? Did you truly believe the *ton* would forgive you?"

Disgust filled him. The skeletons in her cupboard did not merely consist of the fact that she was the offspring of theater people. That, in itself, was disgraceful enough. What riled him more was the ignominy of her parents' deaths, the type of scandal constantly rehashed in the newspapers years after the infamy had occurred. Xander could not chance even the hint of scandal touching Cecily and Lucy. They were who he must consider now.

Not the woman he thought he would spend the rest of his life loving.

"I never set foot on a stage. I am not an actress," she said defensively.

His eyes narrowed. "Oh, I think you are quite a talented actress, Miss Fennimore. You completely fooled me. You acted so very innocent."

"I was an innocent," she said softly, a stab to his heart because he had taken her virginity.

She drew in a long breath and released it. "I never had designs on you, Your Grace. I did develop feelings for you, which I never thought would be returned. Most likely, I would have left your household because of those feelings. Yes, my parents were a playwright and actress. Yes, they died in a scandal of their own making. Yes, I was taken in by Ralph Baldwin so I did not land on the streets. My identity for a decade has been one who is in service, supporting myself on my meager earnings as a companion and governess."

Willa shook her head. "I will admit I was naive and did not even think about sharing my childhood and background. It was in my distant past. You loved me for who I am now. When I realized, though, that you did not know this part of me, I sought to tell you this morning. I did not want to go into our marriage without acknowledging it."

His heart wrenched within him, but he sternly said, "There will be no marriage, Miss Fennimore. I used poor judgment in becoming involved with you."

And believing we had a future together. Believing that I could find love.

She held her head high, tears still coursing down her cheeks. "I understand, Your Grace. You have your nieces to consider. At least you have hired an acceptable governess for them."

He had no idea how he would explain this horrible mess to Cecily and Lucy.

Willa moved to the door and opened it. Her mouth trembled as she said, "I bid you good day, Your Grace." She swallowed. "And a happy life."

Xander nodded curtly and strode through the door.

And out of Willa's life.

CHAPTER TWENTY-SIX

WILLA CLOSED THE front door, knowing she closed a chapter which would be impossible to open again. One which she had thought would bring her a new life. A family. Love. Instead, this chapter would remain only half-written. She would move on, heartbreak her constant companion.

It was as if she had experienced a living death with Xander ending things between them. She had known that this would be a possibility, but had not fully prepared herself for the outcome. A small part of her had believed that when she told Xander about her parents and the sordid past, he would wave it away, telling her it was the past and that he was her present and future. Instead, he had become a full-fledged member of the *ton* and condemned her for her parents' sins.

The life she had hoped to lead with him would never happen now. The love she held for him in her heart would always remain, despite his brutal treatment of her. Still, she could understand why he had done so. Xander had his nieces to consider. Willa had known sharing her background with him would involve him learning of Theodosia and Ambrose's occupations. What she had seemingly blocked out was their violent deaths. Xander might have forgiven her for keeping from him that she was the daughter of a playwright and actress, but he would never forgive her for not telling him about the horrific scandal her parents were involved in.

How could she have been such a fool as to think a duke of the realm would marry not only a governess—but a woman whose parents had caused one of the greatest scandals in London this century?

She would not only need to put together the shattered pieces of her broken heart, but also try to build a different life. How she was going to find employment now was beyond her. She had burned her bridges with Mr. Wainwright and refused to crawl back to him. She could not go to the Plowright Employment Agency to seek work because Mr. Plowright mistakenly believed her to be a duchess. Willa determined that she needed to find a new agency and leave London as soon as possible. The farther the post took her from the great city, the better. Surely, there were other employment agencies in larger cities throughout England, ones where she might apply. Of course, she would not have her most recent reference from the Duke of Brockbank, nor had she received recommendations from Lord Dearling or Lord Appleton when she had abruptly left their service. Her only two references were from when she had served as a companion. Those both came through the Wainwright Agency, and the original letters rested there. She doubted Mr. Wainwright would be willing to share them with prospective employers at a different agency.

That meant Willa was starting at the very beginning. Perhaps she should reinvent herself as a widow and say she was now looking for employment. A fresh start. She had good organizational skills and might even find success as a housekeeper, although she doubted she could land a post as one, thinking they came up the ranks of service.

What was she going to do?

She took out her valises and packed her clothing, removing the sky-blue gown she now wore, one she had been so very proud to wear. She would return it and the other two gowns to Madame Planche and let the modiste know to cancel future orders being made up since Willa would never wear fine gowns as the Duchess of

Brockbank.

Her bags packed, once more wearing one of her shapeless gowns, Willa left Ralph's house and made her way to Madame Planche's dress shop, the three gowns wrapped in brown paper and tied with string.

She entered the dress shop and saw the assistant who had recorded her measurements. Going to her, Willa handed over the parcels.

"Miss Fennimore," the assistant said, frowning as she accepted the bundle from Willa. "We were not expecting you."

"Please thank Madame Planche for her time, and tell her to cancel any gowns being prepared for me. I will no longer be in need of them."

Pity filled the young woman's eyes. "I understand, Miss Fennimore," she said quietly.

"I will pay for any gowns that are close to completion, but it may take me a good while to do so because my savings are meager."

The young woman placed a hand on Willa's forearm. "Madame can always find another client who will want them. Paying will not be necessary, Miss Fennimore. My guess is that you have already paid enough."

Tears welled in Willa's eyes as she said thank you and left the modiste's shop. She decided to go to Ralph's theater next and talk with Jemima James. She slipped into the back row, not wanting to be seen, and watched the rehearsal taking place. The actors were in the second act of *The Provoked Wife*. Willa lost herself for a few minutes in the dialogue being spoken, thinking how talented Jemima truly was.

Ralph called a halt once the scene ended and praised Jemima's performance, while giving a few notes to her acting partner. The director told the cast and crew that they had an hour to themselves before a full dress rehearsal of the play would begin, running from start to finish without stopping.

The actors left the stage, and Willa avoided Ralph, not wanting to share with him the outcome of her conversation with Xander. She skirted the edge of the theater and quickly moved up the stairs, disappearing behind the curtain on the side. This place had been a home to her, and she knew exactly where Jemima's dressing room would be located since her own mother had occupied the same room many times in the past. The door was open, and Willa spied Jemima seated in a chair, wrapped in a dressing gown as she spoke to her dresser. She hovered in the doorway for a moment and then tapped lightly on the doorframe.

Jemima looked over and said, "Willa, what a pleasant surprise. Come in."

As she stepped into the room, she saw Jemima's brows knit together. The actress turned to her dresser and dismissed her, telling her not to return for half an hour and to close the door behind her.

Once they were alone, Jemima stood and came to Willa, enveloping her in a tight embrace. They stood that way for some moments, tears pouring down Willa's cheeks.

Jemima released her and led her to a seat, sitting next to Willa.

"I gather you spoke to your duke."

Willa gave a wry smile and said, "He is no longer *my* duke, Jemima. I tried to tell him exactly who I was this morning before his solicitor went over the marriage settlements with Ralph and me. Xander . . . the duke, that is . . . brushed off my concerns and told me we could speak after I had learned about what was in the marriage contracts."

She paused, wiping tears from her face with her fingertips. "They were extremely magnanimous. To me and any children I might have borne him. When he returned, though, it was a different story. In the time he left me and went to White's, someone told him of my past. Of my parents. Of Theodosia murdering Ambrose and then taking her own life."

Fresh tears flooded her eyes and cascaded down her cheeks. "I think it was his friend, Lord Swanson."

"I know of the viscount," Jemima said. "He is a handsome devil with a cruel streak."

"Swanson came to visit the duke at Spring Ridge and told me that I looked familiar to him. I denied ever having met him but could see I had piqued his curiosity. Most likely, Swanson attended a play years ago and had seen Theodosia perform. The viscount was asked to leave Spring Ridge by the duke. They parted on unfriendly terms. Over me. I believe Swanson is the one who recalled who I was and told the duke."

Willa shook her head. "I cannot blame him. It would have been difficult enough for a duke to wed a governess. Eventually, I think Polite Society would have forgiven him for doing so if I were merely just a governess. But it was impossible for him to wed a woman from the world I come from, one so tainted by scandal. I know very little about the *ton*, only that they close ranks against outsiders. They would have done so against me and, in turn, Cecily and Lucy, as well as my own children. All would have suffered. Truly, it is for the best."

"You still love him, don't you?"

She nodded. "I will always love him, Jemima. I understand why he had to break our engagement, however. No notice was placed in the newspapers. Only you and Ralph—and possibly Lord Swanson— would know of it. Brockbank's reputation will be saved."

Jemima smoothed Willa's hair. "Before he became a duke, he already had a wicked reputation, Willa. Perhaps he will redeem himself as a duke. You say he loved you."

She nodded.

"Then he is showing maturity in giving you up. Sacrificing his own happiness for his nieces." Jemima smiled. "What will you do now?"

"I haven't a clue," Willa admitted.

Jemima looked steadily at her. "You saved my life, Willa Fennimore. It is time I return that favor."

>>>><<<<

XANDER WENT HOME and closeted himself in his study, wallowing in self-pity.

He felt like such a hypocrite.

Xander Hughes had flouted every rule and convention of Polite Society from the time he was a small boy. As a man, he had lived unapologetically, pursuing only his own pleasure and never considering others. He had closed his heart to everyone and everything, knowing he would never love or be loved.

Then Willa Fennimore had come into his life. Suddenly, the day was brighter. Laughter deeper and richer. He had pictured a life with this woman, one he cherished. One he loved.

Now, the thought of happiness with Willa had been ripped away. He hated Gil. He also understood, though, that Gil spoke for the *ton*. Yes, Xander might be the Duke of Brockbank and Polite Society was notorious in forgiving a duke for almost anything.

Almost.

Wedding Willa, a child of enormous scandal, would be an unforgiveable sin in their eyes. He could not let those sins color his nieces' futures. He would need to put aside his own feelings and do what was best for those girls, whom he must protect. Eventually, Xander would wed. It would be a woman from one of the most prominent families in Polite Society. She would be refined. Perhaps pretty and even graceful. She would provide him with an heir to his dukedom.

And he would keep his heart locked up, far away from her. He would never give of himself again so freely, as he had to Willa. He would continue to love Willa for all time.

A knock sounded at the door, and Sewell opened it. "It is time for tea, Your Grace. Lady Lucy and Lady Cecily have a surprise for you."

"I will be there shortly," he said.

The butler closed the door.

Xander would have to address with his nieces that he would not be marrying Willa. He knew they would be hurt, cut off from someone they had come to love.

He went to the drawing room, where the girls awaited him, and mustered a smile.

"I hear you have a surprise for me," he said brightly, feeling empty inside.

"We helped Cook make ladyfingers, Uncle Xander," Lucy said.

"At first, she didn't want us in the kitchens," Cecily revealed. "But we told her how we made scones for you and the Duke and Duchess of Linberry. That Aunt Willa says it's good for us to learn how to do new things, especially if it helps others."

"Then put a few on my plate, and I will try them now," he said, his heart heavy.

"I thought Aunt Willa might come to tea today," Lucy said. "We should save a few for her."

Xander decided being direct would be best. There was no reason not to address the issue now.

"We will not be seeing her anymore," he said, unable to even say Willa's name.

Both Cecily and Lucy froze, staring at him as if he'd sprouted another head.

"I don't understand, Uncle Xander," Lucy said, her bottom lip trembling.

"We found . . . there were some problems between us. That we wouldn't truly suit after all. It had nothing to do with the two of you," he assured them.

Cecily's lips trembled. "But . . . can she still be our governess?"

"No, Miss Janus has been hired for you girls. She will start Monday next."

"I don't want another governess," wailed Lucy, bursting into tears. "I want Aunt Willa!"

Cecily stood, stomping her foot. "It's all your fault. *You* did something to make her go away. You don't want us to be happy."

"I was thinking only of your happiness when I sent Miss Fennimore away, Cecily," he said sternly. "Not my own."

Lucy came to him and took his hand. "Do you still love Aunt Willa?"

"I do," he admitted, wanting to always be honest with them, at least as much as he could. They would never understand why he had to let Willa go. "But there is something in her past which is unforgiveable. Something that would taint the two of you, merely being associated with her. I cannot risk your futures. I want you to have the childhood I never did and go on to be accepted into Polite Society with open arms."

"What did Aunt Willa do that was so terrible?" Cecily demanded, her hands fisted on her waist.

"It is not so much what *she* did. It is what her parents did." He was reluctant to share any details of the affair with them.

Cecily frowned. "You are blaming Aunt Willa for something *they* did?"

"Sometimes, that is the way of the world. Miss Fennimore's parents did something unspeakable. Something which I cannot share with little girls who would not understand."

Cecily's gaze met his and suddenly, she looked much older than her years. "You told us that you would explain about Mama when we are older. Lucy and I already know what Mama did. She loved Papa so much that she wanted to be with him and not us. Even if he was dead. She killed herself. I know that is a sin."

She took his hand. "But do you love us any less, Uncle Xander, because of what Mama did? Mama did a bad thing. Not us. Aunt Willa's parents did a bad thing. Not her."

"I know it seems so simple to you, Cecily, but it is far more complicated than that. If I were to wed Miss Fennimore, members of Polite

Society would not only be mean to her—they would be mean to you girls, too. Not just now—but years down the line. It would affect whether you made a good match or not. I cannot risk your reputations and future happiness. This is hard to understand and accept."

Cecily pushed hard against his chest. "I don't understand. Lucy and I love Aunt Willa. You love her, too."

"Whether I love her or not is beside the point."

"What about second chances?"

He looked to Lucy. "What do you mean?"

"Well, Aunt Willa said second chances are important."

"That's right," Cecily agreed. "You got a second chance to be friends with the Duke of Linberry. And you gave me a second chance when I was always bad." Tears filled the girl's eyes. "Can't you give Aunt Willa a second chance, Uncle Xander?"

If he did as the girls asked, he might ruin their futures. If he didn't, they might be ruined now. All the trust he had built with them. All the love he had poured into them. It might vanish because he had taken away the one person who had healed them all.

Xander wasn't going to let the bloody *ton* destroy what he had built with his nieces. And he sure wasn't going to let Polite Society shatter his own dreams. Dreams of a life with a woman who had made him a better man.

Both his nieces watched him silently now.

"You are right. I was wrong," he told them. "While it is good to care about what others think and hope they hold a good opinion of you, more than anything, you must be true to yourself. We are in this together, girls. With your Aunt Willa."

He knelt and crushed them to him, hoping he now did the right thing.

"Come. We must fetch her and make amends."

Cecily and Lucy began jumping up and down, cheering. Xander knew it very well might just be the four of them in the future who would stand against Polite Society.

But it was a future which must include Willa if it was to be any kind of future at all.

CHAPTER TWENTY-SEVEN

X ANDER CALLED FOR his carriage to be readied and told Cecily and Lucy to go put on their finest dresses.

"Why?" Lucy asked.

"Because you are about to attend a wedding. At least, in a few hours, if I can arrange everything that should be done."

Quickly, Xander went to his study and dashed off a list of things he must accomplish before he could make his way to Willa.

The one woman who made him whole.

While his nieces were changing clothes, he went to the kitchens and told Cook, "You are to prepare the meal of your life. Expect eight to ten guests."

In reality, Xander had no idea who might return with him and merely wanted there to be enough food for what would be their wedding breakfast.

If Willa took him back.

"And bake a cake, Cook. A wedding cake."

She looked dumfounded. "But . . . Your Grace . . . they take days."

"Then make more of those ladyfingers the girls helped you with. They were light and delicious and can take the place of a wedding cake."

He found Sewell and told the butler, "I am off to find Miss Fennimore and marry her. You and Mrs. Sewell are to make sure rooms are prepared and everything is in perfect order for when we return in a few hours."

The stunned butler merely nodded as Xander hurried off.

He went to his rooms and claimed the special license and gathered the girls into his ducal carriage.

"You both look quite lovely," he complimented.

"Are you really going to marry Aunt Willa soon?" Lucy wanted to know.

"Yes. At least, I hope so."

His coachman delivered him to Crockle's office, where he told the girls to wait for him in the carriage. Bounding up the stairs, he breezed past the solicitor's clerk and opened Crockle's door.

"Have you made sufficient copies of the marriage settlements between Miss Fennimore and me?" Xander asked.

"I have, Your Grace. You are a few minutes early, however."

"Early?"

"Yes. Didn't Miss Fennimore tell you that you were to meet here at two o'clock to sign the documents?"

He sighed. "Miss Fennimore and I had a huge misunderstanding, Crockle. I am working on trying to iron things out between us. Put all copies of the contracts into your satchel and accompany me now. We will sign everything—and then you are invited to attend our wedding and wedding breakfast."

Surprise filled the man's face. "Of course, Your Grace."

As the solicitor gathered the papers, Xander asked, "Do you know of a clergyman who might marry us this afternoon?"

"Actually, my wife's brother recently retired from the clergy two weeks ago. He is visiting with us for a month and then will retire to the country."

"Then our next stop will be to gather him and Mrs. Crockle. Do you think they might wish to see a duke and duchess marry?"

Crockle laughed heartily. "I think they would be delighted, Your

Grace."

He wrote down Ralph Baldwin's address and handed it to Crockle. "We will be at this address. Come as soon as you can."

"We will be there shortly," the solicitor promised.

Xander raced to the carriage and gave another destination to his driver before bounding inside.

"Where are we going now, Uncle Xander?" Cecily asked.

"To the newspapers. I must place a notice of my wedding in the newspapers so that all will know."

Lucy frowned. "What if Aunt Willa doesn't want to marry you anymore?"

He tweaked her nose. "That is where my secret weapons will come in. The two of you. If I cannot talk Miss Fennimore into marrying me, then it will be in the hands of the two of you to convince her to do so."

His heart was light as he raced inside the newspaper offices. When he gave his name, a clerk immediately took him to someone who looked important and in charge.

"I wish to place news of my wedding in your newspaper," he said to the man. "I have been in the country and forgot to send in our engagement announcement."

"I would be happy to take your information, Your Grace. When would you like it to appear?"

"In tomorrow's edition."

Xander gave his and Willa's names and said the marriage would take place today and then left the offices, returning to his carriage for the next destination on his list.

"Stay here," he told his nieces again as he left the carriage and entered Madame Planche's dress shop.

The modiste greeted him. "I am surprised to see you, Your Grace. Especially after Miss Fennimore returned the gowns I sent home with her and told my assistant that no wedding would take place."

"A huge misunderstanding, Madame," he said, turning on the charm. "More than huge. But it has been settled now."

At least he hoped so.

"Do you still have those gowns?"

"I do."

"I will take them with me. You see, Miss Fennimore and I are getting married this afternoon. One of those should be suitable for her to wear."

The modiste smiled. "One original dress for Miss Fennimore had already been completed. A lovely day dress in a soft lilac. I thought it would go well with the color of her eyes. Might you wish for that to be her wedding gown?"

"That is splendid news. I will take it with me, along with the others."

"Where will the wedding take place?"

He gave Madame Ralph's address and she said, "Then one of my assistants and I will leave now and take the gowns to Miss Fennimore. She will need help in dressing, and we can make any adjustments if they are needed."

"All right," Xander agreed. "I will see you there."

He raced to the carriage again, all his errands now completed. Settling against the cushions, he put his arms around his nieces and drew them close to his sides. They chatted happily until the vehicle reached Baldwin's house.

"I need you to stay here for a few minutes, and then I will come and get you," he told them. "I need time to grovel before Miss Fennimore."

Lucy frowned. "What is grovel?"

"It means I will kneel before her and apologize and beg for her to take me back."

"If she won't, we will help, Uncle Xander," Cecily promised.

He kissed both girls on their foreheads. "I know you will."

Xander went to the front door and knocked sharply. He waited, no one answering the knock. He pounded on the door, and it flew open. A striking woman of about thirty years of age stood before him.

"Where is Willa?" he asked, the desperation in his voice obvious.

The woman glared at him and started to close the door. He placed his foot so that would be impossible and pushed against the door. She withdrew and he opened it, coming inside and closing it behind him.

"I must see her," he said.

She looked him up and down. "You are Brockbank." Her tone was condescending.

"I am. And I need to—"

"To do what?" she demanded. "Break her heart again? Haven't you already done enough harm, Your Grace? Willa is shattered. She loved you with all her heart, and you threw that love away. You are not fit to wipe her boots, you bloody fool."

He now recognized the woman. She was a well-known actress named Jemima James. He had seen her in a few productions and had thought her quite talented.

"I know I have been an utter arse," he admitted. "Blind fool that I am, I have seen the error of my ways."

"You still wish to marry her?" the woman asked.

"I do," he said solemnly.

"Wait here."

She turned and started up the stairs just as Willa appeared at the top, carrying two valises. She froze when she spotted Xander.

The woman hurried up the stairs.

"Make him leave," Willa said to her. "I cannot speak to him, Jemima."

"I think you should," the actress said.

Willa set down her valises. "And why should I let him rip me asunder again?"

She turned to flee, but by that time, Xander had already raced up the stairs. He caught her elbow and turned her.

Willa slapped him hard and then her hands flew to her mouth.

"I deserved that," he said quietly. "And you deserved better than what I said to you earlier."

He pulled her hands from her mouth and laced their fingers together.

"I bloody well mucked things up, love. I was given a second lease on life with the deaths of my family members. But more importantly, by loving you."

Xander knelt before her. "You are the love of my life, Willa Fennimore. You have made me a better man in more ways than I can count. If I do not have you by my side, I am nothing. No one."

Her mouth trembled. "What of the *ton*? They will judge me harshly for what my parents did to one another."

"Then let them. They will talk for a while. But there is always a new scandal which comes to life. Something else to gossip about. Yes, there will be whispers when the Duke and Duchess of Brockbank appear together in society. We will hold our heads high. We will make friends with those who would judge us not on our collective pasts, but who we are now and aspire to be. The Duke and Duchess of Linberry will stand with us. There will be others who do so, as well."

Tears filled her eyes. "What of Lucy and Cecily? And . . . our children."

"I told you. Gossip will die down eventually. And when the *ton* sees just how devoted the Duke of Brockbank is to his duchess? That she is the light of his life and his reason for living?" He smiled. "They will be happy for us. We will be the grand love story of our time, Willa.

"If you will only say yes."

She bit her lip. "Yes," she whispered.

"Yes?" he asked, rising, bringing her hands to his lips and tenderly kissing her fingers.

"Yes!" she cried.

Xander kissed her, releasing her hands and wrapping his arms about her, knowing he would never let this woman go. He kissed her some minutes, until they were both breathless.

When he broke the kiss, he rested his brow against hers. "I love you, Willa. I love you."

"And I love you more."

Someone cleared his throat, and they turned simultaneously, seeing they had an audience.

Cecily and Lucy stood there, obviously tired of waiting in the carriage. Jemima James and Ralph Baldwin were also present. So were Mr. Crockle and who Xander assumed was Mrs. Crockle and her brother, the clergyman, as well as Madame Planche and one of her assistants.

He turned to his betrothed. "We are to be married now if you but say the word. Crockle brought the marriage settlements for us to sign. Madame has a wedding gown for you. Crockle's brother-in-law is a clergyman. And the girls are dressed in their best." He paused. "I have also come from the newspaper, where I placed the announcement of our wedding today to be run in tomorrow's edition."

Willa beamed at him. "Then I suppose we are to be married as soon as I can change clothes."

Xander kissed her again, knowing he had made the right decision. This woman would be his best friend and lover, a mother to his nieces and the children they would have. She would be both wife and duchess and the dearest person in the world to him.

"Madame? Your presence is requested now," he called down.

The modiste and her assistant hurried up the stairs, carrying the gown his betrothed would wear to their wedding.

"Go, Your Grace," urged the modiste. "We will have Miss Fennimore appropriately garbed as soon as possible."

"Thank you."

Xander descended the stairs and introduced himself to Crockle's brother-in-law, producing the special license from his coat's inner pocket and handing it to the clergyman.

"I appreciate you coming in haste to perform this marriage ceremony."

The clergyman laughed. "I would not have missed this for the world, Your Grace. Nothing quite so exciting happened during my decades with the Church."

"Come into the parlor," Baldwin told them all.

Jemima James stepped to Xander as the others followed the director. "You do love her."

"I most certainly do," he said fervently.

"Willa is very special to me, Your Grace. She saved my life and my career. I would do anything for her."

He studied the actress a moment. "Then my duchess is very lucky to have you as her friend."

Jemima looked startled. "I cannot be friends with a duchess. It simply isn't proper."

"If you are Willa's friend, then you will always be welcomed in our home," he told her. "Gossips be damned to hell."

She laughed. "You are changed from the man I have heard about."

Xander returned her smile. "Willa changed my life—as she did yours." He offered her his arm. "Shall we go to the parlor, Miss James?"

"I would be happy to accompany you, Your Grace."

When Willa appeared in the doorway of the parlor a few minutes later, his heart nearly burst from his chest. She was the loveliest creature he had ever seen. And she would make for the perfect duchess.

The perfect duchess for him.

EPILOGUE

London—April 1823

WILLA GASPED AS Xander thrust deeply inside her, bringing her to the peaks of ecstasy. Ten years into their marriage—and she still found each time her husband made love to her was a moving experience.

Suddenly, Xander flipped them, and she was on top.

"Ride for your life, love," he encouraged, and Willa did that very thing.

They reached orgasm together and both cried out, Willa collapsing atop Xander, her cheek nestled against his chest.

A loud knock sounded at the door. "Your Graces? You simply must let us in or you will be late to the opening ball of the Season," Xander's valet shouted through the door.

She giggled as Xander hollered, "Five more minutes!"

"You said that ten minutes ago, Your Grace," the valet loudly reminded. "You don't want to be late to Lady Cecily's come-out now, do you?"

"All right," Xander shouted. "Five minutes—and I mean it this time."

Willa raised her head and looked into the eyes of the man she loved. Xander had been a good father not only to Cecily and Lucy, but also to the four boys she had produced. She gave him a light kiss and then pushed away from him, climbing from the bed and slipping into her dressing gown.

"I will see you downstairs," she told him.

He leaped from the bed and took her in his arms once more, his voice husky as he said, "We still have four minutes."

After a thorough kiss, he broke it. "Now, you can go," he said.

She went through his dressing room and bathing chamber to her own. Her lady's maid paced the room anxiously, relief on her face with Willa's appearance.

Soon, she was dressed, looking every inch the duchess she had been for a decade. Her acceptance by Polite Society had been less challenging than either Xander or she had imagined. Yes, there had been talk about her husband's wild ways and if he would successfully settle into being the Duke of Brockbank. The *ton* first learned she had been a governess and some thought her simply a fortune hunter who had used her beauty to land a duke. A few recognized her strong resemblance to her mother, and a bit of the murder and suicide was rehashed briefly.

But the *ton* always found new things to gossip about, especially since Xander and Willa had been welcomed by not only the Duke and Duchess of Linberry, but also several ducal couples the pair were friends with. Willa had made good friends with such women as the Duchesses of Westfield, Stoneham, Bradford, and Abington. It didn't hurt that shortly after her first Season with Xander began that an earl had been murdered by footpads, and a marquess was caught *in flagrante delicto* with the wife of his best friend. Suddenly, interest shifted from the Brockbanks, and they had settled into a good life together with Cecily and Lucy and eventually, their growing family.

She left her rooms and went to Cecily's bedchamber, where her daughter was having the final touches put on her elaborate hairstyle by Betsy. The servant had remained with them through the years, not only caring for their girls but the four boys, as well. The two eldest, eight and nine, were now away at school, while the younger two, ages two and five, were fast asleep in the nursery. Willa and Xander had put the boys to bed before they had adjourned to the duke's rooms to celebrate tonight and Cecily's come-out.

"You are looking quite lovely, Cecily," Willa told her oldest child.

Cecily rose from the dressing table, a confident smile on her lovely features. "I cannot wait to dance at the Linberry's ball."

"Well, your dance master has said you are the best dancer of this Season," she reminded. "I think you will prove to be quite popular tonight. But remember, Cecily, it is only one night of many to come. Yes, you may meet the man who will become your future husband this evening—or you may not. Do not force anything."

Cecily grinned. "Yes, Aunt Willa, I know. My heart will tell me who he is." She took Willa's hands in hers. "You and Uncle Xander have told me that enough."

Lucy, who had been sitting on the bed, came toward them and also took Cecily's and Willa's hands. They stood in a small circle of three, happy to be a chosen family.

Sewell appeared in the open door. "His Grace is asking for you, Your Grace."

"Then I suppose we are off to a ball," she declared.

Lucy hugged her sister and made Cecily promise to wake her when she came in, no matter how late it was.

"I want to hear about everything," Lucy said.

Willa slipped her arm through Cecily's, and they descended the stairs. As always, the sight of Xander caused Willa's heart to speed up, never more so than when he wore his black evening clothes.

"Cecily, you are a sight the angels have never seen," he told his niece, enfolding her in his arms.

Then he held up a hand to her. In his palm were a pair of pearl earrings.

Cecily's eyes widened. "These are for me?"

Xander took her hand and slipped the jewelry into it. "They are a gift from your aunt and me."

Cecily hugged Xander and then Willa, thanking them profusely, before attaching the earrings to her lobes.

"Shall we?" Xander asked, offering his arms to both of them and they went to the waiting carriage.

Entering the Linberry's townhouse, they joined the receiving line. Cecily looked about excitedly as Willa told her daughter the names of people around them and pointed out several bachelors.

When they reached their host and hostess, the duke and duchess warmly welcomed them.

Fia said, "It has been a pleasure to see you mature from the young girl we met so many years ago. I hope you find your true love this Season, Cecily." She kissed Cecily's cheek.

The duke teased, "And here I thought you might bring scones you had baked to your host."

"I have been far too busy to bake scones, Your Grace." Mischief lit Cecily's eyes and she added, "Perhaps you might bake some for me and my suitors."

They all laughed, the years of their friendship easy for all to see.

Henry said, "I know the two of you are proud of your eldest child. Would you care to join us at supper tonight?"

Xander said, "We would be delighted to."

The three of them said farewell and entered the ballroom. They did not have to go far. Instead of taking Cecily about the room, others came to them immediately for introductions. Soon, Cecily's dance card was completely filled, and she asked Xander if she might go and join a few of her friends.

"Go and have fun," he told her. "This night happens but once. Enjoy it for all it is worth."

Willa and Xander then moved about the ballroom, greeting the friends they had made during their marriage. The musicians then began tuning their instruments, and they watched as Cecily's first partner, Lord Palmer, claimed her. Henry and Fia also moved to the center of the room, ready to open their ball together. They would dance the first dance before Fia retired to join the orchestra. She would play with it until the supper dance, when she would once more join Henry for the waltz.

Willa told her husband, "Cecily and Lord Palmer make a most striking couple, don't they?"

He slipped an arm about her waist. "Are you already playing matchmaker?"

"No, it is for Cecily to decide which gentlemen she will allow to court her. I do hope she finds love, Xander."

"We have been a shining example to her, love. Cecily is head-strong and stubborn. She will not settle for anything less than love." He gazed down at her tenderly. "Shall we join them on the dance floor?"

"If you do not mind, I would rather simply observe our daughter while she dances her first dance in public."

The musicians struck up a lively tune, and Willa and Xander looked on with pride as Cecily and Lord Palmer danced. Cecily and Lucy were the daughters she never had. While Willa was grateful for bearing four healthy sons, a part of her wished she might have had a girl. At her age, though, just a few years shy of forty, she doubted that would happen.

Then something came to her. She had not started her courses this month. No, they had not come last month, either. Willa realized that she had been caught up in the swirl of preparing Cecily for her come-out and stilled, wondering if a babe might be growing within her.

"What is it, love?" Xander whispered in her ear.

She turned and gazed up at him with all the love in her heart. "You are always so in tune to my moods." Hesitating a moment, she finally said, "I may be with child again."

He chuckled. "Are you just now realizing that? I have known for at least a couple of weeks."

"How?"

He brushed his knuckles against her cheek. "First, your breasts always change. And I am an expert on those breasts. Second, you always lose your appetite those first few months. While you are fortunate and have never experienced the nausea so many women do, your appetite always drops off."

"Why did you not say anything to me?"

"You were busy preparing for Cecily's come-out. Besides, I knew you would figure it out, sooner or later." His palm cradled her face and he added, "Perhaps after giving me all those boys, this time it will be a girl."

The tune ended, and Lord Palmer escorted Cecily back to them, bowing to her before leaving. Cecily's eyes were sparkling.

"Lord Palmer asked if he could call upon me tomorrow," Cecily said in a hushed voice.

"You know any gentleman is welcome to our home if you wish to see him," Willa said.

"I have heard many good things about Viscount Palmer," Xander added. "You do know that I will thoroughly investigate any man who walks through our door with the intention of wooing you?"

"I would expect nothing less, Uncle Xander," Cecily replied saucily.

Then her second dance partner came to claim Cecily, leading her onto the dance floor.

Her husband looked at Willa, love shining in his eyes. "Would you care to dance this dance, Your Grace? After all, you will soon grow too large to do so," he teased.

She playfully swatted his arm and said, "Yes, Your Grace. I would be happy to dance with you."

As Xander led Willa to the dance floor, she counted her many blessings.

About the Author

Award-winning and internationally bestselling author Alexa Aston's historical romances use history as a backdrop to place her characters in extraordinary circumstances, where their intense desire for one another grows into the treasured gift of love.

She is the author of Regency and Medieval romance, including: Dukes of Distinction; Soldiers & Soulmates; The St. Clairs; The King's Cousins; and The Knights of Honor.

A native Texan, Alexa lives with her husband in a Dallas suburb, where she eats her fair share of dark chocolate and plots out stories while she walks every morning. She enjoys a good Netflix binge; travel; seafood; and can't get enough of *Survivor* or *The Crown*.

Made in the USA
Coppell, TX
09 September 2023

21388313R10154